Praise for
SPLIT

"Michael Swartz's gritty novel explores the horrors of learning to survive in a dysfunctional family while battling a unique medical diagnosis. Ethan's internal conflict leads to unpredictable mood swings and identity confusion. You can feel the raw pain and emotion."

—Katrina Mackrides, author of
The Salty Swan and *The Crows Know*

"*Split* is a gripping novel that will keep you turning pages—and questioning the boundaries of identity—until the very last word."

—Deborah Jeanne Weitzman, author of
The Sinking of the Leonardo da Vinci

"Reading Michael Swartz's brilliant new novel, *Split*, put me back in touch with several of the most tormenting dimensions of youth: the brutality of the schoolyard bully, fear of the emerging self, and doubts regarding the limits of human endurance, forgiveness, and redemption. Utilizing his medical experience, Swartz probes these issues through the use of the biological anomaly of a young, human chimera, endowed not with one set of DNA but two. In a fast-paced tale of the struggles between light and darkness, *Split* takes the reader on a climactic ride from love and security to betrayal and its consequences. The future . . . chosen or predetermined? You decide."

—Jim Gulledge, author of
Green Forest, Red Earth, Blue Sea

"Everyone in *Split* is fighting some kind of battle—in school, at home, in the heart and head, in warfare in foreign lands. Events change lives, sometimes catastrophically. A deeply moving reminder that we need each other to survive.

"Michael Swartz has written a painfully beautiful story that moves with the speed of a racing heart. *Split* is a master class in complex family drama, reminiscent of Pat Conroy and Wally Lamb."

—Ron DeChristoforo, author of *This Way Out*

"*Split* is a compelling story that explores the challenges and intricacies of discovering and accepting one's true self during adolescence when born as a human chimera, a fascinating genetic phenomenon. This well-crafted and engaging narrative emphasizes the debate over the importance of genetics versus the influence of family, culture, and life experiences in shaping one's personality, along with the emotional and psychological impact of understanding one's genetic makeup when lacking adequate professional and emotional support. Highly recommended for anyone who enjoys pondering meaningful stories."

—Marie-Claude Gingras, author of
No Stones Left Unturned

Split
by Michael Swartz

© Copyright 2025 Michael Swartz

ISBN 979-8-88824-816-4

All rights reserved. No part of this publication may be reproduced, stored in a retrieval system, or transmitted in any form or by any means—electronic, mechanical, photocopy, recording, or any other—except for brief quotations in printed reviews, without the prior written permission of the author.

This is a work of fiction. All the characters in this book are fictitious, and any resemblance to actual persons, living or dead, is purely coincidental. The names, incidents, dialogue, and opinions expressed are products of the author's imagination and are not to be construed as real.

Edited by Miranda Dillon
Cover design by Catherine Herold

Published by

3705 Shore Drive
Virginia Beach, VA 23455
800-435-4811
www.koehlerbooks.com

SPLIT

Michael Swartz

VIRGINIA BEACH
CAPE CHARLES

SEPTEMBER 1995

LURCHING DOWN THE cement steps two at a time, I'm halfway across the parking lot before the diner's front door slams. But no angry footsteps follow in pursuit. No hands force me to the ground. There is only the soft yellow light from several windows, glowing like the menacing face of a carved pumpkin.

I run, sneakers scuffing against the asphalt, loose gravel flying in my wake. Deep breaths flood in panting waves, plumes of air that bloom and then vanish.

As I surge out of the parking lot, my throat constricts. I *need* to stop. I *need* to take a hit from my inhaler. Instead, my pace increases, moving faster toward where the road splits. To the left, there's the gas station, my high school, the library. I swerve right.

"*E-than!*" A voice demanding vengeance bounces off my ears like a vibrating fist.

I race away, just like my father. How many times did he flee? How many times would he refuse to face the consequences of his actions? If anything is clear after tonight, I am my father's son.

"E-than! E-than!"

The shouts challenge me to twist around, but to face what? The diner's owner carrying a Louisville Slugger or the clenched fists of Jackson VanPatten's friends out for revenge.

Racing forward, the distant growl of an engine carries into the night air. Tires screech, and headlights shine, painting a target onto my back. In seconds, my head start evaporates. I might outrun Jackson's friends, but not a car.

The high beams loom closer, stretching my shadow. The distinct features that make me different are lost. All that remains is a distorted silhouette with unnaturally long arms and legs. A praying mantis—a circus freak.

Hairs on my arm stick upright. The lights must be only yards behind. They're going to run me over. I want to glance back but can't watch the impact. Then I see it. The two closing beams of light point to an adjacent field, and I spring from the road edge, landing in a crouch.

The car passes in a *whoosh* of heavy air, accelerating away. Was that one of Jackson's friends? Will they circle back?

On the road's edge, I'm still visible. Hunched over, I see the dark outline of the woods at the far end of a field. Adrenaline thumps my heart against my chest, and I struggle to catch my breath. Swallowing hard and ignoring the acrid taste of blood where I bit my tongue, I head toward the shadows of the woods while the scene from the diner replays in a continuous loop. My first punch, twisting into Jackson VanPatten's nose. His gaping expression of disbelief. My second punch striking his abdomen, knocking him back, his head cracking against the table edge, his body thudding to the floor.

I slide between thick pine branches, my lungs battling for air. Behind the camouflaged protection of the evergreens, my trembling fingers scrape at the cap of my inhaler. With each failing breath, my windpipe constricts; the whistle in my throat jumps in pitch. Stars, not from the night sky, form at the edge of my vision. My lips tingle, demanding oxygen. Thrusting the inhaler toward my mouth, I bite down on the orange cap. The smooth plastic dimples from the force of my teeth, and like pulling the pin of a grenade, the cover releases. My lips wrap tight around the mouthpiece, and I press hard on the metal cylinder, forcing the chalky medicine into my throat. After the second puff, I crumble, dropping the inhaler.

Curled on my side, I tuck my legs tight to my chest and bundle both lanky arms around my torso. The canopy of trees blocks any moonlight as the medicine opens my lungs, and the sharp, sweet smell of conifer works its way into my nose. It's not a deluge of air, but the drip of a faucet. Minute by minute, my chest gradually expands, oxygen finally reaching my lungs and relaxing the tremor in my hands.

In the distance, the echo of an earsplitting siren rising and falling reminds me of the damage left behind at the diner. My stomach knots; I double over and vomit. Images of my fist colliding with Jackson VanPatten's nose replace my partially digested French fries. Rocking back and forth, my hands press tight into my eyes, shoving the tears away. In my brain, I hear the repeating crash of Jackson's head cracking against the table as he fell backward and then thudding against the diner floor. The two sounds pound in synchrony with my heartbeat. *Crack. Thud. Crack. Thud.*

I picture Jackson crumpled, his legs precariously crossed, his left arm cradling his head while rivulets of dark blood drip into the seams of the black-and-white linoleum tiles. Words I learned at the hospital two years ago flood my memory: subdural hematoma, increased intracranial pressure, near death, could go at any moment. Jackson wasn't moving; was he even breathing? Am I a murderer? If Jackson's friends locate me first, there will be no need for criminal justice.

Sweat pours from my brow, mixing with salty tears. Tugging my shirt to wipe my eyes, even without any light, I fixate on a shotgun pattern of dark spots that crust to the fabric. The marks after my fist cracked Jackson's nose.

Sinking into a bed of pine needles, I lay protected by the woods, feeling caged but secure.

I can't stay here forever. I could keep running, but to where?

My eyes recognize the piles of gray shale several yards away. From somewhere nearby, a trickle of water disrupts the silence. The stream leads to the woods behind my house. My house, where my father's violence began and ended, where I promised that I wouldn't become him.

On my feet, I circle twice before spotting the familiar creek, keeping clear of the shale ledge, slippery from the cold water. My feet shuffle across the route as my mind replays the night's events.

When I see the corn from Henderson's farm, tan and ready to harvest, standing in symmetric rows, I'm home.

At the edge, in the farthest corner of our property, a mound of earth protrudes from the lawn. The box of letters and mementos buried here marked my promise never to become him. My mother's half—the good half—would win over my father's genetics. But the divide between who I want to be and who I am is apparent.

Lowering myself onto dewy grass, I lean heavily onto crossed legs, staring at the heap of dirt.

***

Headlights slice a path through the dark, and car tires crunch against the gravel driveway. Of course, they found me. Coming home was stupid.

My muscles tense. In my head, I'm prepared to face the consequences, but my DNA has me programmed to run. The footsteps are not officer's boots or heavy sneakers out for revenge. They're lighter, more graceful. My heart and breathing slow as jasmine perfume wafts in my direction.

"Ethan, why did you jump from the road?" My girlfriend, Aia, sits close so that our shoulders touch. Her warmth radiates through me, but I resist the urge to fold into her.

"I thought it was Jackson's friends." She shouldn't be here. Jackson's friends could still be after me.

The wind catches several strands of her black hair, pulling them in front of her face. "How'd you know I'd be here?" I avert my gaze, focusing on the ground at my feet.

She slides her hand into mine. "You told me."

Replaying the scene in the diner for the thousandth time, I never said a word when I abruptly fled and ran for the door. My eyes travel from the burial ground of my youth to the tips of Aia's fingers, nails painted a bright purple, that interlock mine. She presses tight against my shoulder. She isn't afraid. She saw what I did to Jackson. She knows who I am.

"Two years ago. You said it's where you buried everything your father ever gave you." Her eyes travel toward the ground, scouring for what she knows is there.

"This doesn't change anything." Her words pull my gaze to her green eyes. "You understand that, right? What happened at the diner, what you did, doesn't change a thing. You are not like your father."

Rumors spread faster than the speed of light in this town, and this fight will be on the tip of every tongue by tomorrow morning. I want to accept that it was a single event. But in my mind, an image forms of the morning patrons at Ronni's Diner sitting on the tall, checker-print bar stools, sipping coffee, and reading the paper. Analogies will spill onto the counter like breakfast syrup, comparing the proximity of an apple after falling from the tree or describing a piece of fabric cut from the same cloth. They're correct, of course, all of them. It's a description of who I am and my biology.

I swallow my question with a gulp, but it wrenches out anyway. "Is he alive?"

PART ONE

September 1990

"It's who we are."

— Phoebe Rivers

CHAPTER ONE

IF THERE'S A place where I'm most vulnerable, it's the cafeteria. It's not the scent of overcooked taco meat or pulsing fluorescent ceiling bulbs. It's the tables of sixth graders on the first day of school, forced to learn about the past-perfect tense or Mesopotamia, who now have a chance to shout and laugh.

The two women in the far corner concern themselves with neighborhood gossip or who made the cover of *People* magazine. This week, it's the cast of *90210*. A slap to the back of the head or a shove to the ground will be lost in the chaos of noise and their inattention.

Beads of sweat drip off the milk carton as my eyes travel over each table, but not for a place to sit. I can't see Jackson VanPatten's spiky blond hair or pink skateboard T-shirt. After checking each table twice, the tight grip around my milk carton relaxes. He's not here.

Two steps forward, my head swivels left and right, hunting for an empty seat near a group of boys. I'll be ignored. I know that. But sitting near a group offers camouflage and some degree of protection. Four tables over, I slide down the bench.

The boy closest, wearing a backward hat, dirty and fraying at the brim, talks about his trip to Yankee Stadium.

When I pull a sandwich from my bag, his story stops. I can feel his attention drifting to me.

Don't look in my eyes. Don't look in my eyes.

Like a movie star trying to avoid a camera flash, I raise a hand to shield my face, but it's too late. The boy stares for three seconds too long. I clear my throat. "I'm Ethan."

He glances at his friends. "Move down."

In unison, the group slides toward the other end of the table.

My heart settles back into my chest while unpacking my peanut butter sandwich.

From several feet away, I hear how Don Mattingly was hurt and that the Yankees lost.

I'm still close enough to feel he's talking to me. Maybe if I ask something, I can slide a little closer to the group. "Did anyone hit a home run?" My voice rattles.

The group doesn't even look at me and slides a foot farther away, leaving me dangling like a piece of bait at the end of a string.

My neck stretches to check each table. No skateboard T-shirts. No blond spiky hair. He's not here.

Alone, I pull Dad's picture from the front pouch of my bag. I touch only the corners as the glossy photo shimmers in the light. He smiles in his military uniform, his tie tight against the collar of his shirt. His awards, two rows of bold-colored blocks, are pinned to his uniform above his left chest. Huddled over the cafeteria table, I rest my head on my arm, my eyes inches away from the paper to copy the exact dimensions and shade the square corners of the colored blocks. In my head, the conversation from the other end of the table gets quiet, and I can only hear the pencil scratching against the paper.

A hand swats the milk container on the table, puddling white drops over the once-glossy picture. The pencil markings from the drawing smear, and the paper turns translucent, bubbling up as it absorbs the thick liquid. My throat constricts, cutting off a scream as Jackson VanPatten laughs. The carton rests on its side, dripping into a lake of milk that trickles off the table and onto my shirt.

Fingernails from my fist pinch sharp into my flesh. When Dad yells at Mom, her fingertips curl tight into her palm, leaving four little lines. Her eyes get wet, but no tears fall. That works for me, too; the slight rush of pain prevents me from crying.

"Sorry," Jackson mocks.

My breath quickens, my lungs needing gulps of air as thoughts about the ruined drawing and my stained shirt surge. The lunch ladies across the room, monitors supposedly in charge, remain in their quiet conversation, pointing at the pages of *People*.

"How was the circus, Freak Show?"

He licks his lips like a cat moving toward a mouse in the corner. He's enjoying this.

"How many people came to see Ethan, the skinny midget with two different colored eyes?"

Murmurs of laughter erupt from the neighboring group. Heads swivel anxiously, watching the unfolding spectacle.

My hands flutter as I bury my head. Everyone notices my eyes, one dark green and one light blue. They're the reason Jackson has tortured me since first grade. They're why I don't have anyone to sit with at lunch. They're not special. They're different. I'm different.

I hate it.

Jackson pulls out his eyelids, and the laughter swells. His eyeballs bulge outward. "Come and see the circus freak. A midget with two different colored eyes."

He leans forward, pulling a tuft of my curly hair and twisting my head in his direction. His wide smirk reveals the remnants of the bologna sandwich still stuck in his teeth.

My lips twitch. I want to tell him to leave me alone. I want a seat closer to the lunch monitors so he won't bother me. Instead, I sneeze, splattering a fine mist on Jackson VanPatten.

This is bad. This is very, very bad.

He recoils, turning red, clenched teeth replacing the once clown-like smile.

"Gross!" he yells, wiping his face with his shirt and stretching across the table to punch my arm.

I don't scream. I don't cry. Instead, I wrap my hands around my chest.

The lunch monitors squint in our direction, and Jackson heads for the door.

I'm stuck with his insults echoing in my brain. I'm a circus freak. I peel the ruined drawing and soggy sandwich from the table, and the cafeteria stares as I drop them into the garbage.

Jackson bullies half the school, but I'm his prime target. During homeroom, he found an empty seat next to mine. After kicking my bag and scattering books over the floor he said in a low monotone, "We'll spend the year next to each other." Somehow, I thought the first day of sixth grade would be different.

Staring at the floor and trudging down the hall toward the gym, teachers pass, but no one questions my downcast face or hears my growling stomach. I spend the remainder of lunch circling the hall, filling the time.

In gym class, the teacher plans to assess our physical fitness. I'm the last to go and, of course, partnered next to Jackson. He scrambles up the rope; I barely rise a foot off the ground. Sprinting the relay is even worse. He's done before I reach my last lap, laughing with the class as my short legs cross the finish line.

By the end of class, I can't breathe. I mean, legitimately can't breathe. I'm trying to force down gulps of air like someone who has spent days in a desert and just found water. The only problem is the air isn't going down. With each successive gulp, I feel thirstier. My heart pounds, racing against my lungs. I shut my eyes, trying to concentrate. *Breathe in. Breathe out.* I've had asthma attacks before, but never this bad.

My inhaler is at the nurse's office. A few quick puffs and I'll probably feel better. But what if someone sees? One word from Jackson and the entire class will be convinced that I'm weak. Taking a hit from an inhaler doesn't make me special. This is sixth grade. A kid who can't summon the ability to breathe is doomed.

I step into the center of the line as we head down the hall to science, lowering my head and trying to appear normal. The last thing I want is for Jackson to see me gasping.

Mohamed, a dark-haired kid in my class, glances back in my direction. "You okay?"

I nod, hunching my shoulders, trying to appear invisible.

The class pours down the hallway, heading to Mrs. Trayne's science class. Hopefully, she'll stand at the front of the room in her bright green dress, the color of a traffic light, and continue waving her arms and hands like she's swatting at flies like she did during homeroom. The perfect distraction as my lungs strain to breathe.

I'll rest at my desk. If I can stay still, things will get better. I drop my head on the cool desk, lines of sweat slipping off my cheeks. But my mouth feels dry, a desert with no oasis in sight. The desk next to mine slides closer. Looking up, Jackson sits, showing all his teeth. Defeated, I lower my head to my desk.

"Now, class," Mrs. Trayne says, stepping toward the blackboard, gripping a piece of chalk. "This year in science, we—"

A voice interrupts, "Look!"

With no energy left, I can't lift my head and can't see why my classmates are gasping. Mrs. Trayne's voice rises above the clamor. "Please raise your hand."

"No," Mohamed shouts even louder, stomping his foot. "Look!"

Mohamed's blurry finger points toward my row of seats. To my left, Jackson looks straight ahead. On my right, a girl I don't know glances toward Mohamed. I don't care what he's pointing at. My head drops on the desk, cushioned by my cradling arms.

Mrs. Trayne pauses before she drops the chalk. "Oh, my God!"

Her high heels clap loudly against the floor.

It's only then that I realize how much trouble I'm in.

"Your lips are blue!" Mrs. Trayne cries. "Mohamed, help me get him to the nurse."

CHAPTER TWO

"**Y**OU'RE GOING TO be okay. You're going to be okay." Mrs. Trayne strokes my back like she's petting a cat.

Breathe in and out. That's all I need to do. But the taunting eyes of the class bore into me, and my throat tightens further.

Mrs. Trayne leans close, but not close enough so the entire classroom doesn't hear. "Do you need me to carry you?"

Soft laughter builds within the room, and a flush inches across my cheeks, but not because I can't breathe. I *still* can't breathe. She's treating me like a baby who needs coddling, an infant who requires a teacher for safety. I lower my head, wanting to disappear.

As she and Mohamed escort me toward the door, Jackson's nostrils flare, and his mouth sneers. "Hurry back, freak." I fold deeper into Mrs. Trayne's green dress.

Her heels click clack like a galloping horse, and she yanks at my shoulder with one hand as her second flails in the air. As we parade down the hall, Mrs. Trayne shouts, "Nurse Richardson! Nurse!"

The nurse awaits with arms extended as we gallop down the hall.

She has my inhaler in hand and two puffs later, my color returns.

Mrs. Richardson leaves me in a dimly lit room, thinking I need a nap. I don't. I just want to be like the rest of the class. Have two eyes of the same color. Have the ability to breathe. Most important, right now, I want to be left alone.

Unfortunately, Mrs. Trayne tells Mohamed that I need someone to keep me company.

He's sitting in a chair across from my cot, his eyes wandering around the room. I just met him today in homeroom, so he probably went to one of the different elementary schools last year. I can only imagine he's trying to escape from this cell, ready to tell the class how I was crying after I got my inhaler.

The paper wrap on the mattress wrinkles and crackles beneath my weight, muffling Mrs. Trayne's voice in the hall.

"I didn't know if he was breathing and rushed him right down," she tells Nurse Richardson.

"Oh my. He's lucky you acted so quickly."

"Well, I just did what anyone else would've done," Mrs. Trayne says, in a tone falling well short of humble.

Mohamed leans forward and snorts. "Oh *yeah*," he says, overemphasizing the words. "She deserves a medal." He pulls at his hair, bobbing his head back and forth, speaking two octaves too high. "Ethan, you're going to be okay. It will all be okay."

His exaggerated impersonation is horrible and sounds like he's been sucking on a helium balloon.

Several coughs stifle a short laugh. Mohamed ends his performance, his head twisting toward the doorway that leads to the nurse.

"You okay, Ethan?" Nurse Richardson ducks into the room, her dark spectacles hanging low on her chest.

"Good." I raise a thumb and nod.

Her gaze hangs on both of us for an extra second before retreating to her desk.

"Sorry." Mohamed stares at the floor like he's apologizing for his performance. "Why didn't you just go to the nurse?"

Rather than answer, I begin ripping at the paper covering on the cot. A pile of six or seven strips forms before Mohamed answers his question.

"That Jackson?" Mohamed murmurs, despite my continued silence. "He's a jerk. I saw what he did at lunch."

My mind wanders to Dad's photo, and I gag at the scent of sour milk.

"I'm Mohamed Alsoufi," he says, ignoring my reaction.

Lost in my thoughts, I barely hear his name. *"Mouhoumid Alsooofeay?"*

He grins, showing his teeth and shaking his head. "No, no. Mo—"

"Mo!" Interrupting him before he exaggerates the next syllable.

His face brightens, probably turning the name over in his head for a moment before agreeing that it fits. "You can call me Mo."

"I'm Ethan Rivers."

"No," Mo snorts. "If I'm Mo, you're Curly." He points to my wild curls.

"*The Stooges!*"

Mo's grin deepens, nearly reaching the corners of his eyes.

And then he doesn't stop talking. His parents are from Iran but left to go to school in America. I want to tell him my dad is in Saudi Arabia, two countries away, but Mo doesn't breathe while speaking about his mother and father working at Carrier, the factory that manufactures air conditioners, and about his twin sister, Aia.

***

Mo is still speaking when footsteps rapidly approach, along with the unmistakable sound of B's black purse banging against her hip.

When I was a baby, after days of failing to pronounce the word *Mom*, Dad said, "Phoebe, give the kid a break," and I echoed, "B," pointing my finger in her direction. Of course, I can pronounce Mom now, but keeping her name to a single letter is special to us. Sort of like a secret handshake. A club where only we belong.

On the phone, the nurse used terms like *perioral cyanosis* and *respiratory distress* and said that B needed to come to the school even though my throat's tight, clenching feeling disappeared.

B leans against the wall. Her wrinkled blue scrub shirt hangs askew, and she's panting like *she* needs an inhaler. Mo springs from the chair, turning sideways through the small doorway. "And I guess I've been relieved. See you tomorrow, Curly."

As he bends the corner, I wonder if he's just being polite.

B slumps against the doorframe, examining me. "Ethan, are you okay?" She draws a deep breath, releasing the tension in her shoulders.

I stare, and B spins, her shoulders square to face Nurse Richardson, whose back arches like a boomerang.

"I thought you said Ethan was cyanotic?" B examines me for a second and third time before glancing back at the school nurse.

The nurse rubs her hands together. "He was. He's gotten his color back since he's taken his inhaler. I can't send him back to class. He needs to see the doctor."

The two nurses butt heads, like rams charging at one another. It isn't until I croak that they stop their advance mid-step and look at me.

I'm not proud of my actions. Seriously, if I had a chance to turn back time, I'd tell the nurse that I did feel fine. That there's only an hour left. That I can finish school, catch the bus home, and take a puff from my inhaler at the first sign of trouble.

I picture returning to class and sitting next to Jackson VanPatten, waiting for his inevitable advance, and a croak escapes my open mouth. When B and the school nurse take notice, I repeat the noise.

Nurse Richardson places one hand on her hip and points with her other, palm upright, like she's supporting a dinner plate and presenting my croaking sound as the main course.

That's how we end up at Dr. Taylor's office, the doctor who's been treating my allergies and asthma. He isn't much taller than B, but wisps of gray hair band the edge of his hairline, and the skin on his face appears stretched and almost orange.

Two months ago, Dr. Taylor and Nurse Suzy drew a tic-tac-toe board on my back.

"We're just going to do a skin test," she said. "We'll put some common substances on your back and figure out what causes your allergies so we can better prevent your asthma."

It was like a Q and A for my immune system. My body held information about my allergies and asthma attacks, and the nurse was asking for the evidence.

I didn't realize it wasn't a friendly inquiry. She wasn't a detective. She was a gangster beating a prisoner until he snitched. After Suzy drew the grid, she pricked my back sixty-four times. Some of the substances in the middle of my back gave only a half-reaction, so she gave me fourteen shots in my arm. After the fourteenth shot, I puked all over Nurse Suzy's shoes.

"Ethan," Dr. Taylor says, flipping a page in a folder, "how are you feeling?"

I feel fine now, but my hands curl around my shoulders to protect my arms from the threat of any future shots. Dr. Taylor doesn't look up from the messy blue scribbles and the pictures of my previous allergy test.

"I'm good." My voice quivers, and my legs dangle over the exam table, swinging back and forth like I'm treading water.

Putting down the chart, Dr. Taylor places a hand on my shoulder; the warmth of his grasp isn't comforting.

"I thought the Seldane we started a few months ago would've helped. Let's have a listen."

When his patients can't breathe, I imagine his ears search for the hidden squeaks or lurches. Of course, I can breathe now, so there's no point. I've been to his office a couple of times, but this is the first time he's listened to my lungs. Most of his time is spent talking with B.

He moves his stethoscope like he's playing a board game on my back before finally releasing his grip and looking at B. "He has wheezing throughout."

B offers no response, clasping her hands tight. We're only a few feet apart, but there's a world of space between us, and it's been expanding ever since Dad left. She can't think about anything other than him, which I guess isn't too different from me.

Dr. Taylor examines my nose and my eyes with a light. The bright beam remains suspended, shining into my face, and I feel like a frozen deer, unable to dart out of the way of an oncoming truck.

His mouth opens, and his head tilts to one side. "Ethan has two different colored eyes." He steps backward as if he just tripped on a rope.

Yes. I have two different colored eyes. I've always had two different colored eyes. I had two different colored eyes during my allergy test. I have two different colored eyes now. But I'm here for my asthma; I don't need Dr. Taylor piling onto Jackson's insults.

B stares at Dr. Taylor with a crease on her brow. "Is that a problem?"

"No."

Inching closer, he touches my hair, pulling gently on a tuft, first on the left and then on the right, pinching several strands between his fingers and thumb.

His brown eyes open wide, and his mouth hangs ajar. He looks like he's found the eighth wonder of the world in my scalp. Dr. Taylor spent less than two minutes explaining the allergy test results at the last visit. Today, he's spent more time gawking at my eyes and combing through my hair.

"Ethan, can I see your back?" His voice is quiet, without inflection, like he's caught in a trance.

I twist, facing away from B. His hand traces the center of my spine, and under his breath, I hear, "Amazing."

I turn to face B, not caring if Dr. Taylor is finished with his exam, and catch worry creeping into her eyes.

"Was Ethan lying on his side in the sun?" Dr. Taylor sits on his rolling stool, re-examining the pictures of my allergy test.

"No." B leans forward off her chair.

"On the left side of Ethan's back, it's a little darker, almost like he got a sunburn." Dr. Taylor flips the pages back and forth.

I've noticed the patch. It's not over my entire back, just toward the middle. It's been there forever.

"Give me a thumbs up," Dr. Taylor instructs.

With each question, I'm traveling farther and farther down an unknown path into a dark forest. With each question, there is increasing danger. Still, I raise a thumb. *What is he looking for?*

"Sorry, give me two thumbs up."

My left thumb rises alongside my right. He steps closer, his head nodding almost imperceptibly before returning to the chart. My thumbs remain awkwardly raised.

B sees it too. *"Wh . . . what?"* she stammers.

"I heard of this at a conference a few years back. It would explain Ethan's asthma and allergies. But I didn't think—" His voice trails off, his gaze focusing on the pictures in the chart and then back at me.

"I think I can explain Ethan's allergies."

His tone is confident, and my head jerks upright, ready to listen.

"But what I'm about to tell you is very new. I mean, *very* new."

I lean forward for his answer. If he knows why I have asthma, he can fix me, and there's a chance I can be just like everyone else.

Dr. Taylor swivels to look at me, and I stare at my dangling legs, but my ears hang on every word.

He faces B. "Ethan is what we call a *chimera.*"

I lurch backward.

Dr. Taylor didn't say, "Ethan has a disease called asthma *3.7,*" or "Ethan has a special kind of allergy." No, Dr. Taylor used the word *is* to describe what I am. Whatever *chimera* means, it's a label. It's a mark. Whatever he says next will further separate me from the rest of the class. A bead of sweat trickles from under my arms.

"Let me explain," Dr. Taylor continues. "A child is a mixture of both the mother's and father's DNA. Sometimes during gestation, there can be a set of twins, usually fraternal, meaning non-identical twins, so they don't look like one another. Rarely, and I mean *rarely*, one of the twins dies and gets absorbed by the other in the womb."

B's face stretches somewhere between a grimace and pure horror. Dr. Taylor pauses, perhaps debating if he should continue, but like a runaway train, he keeps going.

"This isn't bad." He raises his hand, outstretched as if ready to stop an oncoming bus. "But each twin has their own unique set of DNA. The DNA from the dead twin is incorporated into the one that lives. The result is that instead of having only one, the living twin has two completely different sets of DNA. Sometimes, one is on the left half of their body, and a second different set is on the right half of their body. We consider that a chimera when two different types of DNA are within a single person. It's an old Greek term from a myth about a goat and a lion. I actually can't remember the whole story."

Dr. Taylor takes a breath, but it only lasts a second before he continues.

"A fetal chimera looks mostly just like the rest of us. But there are some subtleties. Ethan's eyes, for example, his right eye is green like yours," he points to B, "but his left is blue."

"Like his father's," B whispers.

"Yes. Yes!" Dr. Taylor leaps from his stool, gawking in my direction like I'm a sideshow, a circus freak. "And his thumbs. Look at his thumbs."

Staring quickly at my thumbs, they look identical, like two ordinary-looking thumbs.

"The one on the left bends backward. That's called a hitchhiker's thumb. But the right doesn't do that."

B raises her thumbs, both of which stand straight at attention. The veil tears away, and suddenly, I see the difference too. I try to force my left thumb straight, but it can't. It won't.

"Also, his hair has more curls on the left side."

B has straight blonde hair. Dad's hair is curly. Swallowing hard, I resist the urge to search my scalp, hoping against all odds to uncover a straight hair on my left side.

"But, maybe most importantly, do you remember the strange reactions in the middle of Ethan's back when we gave him different allergens? He has a patch of light skin to the right of his spine. The half-reactions were probably because of the difference in skin tone. It's common in chimeras. It has a special name, but honestly, I can't remember."

Dr. Taylor's words begin to cut in and out.

"We need to examine Ethan's DNA to prove he's a chimera."

I imagine the needles required for that experiment and cringe.

"Often, chimeras have allergies and asthma that don't respond to medication, just like Ethan."

Dr. Taylor's eyes lock onto mine, and there's something in his expression that I can't read. It's not regret, like he's handing out bad news. There's a twinkle, and he's speaking faster. Like uncovering who and what I am for him is exciting. Like he's won a medal, except I want this award reburied.

"All kids have their parents' DNA, and you do too. But you are different. Very different."

I want him to stop, and yet everything is starting to make sense. Worst of all, Jackson VanPatten is right. I'm a circus freak. I'm not just a midget with two different eyes, I'm a chimera.

"I imagine you haven't studied this in school yet." Dr. Taylor crosses his fingers into a twist. "DNA looks like this. It's two strands of nucleotides. People have one set of DNA in each of their cells, two strands of twisting stacked *nucleotides*." He holds up his fingers again. "You have two sets of DNA, just different sets on each side." His other hand waves, and his index and middle fingers cross into a double twist. "Children are the combination of their parents' DNA. DNA is the genetic material that Mom and Dad pass on to their kids. Usually, it's like putting Mom and Dad's DNA in a blender, and the child's DNA is a mixture. Sometimes the child looks like their mother. Sometimes it's more of an equal split. I'm sure you've heard about babies having their mother's eyes or their father's chin. We categorize or catalog these traits. Ethan is still a mixture of both you and your husband."

I take a moment to look down at my thumbs, flexing them slightly to see the curve on the left that I'm certain aligns with Dad. Now, there is a scientific term to describe how I'm different. Not circus freak, two eyes, or any other name that Jackson VanPatten concocts. An actual scientific label. *Chimera.*

"Ethan is two different mixtures. He's split in two. The blend on his left half resembles his father, and the blend on his right resembles you." Dr. Taylor points to B. "If we study Ethan's DNA more closely, we can prove that. It will show us that his DNA differs between his left and right sides." Dr. Taylor's eyes light up.

The weight of his words pile on one another like heavy stones. I shoulder the first, but with the increasing weight, I break. B doesn't see it. Neither does Dr. Taylor.

"For now, though, I'll write you a note so you can keep your inhaler with you." He pauses, his face puckering again as if he were sucking on a lemon. "And probably no gym for a few weeks."

B isn't moving. She's a mannequin, and I want her to shift. I want her to say something because I don't know what this will mean for us if she stays silent.

Vaulting off the exam table, I grip my inhaler and take a puff. It's all I can think of to interrupt Dr. Taylor. B stares at me but focuses on only my right eye. She isn't looking at me anymore. She's focusing on *what* I am.

"Your left half is like your father, and the other half is like your mother." Dr. Taylor's words repeat in my head over and over again.

CHAPTER THREE

MY FINGERS CLAMP around B's hand, pulling her outstretched arm through the waiting room.

From the reception desk, a voice hails, "Mrs. Rivers, we can schedule your next appointment."

B's feet shuffle, and she mutters, "I'll call the office," as we storm into the bright September afternoon sun. She's like dead weight, and when we reach the car, I'm thankful for the earlier inhaler puff.

Her torso folds, collapsing into the driver's seat. I hope the tires squeal as we speed away with the urgency of robbing a bank. Instead, B massages her temples, her head resting on the steering wheel, the car idling.

"B?" The hum of the car engine drowns out my whisper.

She doesn't answer, and I tug at the sleeve of her scrub top.

A car pulls into the spot facing us. The driver stares three seconds too long at B, crumpled in her seat, before he pops out of the car and walks away.

When he returns, and we haven't moved, a single eyebrow

arches high. I lean forward, inspecting his face like a detective, thinking that maybe he's like me. Even in the fading afternoon sun, I can tell both his eyes are blue. His hair, though cut short, appears the same on both sides.

"B?"

I'm trying to close the distance between us. I know this is too much. Dad is in Saudi Arabia, she left work early, and now I'm a genetic freak. The mounting problems form a tower so tall she can't see the top.

Her hands lower from her temples as she leans into the seat with a heavy sigh.

"This is good news," she says, but her voice stays low. "Now, we have a reason for your allergies and asthma."

My chin drops to my chest. Her fake smile doesn't disguise how she feels. *I'm different.* But not just different from other kids in my class or school. I'm like one in a million. Maybe even larger. I stare at my shoes. There's a name to catalog what I am. *Chimera.*

"I'm a circus freak." Jackson VanPatten is right. I'm a sideshow attraction.

"You're not."

Despite the sharp response, B's flat expression proves she's not convinced.

"This isn't something to broadcast to the world." She pauses, clasping my hand and squeezing it tight. "This just explains who you are."

Her familiar catchphrase. It's her answer for why I don't have any brothers or sisters, why she and Dad yell at each other, or why we live so far away from everyone. It's just who we are. It's better than *because*. But I have no idea what, *"It's just who we are"* means.

She shifts the car into reverse but keeps her foot on the brake. "We'll talk about this later."

B never talks about anything later, later means never.

The car lurches as she pulls her foot off the brake. As she drives, the uneasy silence builds, so she turns on the radio to fill the void. She stares straight ahead, refusing to look in my direction when the car stops at a light. She doesn't tap the steering wheel with her thumbs or move her lips with the song. She's retreating again. This time, I let her go.

B is in the house before I can get my bag from the back seat. Beyond the surrounding cornfields, Mr. Henderson sits on the green dot that is his tractor, appearing as only a speck on the horizon. He's our closest neighbor. Past the cornfields, I imagine the homes ten miles away. There, kids play kickball on a quiet street. But just as I recognize their faces, I blink and am back alone at my house.

The front door is wide open, and there's a small hope that B will be making dinner. But the kitchen is empty, and her bedroom door is shut. Even though the living room is only big enough for a couch, a chair, and a small TV, the walls seem to expand. I spin, looking for someone, for anyone.

"I'll be upstairs." The words echo, but no one listens.

Beneath my foot, a piece of plastic cracks, and a Lego sits fractured within the strands of the golden yellow carpet. The edge of the blue rectangle, busted nearly in half, is as sharp as the memory of Dad screaming at three in the morning.

Before he left, he paced the house in the dark, accidentally stepping on a Lego. B scrambled to the living room while I overheard from upstairs. In the dark, Dad sat on the couch, rubbing his left foot.

"What happened?" B quivered in a soothing tone.

"I stepped on another one of his Legos. I should wake him and force him to walk on it."

"I'll talk to him in the morning. Just come back to bed."

"Can't sleep," Dad said, his voice sharp.

"Then just try to lie back down next to me."

Shaking the memory from my head and dropping the Lego pieces on the bookshelf, my eyes travel to the books from Grandma and Grandpa, and my fingers tap against *A Wrinkle in Time*. The pages are musty, and the words are gray. But after several minutes, I'm transported into Meg's story. Meg gets bullied at school and her father also isn't at home. Pages flip, and soon I've forgotten about Dad, about B isolating herself, about being a freakish chimera.

Thirty pages later, the sun nearly set, B yells that dinner is ready.

On the couch downstairs, I sit on the cushion with the jean patch that keeps in the stuffing. It's a target, and I'm helping the patch with my weight.

When I asked why we couldn't get a new couch, B, of course, replied with her answer for everything: "It's who we are."

Tucking my legs close against the yellowed fabric creates room for the TV trays. B plops onto the couch with a sigh, handing me a plate of macaroni and cheese. The sofa squeaks and groans.

There's a small hope that maybe she'll explain that a chimera isn't so different. Maybe she saw a kid with the same thing just last week. But we slowly eat our dinner, waiting for the national news with Tom Brokaw.

The meteorologist forecasts sunny, warm days ahead, suggesting that he may be partly responsible for the excellent weather. But his words are muffled by my repeating thoughts.

I want B to talk with me. Questions about who I am and what's a chimera stay lodged in my throat. Instead, my mind travels to Dad. "What time is it in Saudi Arabia?"

She doesn't seem to hear me, even though we are only inches apart. Dark circles rim her eyes, and deep lines crease at the corners of her mouth. They weren't there in July.

"It's after 6 p.m. now," she sighs, "so it's about two in the morning in Saudi Arabia."

I nod, imagining Dad in Saudi Arabia.

Before working for the fire department, Dad was in the Army and is now part of the Army Reserves. President George Bush activated Dad to protect the people of Saudi Arabia. He's like a bench player for the Army, and it's his turn to play.

"You know," B says, "maybe I could get you a pair of watches for your birthday. That way, you'd always know the time in Saudi Arabia."

"I could put one watch on my left wrist and the other on my right. Synchronize watches," raising my naked wrists.

B's gaze returns to the TV.

"B?" Searching for the words and the courage. "What am I?" I don't know how else to ask. Before today, I was a skinny midget with two different colored eyes and asthma. She pats my leg. "A boy. You're a boy. That's it. No more, no less. Whatever Dr. Taylor said today is not something for you to worry about. You're a boy. You're my boy."

The horns announce the beginning of the *NBC Nightly News* interrupting our conversation, and B's focus shifts.

Dad has only been gone a few weeks, and already I feel like we entered a different world. When it was quiet and he was working, we would meet him at the firehouse, deliver him dinner, and eat with the other firefighters on duty. At home, we always ate at the kitchen table. Dad would sit in the corner, leaning back on his chair, describing his most outrageous calls. Once, two neighbors got into an argument and fired model rockets at each other, catching a shed on fire. Another time, a college student built a bonfire to lure one of the firefighters to her apartment, hoping for a date.

***

With Dad gone, Mom and I eat on the couch, hoping to see him on TV. I'm not so stupid to think that Tom Brokaw will interview my father, although that would be great. But maybe Dad will casually stride past during a broadcast, or we'll catch a glimpse of someone from the Fourth Quartermaster Division.

The music builds, and we shift to the edge of the couch. "Good evening," Tom Brokaw says, wearing a crisp gray suit and sitting behind a desk. "We begin our coverage tonight from the United Nations." We both slide back. The president demands that Iraq leave Kuwait. Experts talk about what they think might happen next, but there's no footage of the troops.

"Go upstairs and write your letter," B says, heading to the kitchen with our dishes. I trudge upstairs and pull a pencil from my desk.

I write Dad a letter daily, and B mails them in batches on Mondays. She says he should get them in a day or so. B writes several pages a week that she places with my letters, but I don't get to see hers. I've been afraid to sneak a peek.

Sitting at the table that is my desk, I lean back in the chair, thinking about what to write. There's paint on several legs, but it still works fine. I shove aside the thought of telling Dad I'm a chimera or had an asthma attack.

Dear Dad,
Today was my first day of middle school, and I climbed higher than I ever had up the ropes. I met a new friend today. B and I looked for you on TV but didn't see you tonight. I miss you.
Love,
Ethan

Settling under the blankets, I imagine Dad driving in a Jeep, keeping the Saudi Arabian people safe, big clouds of sand and dust flying from beneath the wheels.

The stairs creak, pulling me out of my thoughts.

"Good night, Ethan," B says quietly, kissing me on my head.

"I'm sorry about today." I stare into her red eyes.

"It's not your fault." She kisses the top of my head again for good measure. "We'll have a better tomorrow," B says, closing the door. I desperately want to believe her.

CHAPTER FOUR

THE THIRTY FEET from the school's entrance to homeroom takes five minutes through the traffic of lockers opening and closing. Leaning a shoulder against the cold brick wall, I shuffle down the hall. Even at the edge, backpacks and bodies prod me forward, and like a grain of sand tumbling along the ocean floor, I'm deposited in Mrs. Trayne's room.

I expect that Jackson will somehow know about my diagnosis, that chimera will replace circus freak. Maybe Dr. Taylor phoned Nurse Richardson about my gym excuse while Jackson lurked in the hall. Or maybe Jackson's father and Dr. Taylor are friends, and their families talked about an interesting patient over dinner at the country club. When Dr. Taylor described how the boy had two different colored eyes, Jackson stayed quiet, eating his steak, his grin stretching wide.

Either way, today I'll have a new name. Not that Jackson will know what it means, but it won't matter. This time, the insult won't be an idea in his head but a scientific fact.

Gulping down the powdery medicine from my inhaler, the chalky taste slows my breathing. An easy breath in and out, and my fidgeting hands relax. Two steps through the door, I see the empty desk next to mine. My eyes scan the room, but Jackson isn't inside. Spinning to face the hall, expecting his menacing grin, he isn't there.

With stumbling feet, I slide into my desk. The legs scrape against the floor after I push the desk two inches farther away from where Jackson sat yesterday. It won't make much difference, but I have to try something.

"Hey," a voice shouts from the back of the room. My head jerks toward the noise, but it isn't Jackson.

Rhythmically tapping my foot against the linoleum floor, the commotion of bags dropping and voices echoing around the room drowns out the noise. Mrs. Trayne sits at her desk, twirling a pencil between her fingers, unfazed by the turmoil.

Waiting for Jackson to begin day two of my torture, I bury my head back into *A Wrinkle in Time*, hoping to lose myself for a few seconds in a different world—a place where Meg also misses her father and feels alone.

My head pops up from the pages. Mrs. Trayne still appears uninterested in the boisterous class rants—or my safe return. She's staring out the window into the school parking lot.

The chair to the right moves, and the words of the page blur as my nose nearly grazes the print. I can't see what he's doing but feel his hot breath on my neck. I swear he's trying to decide where to strike. I wait for his first blow—an insult about being a chimera, a punch, or worse.

"What's wrong, Curly? You still can't breathe?"

I bolt upright, closing the book with a loud snap. Mo drops his bag next to mine.

"Listen," he continues, "Mrs. Trayne told me to sit here for the rest of the year. She kept babbling that I should watch out for you during homeroom and science because you tried to *die* yesterday."

He shakes his head, emphasizing the word die. "No joke, she actually used the word die. Anyway, I told her I'd be happy to help."

"Really?" My voice trembles, expecting a trap. We just met yesterday.

Mo shrugs. "Why not? It's better than sitting in the back next to Alyssa Eager. That girl needs deodorant."

He slides into his desk. "What's your first class? I've got math with Mrs. Korsik."

"English." My voice is barely above a whisper.

"Alright, we'll meet up at lunch."

Jackson passes his old desk, heading several seats back. He glares, pounding a fist into his open palm.

There's the faintest drop in my shoulders. Jackson can't reach me.

***

At lunch, Mo unpacks his sandwich. "So, what's the deal with you turning blue anyway? Are you gonna try that every day or just most days? I want to be ready."

He pulls the wax paper back from a turkey sandwich and takes a giant bite. Large crumbs drop into his lap as he waits for my answer.

Each time Mo speaks, it's like he's delivering the punchline of a joke. He has this wild and eccentric way of talking, no matter how serious the question. "I don't know." I shrug. "It happens. I get to carry my inhaler now."

He snatches the yellow cylinder with the bright orange cap. "Can I try it? It won't kill me or anything, right?"

"You can try it." I take a bite of a sandwich. "But if you die, Jackson will sit next to me again."

"Funny, Curly."

He pops the cap and presses down on the vial. His face scrunches into a prune, and he pulls away.

"That's disgusting. It's like breathing chalk." He pushes out his tongue, scraping it against his teeth, trying to rake away the taste.

"I didn't say it tastes like chocolate cake."

"Yeah, but you didn't say it was like breathing sand." Mo jerks his head from side to side. "Now I know why you didn't go to the nurse straight away." He tosses me the inhaler, returning his attention to his half-eaten sandwich.

"Man, I thought Mrs. Trayne was going to piss herself yesterday. Did you see her arms?" Mo whirls his arms in circles, trying to imitate Mrs. Trayne, and I can't help but laugh. Taking the encouragement, he bounces from his seat and flies around the table. He lets out a squawking sound from a radio. "All units, we have a boy who cannot breathe. Please activate Mrs. Trayne." For once, the lunch monitors from across the room point for Mo to sit.

Finishing my sandwich and apple, I stare at his half-eaten buffet.

"That's all you got?" Mo opens his second bag of Doritos.

I've had the same lunch since kindergarten, a sandwich, and a piece of fruit. Only on rare occasions does B pack anything else.

Mo tosses over a bag of Doritos. "No wonder you're so skinny," he says, taking a cookie. "If I don't eat, I get cranky, and nobody, and I do mean nobody, wants to see me cranky."

I crunch down on a Dorito, enjoying the nacho cheese flavor, but pause mid-bite.

"Look, Circus Freak is friends with Brown Boy," Jackson's voice rises above the crowd. Mikey and Jonny stand on either side, laughing. After yesterday's show, most of the cafeteria whirls, ready for round two. The lunch ladies gab to one another, no longer paying attention.

That happens all the time. The lunch ladies and teachers always seem to turn their backs when Jackson is causing trouble, which, of course, happens every day. For anyone else, they'd insist he move on. But Jackson's father is a lawyer on the school board. His picture in the glass display case in the school lobby is a constant reminder of Jackson's protective status.

Mo stands, his eyes popping out of his head. "Wow, Jackson," he says emphatically, "you can see!" He loudly emphasizes every syllable, like an evangelical minister. "It's a miracle. Praise the Lord." Mo raises his arms toward the heavens as his voice echoes across the cafeteria. The two lunch ladies can't help but interrupt their story.

I sit paralyzed in the center of their gunfight. The two outlaws stand motionless, their fingers playing piano in the air next to their holstered weapons. Who will draw first? Jackson narrows his gaze at Mo.

"Yeah, whatever." Jackson walks away with his two goons, and there's a quiet groan from the spectators as they return to prior conversations, missing the opportunity for another show.

"That was amazing," I whisper.

Mo sits, popping an Oreo in his mouth. In between large chomps, he says, "I've dealt with bigger fish than him before. A few years ago," he pauses, wiping his mouth with his sleeve, "there was this kid named Scottie. No joke, it was his second time taking third grade. Before he moved, that kid was brutal. Jackson," Mo sloshes his head, "he's a small fry."

Those words stick with me throughout the rest of the day. On the bus, I think about Mo defending me. He said all the things I'd wanted to say to Jackson to make him stand down.

***

At home, pacing through the house with unbound energy, I want to tell B about my day. The two outsiders, the Stooges, the two kids who are different, are friends.

Outside, sheets of water pour off the porch roof, so I pace around the house, constructing a loop between the couch and Dad's lounge chair, toward the kitchen, and past the table in the corner to the sink. Then, back through the kitchen, down the hall toward B's room, and finally past the backside of the couch. I don't bother climbing the stairs; it's only my room, and no windows face the front of the house. After my sixty-seventh lap and the tenth time pulling aside the front curtain, the tires of B's yellow Buick hit the gravel driveway. Flying toward the door, my heavy footsteps cause the dishes in the kitchen to rattle.

B shuffles in, her eyes puffy and cheeks red, and the happiness surging inside evaporates, leaving me hollow.

"What's wrong?"

B drops her purse and heads toward the kitchen without a word. The front door hangs ajar, letting in the sounds of rain pelting the roof.

"Everything okay?" I ask, moving to close the distance between us.

"Just tired, that's all. I'm going to lie down."

"Are you sick?" The space between us expands.

She shakes her head and locks her bedroom door, leaving me alone to focus on the paneling and imagine what's wrong.

CHAPTER FIVE

"CURLY, YOU GOTTA blast 'em." Mo raises on his toes, dipping one shoulder to the side, imitating the movements of Cyclops. As he punches buttons, the cord connecting his controller to the Nintendo console snaps like a whip.

I tap the button to fire. Multiple percussive pings from our lasers obliterate the computerized notes from the game's background music, and Sabretooth falls.

"There you go." Mo grins. Without a pause, we are on the next level, maneuvering around barricades and blasting the evil mutants to save the world.

Mo's partial reflection stares back from the screen; his wide eyebrows cinch together into a straight, tight line. He's so close to the TV I can't see my character, and I take a step forward so our shoulders are level.

It's been a month since we first met. A month of sitting with someone at lunch. A month of Jackson VanPatten no longer next to me at homeroom or science. A month of having a friend.

***

Mo's house is just fifteen minutes away, but his neighborhood looks like a different world. There aren't cornfields or far-off sounds of a tractor. The distance between neighbors is measured in feet—not miles. Houses made of brick, and even a few wrapped in stone, evenly space his street. Paved driveways and flower gardens line front yards. Inside, carpet is everywhere, even on the stairs, and I need to remove my sneakers at the door.

When Mo switches on his Nintendo, inserting his favorite game, *X-Men,* my arms pull tight across my chest. Thoughts about my own mutant DNA rush forward. How did he know? Maybe B told him? But he doesn't notice the flush in my face or the change in my breathing.

"I love the comics, so Dad got the game," Mo says.

Selecting through the characters, a grainy image of Cyclops fills the right corner of the screen.

Mo leans closer, snagging my controller. "You'll probably want Wolverine."

There's no mention of my genetics, chimeras, or changes in my DNA. It's only a game. Just a game.

In first grade, a girl named Jennifer needed to see a specialist, or at least that's what Mrs. Anderson told the class when her parents picked her up early. The next day, Jennifer showed the purple bruise on her arm where her blood was taken. Hours later, her mother and father took Jennifer to the hospital, interrupting her drawing. She would miss school, sometimes for weeks at a time, getting her cancer medicine. From that moment, she was the kid with cancer. If she wasn't at school, it was because of cancer. If she looked sick, it was the cancer. Mrs. Anderson said cancer wasn't contagious, and we couldn't catch it, but she had also told us that chicken pox wasn't a big deal, and earlier in the year, half the class was covered in red blisters.

Jennifer doesn't go to our school anymore. She moved to New York City, closer to a big hospital. But her label had stuck for the next three years. She ate alone at lunch. Most kids pulled their desks a little farther away from hers. The last thing I want is for Mo to learn about my label.

"You've heard of *X-Men*, right?" Mo lowers his controller, taking a breath after we finish another level. "X-men are like humans but born with an x-gene, giving them extra abilities, like Colossus who can transform himself into a stronger version, almost like the Incredible Hulk. Magneto commands the bad mutants. Xavier leads the good mutants, trying to protect the world from Magneto and his gang."

"How does Xavier know who's a mutant?" Maybe everyone is tested for the x-gene, just as Dr. Taylor suggested a month ago? He'd phoned the house twice, reminding us about the importance of a follow-up visit and DNA test. Fortunately, B was so distracted that she told him no.

Mo switches his character to Iceman. "Oh, that's easy," he says, selecting the next level. "He has this machine, Cerebro, that tells him if someone has a mutant gene." Mo snaps his controller to attention. "Be ready. There's a mutant."

I jerk the controller close to my chest.

Mo offers a friendly nod. "We'll get through this. Don't worry," he says as his thumbs move faster.

We take a break for dinner, and Mo's twin sister, Aia, trots down the stairs. Mrs. A. places a massive pile of rice with chicken, beef, and a brown sauce on my plate. I take a quick sniff, thinking about how to dispose of the meal without attracting attention. It doesn't look like anything I've ever eaten. The food smells like peppers, and after a quick prayer, I poke my fork at the chicken. It is nothing like the macaroni and cheese B makes for dinner. It's better. The meat dissolves in my mouth, as I take a second forkful. Mr. A. leans his heavy forearms against the table. His enormous hands resemble

Juggernaut's boxing gloves. But despite his size, his voice is quiet, the opposite of Mo's. He talks about how the SU basketball team looks good this year. Aia says she wants to try playing tennis. There are no TV trays in the living room. There's conversation rather than the necessary silence to watch Tom Brokaw, hoping to catch a glimpse of a soldier from the Fourth Quartermaster Division.

"Thank you for dinner." I use a piece of flatbread to soak up the remaining sauce. If there's one thing Grandma taught me, it's to leave the plate spotless.

"Such a polite young man." Mrs. A. takes my plate with a warm smile, stacking it upon her own. "Maybe you could help Mo with some of his manners." Aia grins, until Mo kicks her under the table, and her eyes narrow.

After dinner, we play *X-Men*, defeating Magneto in the last level despite Aia blocking the screen. Mrs. A. gives us gooey brownies for dessert, and on the way home, we talk about beating Magneto and what superpower we'd want if we had an x-gene.

"I'd want invisibility," Mo says. "That way, I could sneak around. What about you?"

I think about all the powers—weather, magnetism, invincibility. "Strength." I wouldn't depend on Mo's protection if I were strong like Colossus. Jackson and his friends would leave me alone. But I don't want to look different from everyone else. Colossus is a giant; he would never fit in my bed and probably not even in my room. I'd rather be like the Hulk. Bruce Banner appears like everyone else until he needs to defend himself.

***

The minivan lurches over the gravel pits of my driveway. There is no plush lawn, only scattered clumps of grass that bunch together among the weeds. Instead of large windows looking into a well-lit living room, there is only the outline of a tiny window as light escapes around the shade.

"Maybe next time, Mo can come to your house?" Mrs. A. puts the car in park.

She must not see the difference. She doesn't notice that our house is closer to an abandoned shack when compared to hers.

My chin anchors to my chest. There's no hiding where I live. "I don't have a Nintendo."

"That's okay." Mo's front teeth glow white in the dark car. "We can play tag in the corn!"

My face brightens. If there's one thing my house offers, it's corn. I've hunted inside the rows, getting lost trying to discover a stalk different from the rest—the one with two different colored tassels. The one like me. So far, there's been none.

"I'll see you tomorrow. Thank you for dinner, Mrs. A."

As I shut the car door, I hear her say, "You see Mo. Polite," followed by Mo's muted voice, "Yeah, yeah."

Inside, B lies on the couch facing the TV. "Did you have fun with Mo?"

Her head doesn't turn, and her voice is deep. Months ago, her voice would rise an octave, talking about work or telling me about how, as a kid, she would sneak out after dark to go swimming with her friends.

"Yeah, we played this cool video game *X-Men*." I wait for the recognition that X-Men are mutants. I'm a mutant. But her face is flat, her eyes dull.

"Good." She stretches her arms. "Go write your letter to Dad. I'm going to bed."

***

It's late, but I'm still thinking about destroying Magneto. My letter to Dad describes the game and how next time I'll play Mario Brothers when I'm over at Mo's house.

Downstairs, I flip on the kitchen light and see the empty soup can next to the sink and the stack of letters blending into the white Formica countertop.

For the past seven weeks, B mailed her letter with mine, and I haven't had an opportunity to peek. Tonight, she hasn't sealed this stack yet. My fingertips curl around the off-white stationery. Glancing around the room, I'm breathing faster as B and Dad stare back from their wedding photograph hanging on the living room wall. I turn my back to the picture.

Unfolding the pages, I press them to my nose to read the tiny letters of B's flowing cursive.

Spence,

I breeze through the first line of each paragraph. Apparently, Dr. Carter's office is threatening to cut B's hours if she can't stay late, but that's not why I'm snooping. I scan for something about my diagnosis, but there's nothing. I lose hope of discovering anything useful until the middle of the last page. The final paragraph appears different from the rest. The sentences crammed in after B signed her name.

I keep thinking something terrible is going to happen. You've told me you are well out of harm's way.

***

I remember last Sunday, sitting on the couch with Grandpa watching *Murder, She Wrote*, and what I overheard in the kitchen.

"I mean, it's so hard," B said. "The house is so quiet. Ethan is always in his room or outside. I lay awake in my room thinking about what could be happening right now."

Her admission confirmed that we are two peas in a pod, each thinking about Dad. But since Dad left, she seems to be moving farther away into a deep space where she can't see me.

"I mean," B continued, "not that a firefighter is the safest job in the world, but it seems safer than fighting in another Vietnam." *Another Vietnam!* Was that what B thought? Dad will be in Saudi Arabia for years. That war lasted forever.

"He'll be okay, and maybe this is a good thing. Now, you and Spencer can have some time apart." I pictured Grandma stroking B's back with one hand while her other cradled a mug of coffee.

"Yeah, maybe, but I mean, shit. What if?" B's voice trailed off, and I nearly fell from the couch. B never swore. Grandpa seemed unaware of the conversation in the kitchen. He was mesmerized after learning that a sneaker the sheriff just found might be the key to solving the murder, at least according to Angela Lansbury.

"It won't. That's enough of that," Grandma said.

Between several quiet sobs, B said, "I would give anything, and I do mean anything, to get him back in one piece. I wouldn't wish for another thing as long as I lived. I mean it. As long as he comes back alive, I will be happy for the rest of my life."

"How many years did the Vietnam War last?" I asked Grandpa, diverting his attention away from the TV.

"Look it up." His voice was gruff, annoyed at the interruption.

My eyes traveled the room's perimeter, moving from the wood stove to the bookcase.

"On the shelf." He pointed to a set of encyclopedias on the far wall. As my fingers ran across the spines, Grandpa said, "I forgot, those aren't going to help. They're from '63, when your mother was little. The war barely even started."

My mind returns to the present, and my eyes travel to the letters on the page.

I'm afraid I might lose you and that I'll be alone. We've had our problems lately, and I know I sound pathetic, but please stay safe and come home soon. I need you.

CHAPTER SIX

FOR THE NEXT two weeks, I pretend that I don't know about B's worries. Two weeks of watching TV news analysts suggest that only bullets will force Saddam Hussein from Kuwait. Two weeks of B picking at her dinner, pushing the food around her plate like a two-year-old ordered to eat broccoli. Each morning, she withdraws deeper. By early November, she's barely standing.

Each morning, I expect to see her shoulders hunched and her elbows leaning heavy against the kitchen table, staring into a mug of steaming coffee like it's a black hole.

This morning, B leaps from the hallway, nearly knocking me over.

"Happy Birthday!" she shouts with the energy of a cheerleader. But her smile seems painted, stretching to the edges of her ears, her cheeks straining against the force of an oncoming frown.

"Are you excited?" Her low voice doesn't ascend two notes higher with each word.

She's trying, and I put on my own mask, pretending that I'm a boy who hasn't spent the last two months with a father thousands of miles away and a mother whose thoughts are even further in the distance.

"Do you want your presents?" B palms two blue boxes, each the size of a baseball. My eyes bounce from box to box, acting like a puppy waiting for a treat. Maybe she's trying to compensate for Dad's absence. He usually takes me to the movies every year. Last year, he snuck me into *Indiana Jones and the Last Crusade* despite its PG-13 rating. Either way, she's making an effort.

"Which one should I open?" My head bounces from left to right.

"Doesn't matter." Her voice lacks any brightness.

I concentrate, forcing a smile upward. I put one box on the table and tear at the paper in my right hand like it's Christmas morning. Paper flies in the air like arcing confetti.

B's head twists away, ignoring the mess, her glow fading.

My hand falls. I don't need to keep panting with enthusiasm or staring with wonderment at the dark leather box. The charade is over. A shred of wrapping paper clings to the box's edge by a small remnant of tape.

I open the leather box like a seashell. Inside the second hand of a watch bounces around the silver and white face in jerky movements.

B glances back, the energy from minutes earlier drained, and I rip the paper around the second box, folding it into a flat sheet and placing it neatly on the table. It's another hinged box and inside another watch, except it's digital with a camouflage band. The black numbers blink on a pale green face, but the time is wrong. It's several hours ahead. I strap a watch around each wrist, pumping both fists in the air. "It's the time in Saudi Arabia." Taking two quick steps, I wrap my arms tightly around B's waist. "These are great!"

Her arms hang limply on my back, and she kisses the top of my head but doesn't squeeze. She doesn't promise this will be the best birthday ever or that I'll be a teenager next year. She's slipped into her own world.

I pull back and shoulder my bag for school.

"Grandma and Grandpa are coming for cake later tonight," B says before she pulls out of the driveway so that she'll get to work on time, leaving me alone.

***

I'm well past the age of cupcakes or parties at school, but Mo brings an extra package of Twinkies at lunch. Mrs. A. thwarted his plan of using lighted candles, catching him trying to sneak a box of matches into his bag. Other than Mo, I'm not sure anyone at school knows it's my birthday.

Today in science, we are presenting our projects about different parts of the animal cell. Mikey and Julie talk for five minutes about the cell's powerhouse, the mitochondria, while pointing to a large potato-looking piece of construction paper.

Last night, Mo and I constructed our DNA model by painting marshmallows with blue, red, green, and yellow frosting and linking them with Twizzlers. I pretended to act intrigued as we read about the helical structure of DNA while picturing Dr. Taylor's twisted fingers.

When it's our turn, Mo explains how the marshmallows in the center are the different nucleotide bases, and I describe the twisting helix and that DNA contains all the genetic information that codes who we are.

Jackson VanPatten raises his hand. "Does the DNA twist that much?"

I wait for the snide remark, for the moment his question changes into a veiled insult. But he actually seems interested. Maybe he isn't always so evil. I explain that DNA twists every ten bases, a fact I learned from the encyclopedia in the library.

Mrs. Trayne thanks us and lowers her head, writing notes on our grading sheet as I carry our model to the back of the room.

With one step forward, the DNA model held in my outstretched hands, my left foot hits something in the middle of the aisle. My breath and heart catch as my eyes widen, losing my balance; the DNA arcs high into the air. Tumbling forward, I glance down, trying to catch my balance, and see Jackson withdraw his foot safely under his desk. The DNA model lands on the floor in a splat, ripping apart pieces of marshmallow and Twizzler. I try to catch my balance, but I'm too far forward and twist, falling on my side.

The camouflage watch smacks first and splinters against the floor as my body lands hard on the model, sections of soft marshmallow and frosting squishing beneath my weight. Pushing to my knees, a multicolored pattern of frosting crusts my shirt.

Jackson flashes a malicious grin.

I want to be Colossus. I want to change into the Hulk. I want the strength to stand up to Jackson and defend myself. But the spiderweb cracks on the face of my Army watch deflate any bravado. The blinking black numbers from the corner are gone. The green background is dark.

I feel for the security of my inhaler, breathing faster. Tears work to the corners of my eyes. Frosting on my shirt and pants drops in clumps at my feet with a splat, and in the back, Margaret Rucker laughs.

"What happened?" Mrs. Trayne faces the class.

Jackson stands and points at me. "He tripped on my desk," and quickly lowers himself back into his seat. The case made. The truth rewritten.

Mrs. Trayne's head tilts to the side. "Oh. Ethan, I'm so sorry."

Two feet stomp, cutting short her soothing words.

"That's not true." Mo's stiff arms press to his side like a toy soldier. He points to Jackson. "That big jackass tripped him."

Mrs. Trayne gasps, concealing her mouth with a hand. Her head jerks ramrod straight, and her eyebrows draw together. "Mohamed!" His name spoken sharp. "I am certain that Jackson would never do such a thing, and *you*," she emphasizes the word "you" for several seconds, "you, young man, can march to the principal's office and explain the language you used in my classroom."

On shaky legs and with a trembling voice, still breathing heavily, I echo, "It's true. Jackson tripped me."

I can't believe I'm speaking, but Mo is defending me. Standing straight, I step toward him so we are shoulder to shoulder. The two of us. The Stooges.

Mrs. Trayne squints at all three of us before her gaze lands on Jackson. "Jackson, did you trip, Ethan?"

Jackson sits upright. His hands folded neatly on his desk. "No, Mrs. Trayne. I wouldn't do that." Jackson shakes his head, emphasizing his innocence.

"I thought not." Mrs. Trayne crosses her arms.

Jackson continues, "But I'd be happy to help you clean up Ethan's mess." He tilts his head to the side just a little.

I can almost see Mrs. Trayne drawing a halo over Jackson's head and patting the angel wings that she sees sprouting from his back.

"That's very nice of you, Jackson."

Mrs. Trayne's head swivels, and her once smiling face turns sour as she refocuses on Mo. "Mohamed, I told you to go to the principal."

No matter the superhero, I'm powerless. I don't have the strength to defend myself. I don't have the power to protect my friend.

Mrs. Trayne's finger points to the door, and with a heaving sigh, Mo lowers his head and shuffles out.

Mo's back is barely through the door before Mrs. Trayne turns on me. "Perhaps you should tell the truth next time instead of defending your friend. Go to the bathroom and clean up."

"But—" I stammer as a small piece of frosting plops from my shirt to the floor.

"Go!" Mrs. Trayne points her finger toward the door.

I use my hand to push the remaining globs of frosting into the bathroom garbage, but the light blue and green stain smears across my shirt. All I can smell is the too-sweet smell of sugary frosting.

I can wash my shirt. But the watch, the gift from B, so I know the time in Saudi Arabia, is beyond repair. My throat constricts, but it isn't asthma.

Ignoring Mrs. Trayne's instructions, I head to the principal's office. Mo's outstretched legs extend into the hallway, while his body slumps in a chair. Above his head, the picture of Mr. VanPatten looks down with a smirking expression.

"Curly, what are you doing?" Mo's voice lacks its usual snap. The punchiness deflated.

"I came to tell the principal what happened." I try to sound confident. If Mrs. Trayne doesn't believe me, maybe Principal Andrews will.

Mo's head jerks upright. "Don't bother. He's already called my mom. He didn't want to hear that Jackson isn't perfect." Mo smirks. "Mr. Andrews even told me *my kind* always tries to start a war."

"Your kind?"

"Helloooo," Mo draws out the word, "You know. Your father's in the Middle East. Saddam Hussein invaded Kuwait. I'm Arab."

There's anger in his voice. Mo was telling the truth and getting in trouble. What's worse is that now Mo's going home, not for what he did, but because he's Arab. Would Mr. Andrews have sent me home?

"If you're hungry, I saved you some frosting." Pushing forward my shirt and a speck of green frosting, "If you don't like what's in the front, there's probably more on the back sleeve."

Looking up from his Nike's, the anger melts from Mo's face. For the first time, my friend, the comedian, laughs so hard that he coughs.

"I'm gonna need your inhaler," he says between cackles. "You're alright, Curly. Get back to class before they call your mother."

***

At home, I huddle on the porch steps, looking past the pages of my new book, *The Lion, the Witch, and the Wardrobe*, with my knees bent and elbows resting heavy on my jeans. It's another one of B's books about Lucy fighting the evil white witch.

The sky darkens from gray to black, and the words on the page blur until a car's headlights beam toward our house. The broken watch presses against my thigh, reminding me of the day.

"Ethan," B creeps toward the porch. "You want to talk about it over fries?"

Is it a mother's intuition that she knows something is wrong, or did the school contact her? "I'm not hungry." My eyes focus on the blurry words on the page.

She forces me up. "C'mon, let me change, and we can go to Ronni's."

I nod, hiding my naked left wrist behind my back.

Sitting in the diner booth, I tell B the entire story. How Jackson VanPatten tripped me and destroyed our model, and how Mo defended me but got in trouble.

"This boy, Jackson VanPatten, is his father the lawyer, the one with the commercial on TV?"

"How did you know?" I've never spoken about Jackson or his bullying.

"Lucky guess."

I expect more, but she sighs and reaches across the table to rub my shoulders. "I'm sorry you had a bad day. Jackson, like his father, doesn't sound very nice."

"You know Jackson's father?"

B glances around the diner like she's about to divulge a secret. We're alone except for an older couple drinking coffee and eating pie at the counter. B focuses back on me. "I've met him a few times. Let's say the apple hasn't fallen far from the tree." She reaches across the table squeezing my hand. "It doesn't make it right, but it's who they are."

"It's not who I am," I stammer, paraphrasing B's stock line.

"No, it's not who you are," she leans over the table to hug me from the bench seat. I'm a good person, like Meg and Lucy, the characters in the stories I've read.

***

Back at our house, in the kitchen, we meet Grandma and Grandpa for chocolate cake. My eyes focus on the massive red box on the counter. I can't even imagine what's inside. There's no way Grandpa and Grandma got me a Nintendo, but what else might be so big?

I blow out the candles, and as Grandma slices the cake, B hands me several cards from my Uncle Jack and Aunt JoJo. They both still live in Pennsylvania, where Dad grew up, so I rarely see them. Each card contains a twenty dollar bill, and I feel rich until B plucks the money from my hand, saying it's for my savings account.

"You want the one from us?" Grandpa pulls at the box on the counter. It doesn't budge. B and Grandpa both lift it onto the floor. Pulling back the paper, there's a brown, sealed cardboard box with twenty-two tightly packed books, each with a crimson edge. I pull one of them out from the center, and the box releases a *ffftt* sound. A gold border shines bright on each page in the kitchen light. Across the top, in bold gold letters, I see the title, THE WORLD BOOK ENCYCLOPEDIA. These books hold the answers. It's not a Nintendo, but these volumes contain the answers to my questions. Questions that B answers with, "It's who we are." Questions about a chimera or Saudi Arabia. Questions I can now answer myself.

CHAPTER SEVEN

ENCYCLOPEDIA VOLUMES SPREAD open across the floor. Volume H has a diagram of the heart. There are two sides—one left and one right. Volume B shows the brain, again, two sides. There are two of almost everything—kidneys, lungs, hands, arms, and legs.

Spreading Volume D, the famous work of Leonardo daVinci comes into focus. *The Vitruvian Man*, an example of how the body is symmetric with a line drawn down the center. I imagine my own line. On the left is Dad's side. On the right, there's B's. But there is no mention that people can be chimeras. No discussion of what it might mean. There is only a vague reference to Greek mythology.

***

In mid-January, the coalition forces bomb Iraq. On the news, grainy video of a warehouse or building full of weapons lies in the crosshairs of a Tomahawk missile before the image explodes and goes black. Anti-aircraft guns fill the night sky like green fireflies, but the US fighter jets slip in and out of Iraq without a scratch. When Saddam Hussein fires rockets at Israel, Patriot missiles smack Iraqi SCUDs from the air.

This isn't war. This is a video game. Saddam's army is getting destroyed. This isn't Vietnam. There aren't nightly body counts or pictures of soldiers blanketed in Agent Orange. US soldiers sit hundreds of miles away in a command center on the USS Missouri or in the safety of their barracks. There's no hand-to-hand combat. In a matter of weeks, the destruction will be too much, Saddam will leave Kuwait, and Dad will return home.

B isn't convinced. It doesn't matter that Dad and the US soldiers aren't in harm's way. She flinches, her arms and shoulders contracting tight, with the image of each missile strike.

"Dad isn't near any of the explosions," I remind her. But she doesn't—or can't—hear me.

Dad missed Thanksgiving, Christmas, and New Year's. But he usually works at least two holidays at the firehouse, so this year doesn't feel much different. But the 194 consecutive days he's been away are getting harder. Each night, I etch another imaginary slash into my mind, like a prisoner carving another year into the jailhouse wall.

Writing letters helps, but it's only half the story. I write about the Rubik's Cube I got for Christmas but omit that B didn't open her presents. I include the A-plus on my math test, but don't mention that B didn't get home until after seven that night because of several late appointments, leaving me alone for hours.

Dad received all my letters but has only had time for nine replies. I keep the letters in a pencil case to read each night. In my head, I try to remember how he pronounces words. Instead of *down*, he says *dahn*. There's a phrase he uses sometimes: "It's like I'm trying to herd cats with a pole." But I know that I'm mixing up several of the words.

The gaps in my memory of how he sounds and talks fades. It's like the edges of Dad are fuzzy, like a weird abstract painting. I can see the image, but it's not crystal clear. My new memories are blocks in a wall that replace older crumbling bricks that are gone forever.

Unfolding the crinkled paper, no large black lines strike through sentences or paragraphs. There's no need for censorship, like in the movies. Either the government decided Dad wasn't giving away any secrets, or there wouldn't be spies in central New York.

> *Ethan,*
>
> *Our division decorated a Christmas tree today, but it doesn't feel much like Christmas when it's eighty degrees in the desert. The sand gets into everything. The sand even gets into the fake needles of the Christmas tree, and someone has to sweep the tree every day. Can you believe that? I bet there is probably Saudi Arabian sand in this letter.*

Reading the paragraph, I brush my hand over the page, trying to expose some of the gritty substance, and a tiny jewel of sand catches the light—the smallest of diamonds.

> *We are still just waiting. Bryce, one of my friends, and I play Trivial Pursuit for half the day to pass the time. He's outstanding. He tries to get the others to bet against him. Most of the time, someone takes his bait, and Bryce gets $20.*
>
> *I know you're not the biggest fan of baseball cards, but they circulated some special ones just for us. Enclosed is a pack. Maybe it'll be worth something someday.*
>
> *Anyway, I miss you and your mom. I think you both are going to Grandma and Grandpa's for Christmas again this year. I'll miss you all.*
>
> *Love you, and goodnight.*
> *Dad.*

Carefully, I fold the letter and neatly arrange it with the others back into the box. Dad plays board games. He's sweeping Christmas trees. He's not fighting. He's not in a war; he's only near a war.

***

Shuffling downstairs, B sits on the couch, the remnants of dinner stacked on two plates, the TV trays pushed to the side. "Did you see him?" I ask, already knowing the answer. If B had seen even the resemblance of Dad, her excited screams would have carried to Mr. and Mrs. Henderson's half a mile down the road.

"No." Her deep voice is quiet.

"He's probably busy sweeping the Christmas tree." B doesn't acknowledge my joke. "Or maybe he's playing Trivial Pursuit with Bryce."

She sighs, lifting her shoulders into her neck. "You should be in bed."

"No." Looking into her wrinkled brow, I plead, "I figured you'd want some company. It's not a school night."

"Breaking news tonight," says Tom Brokaw, and we bolt upright. This is it. This is when Saddam admits defeat. Where he surrenders, returns to Iraq, and leaves Kuwait. This is how Dad comes home. This is how B returns to normal; how we will return to normal.

"We bring you to the White House and President George Bush." I squish tight toward B, feeling her warmth. President Bush stands in a tan suit. His voice is clear, and his manner direct.

"Do you think it's over?"

B shushes me and snatches the remote, increasing the volume.

"Good evening," says the president. "Yesterday, after conferring with my senior national security advisers and following extensive consultations with our coalition partners, Saddam Hussein was given one last chance, set forth in very explicit terms to do what he should have done more than six months ago: Withdraw from

Kuwait without condition or further delay and comply fully with the resolutions passed by the United Nations Security Council."

No. No. No. Saddam should be leaving Kuwait. The president isn't smiling. He isn't giving a victory speech. He isn't describing how air strikes have liberated Kuwait.

"I have therefore directed General Norman Schwarzkopf, in conjunction with coalition forces, to use all forces available, including ground forces, to eject Iraq's army from Kuwait."

There it is. What B knew was going to happen. What B was afraid of. Another Vietnam. A ground war. Hand-to-hand combat.

"May God bless and protect each and every one of them, and may God bless the United States of America. Thank you very much."

The image of Tom Brokaw fills the screen. I don't hear anything else, and B doesn't either. The video games are over.

CHAPTER EIGHT

THE NEWS CYCLES the same images of Iraqi soldiers with their hands raised high in the air as tanks roll through the desert sand dunes. Maps show the advancing coalition forces gaining ground over Iraq's retreating army. B doesn't miss a second. In the morning, she still reclines on the couch, a blanket curled around her as the TV emits a soft glow, the volume low. Dark circles rim her barely open eyes. Last night, at four in the morning, when I needed to go to the bathroom, I heard her shaky breaths while watching an Iraqi soldier firing an assault rifle.

Monday morning, I expect B curled in her spot, nearly comatose. As my bare feet touch the cold wooden stairs, it's worse.

She sways back and forth in the kitchen, cradling a spatula. I gag at the smell of eggs burning. There's an updated map on the TV, the arrows show the coalition forces advancing.

B staggers, the spatula hanging limp in her hand, and a small piece of brown crust floats to the floor. "I made eggs. You'll have to buy lunch."

Her voice is hoarse, like she's been smoking cigarettes. She doesn't try to smile.

I can't go to school. I have to stay home. We need to stay home. There's a ground war. School can wait.

B takes my silence as an objection. "You have school. I have work." Her head bobs toward my bag, and I sit at the table and start picking at a piece of brown egg with my fork.

***

At school, Mo slaps the top of my desk. "What's wrong, Curly? It looks like someone just ran over your dog." He bounces in his chair. For him, it's another day in paradise.

I don't look up. Don't even raise my head. "Shut up." My barbed words are sharper than I meant. But he doesn't understand. His family is intact. Even if Mr. and Mrs. A were gone, he'd still have his sister. I have no one.

"Crap, did your dog die? Cause one time, my mom was crying when I got home from school, and I asked, 'Who died?' and sure enough, it was Aunt Tara." Mo shakes his head. "Not my finest moment."

"The ground war." It's the easiest thing to say of all the things in my head. The words feel heavy in the air, like a blanket wrapping tight.

Mo's rambles evaporate, the excited demeanor going flat.

"He'll be okay. Just wait and see. He'll be fine."

He doesn't understand that it isn't just Dad. B is only a shell of her former self. She is more like a zombie than my mother. And there's a part of me still trying to understand if my diagnosis isn't part of why she's so quiet. The visit to Dr. Taylor was essentially at the same time Dad left. Maybe she won't talk to me because she isn't sure what I am. Who I am. Who we are.

At lunch, Mo doesn't try to entertain me with stories about his latest Nintendo conquest or how he's sure that Aia stole his Nerf gun for the fifth time. He only chews a sandwich and silently offers me his cookies.

When the school day ends, I shuffle in line to get on the bus. The engines rumble loudly in the cold air. Mo and Aia stand two lines down. They're about to climb the stairs when Aia breaks away, heading toward me. Mo shakes his head, glancing between his sister and where I'm standing, trying to decide whether he should stay in line.

"Ethan." Aia's face comes into focus, and other students prod me to the side like a pinball. The cold has turned her nose and cheeks red, and two dark braids hang underneath a bright orange hat.

"Your dad will be okay. In fact," she pauses, "I know he will." She touches my arm, her purple glove pressing on the fabric of my jacket.

I swallow, focusing on the weight of her purple fingers. "It's going to be okay," Aia says.

I hear the rumble of the buses again only after she's back in line with Mo, and the kids in the back of my line propel me forward.

At home, I drop my bag by the door and go upstairs, not wanting to turn on the TV alone. I stare at my left thumb, the one that bends backward. My dad's thumb. My father's half. Dad is right now in Saudi Arabia, not Iraq. He's not fighting. He's stationed with the quartermaster. But images of Dad cruising around in a Jeep, clouds of sand rising behind him, are replaced by gunfire and chaos. I imagine Dad ducking behind and underneath a Jeep for cover. Just when the images become too vivid, Aia's hand rests on my forearm, and her voice soothing like a blanket. "It's going to be okay."

The front door shuts, and B shouts, "Sorry I'm late."

Her voice is tired but not defeated. I sprint down the stairs, taking two at a time, nearly tripping over her black purse, and darting into the kitchen.

B kisses me as she jogs past. "Can you turn on the TV?"

Pots rattle against one another in the kitchen. On TV, there is a picture of a burning warehouse. I swallow hard, trying to get the words out. Force them from my throat. It's only a croak. The muffled sound silenced by the noise of water hitting the bottom of a large stainless-steel pot.

"Where's Dad stationed?"

B sways into the living room, opening a box of spaghetti. "Ethan, you know that!" She pauses. "In Dhahran." Her words trail off into almost a whisper as she looks at me and then at the TV. The box of pasta plummets, dried noodles scattering to the edges of the room, and she shrieks, confirming what I already know.

The TV screen is split. On the left, Jane Pauley sits behind a news desk; on the right, Tom Brokaw stands in the desert. The caption reads *Dhahran, Saudi Arabia*. Tom Brokaw's image is replaced by burning wreckage. "A dozen are dead, and more than forty are missing as a SCUD missile made a direct hit on an Army barracks."

B steps back into the kitchen doorway. Her blue scrubs pull tight as she leans against the white door casing. Her body angles to the side, but her wide eyes remain fixed on the TV. A tremor overtakes her, first on her lower lip, then descending into her arms, and finally, her legs that look like teetering stilts.

I gulp, trying to swallow my thoughts, but they keep returning. *Dad is in Dhahran.* "I knew it," B mumbles. "I knew it." She swallows, breathing heavier.

"Mama," my voice cracks as she slides down against the door frame, her legs bent and her head hanging loosely to the side.

Hurdling from the couch, I cup her face between my hands and see the black centers of her eyes as small as pen tips. "Mama," I yell, hoping she'll hear my screams.

B collapses to the floor, and I am alone. The phone hangs from the kitchen wall, its white cord a possible lifeline. I yell again, my mouth nearly touching her ear.

She answers only in deep gasps, the kind I have after an asthma attack. There isn't enough air in the world to fill her lungs, and she's begging for more. Her face slumps forward before she crawls across the living room floor. The yellow shag carpet shifts underneath her weight, rippling like a tide pulling her toward the couch.

The news shifts to reports at the Pentagon about a possible ceasefire brokered by the Soviet Union. *Why didn't they continue with the story from Dhahran? Why stop reporting? People are dead. Soldiers are dead.* I can't finish my next thought and clench my teeth and bolt my eyes shut to block it from my mind. Despite my efforts, the idea weasels its way into my brain. *Dad is—*

I glance toward the living room wall. In my parents' wedding photograph, Dad and B smile back.

The news coverage continues about the Soviet peace negotiations and how the president played paddleball when he learned about the proposal. Dad might be dead, and Tom Brokaw wants to talk about the president playing paddleball? B must feel the same way. She's bent, her shoulders slump forward like her backbone has been surgically removed, and she is now only a blob of jelly.

Tom Brokaw returns to the entire screen, and my body goes numb. "This is what happened. A SCUD missile made a direct hit on the barracks of a corps of Army reservists tonight. We don't know the unit, but twelve were killed, and forty are missing."

Reservists. Not Marines, not enlisted men. Dad is a reservist in Dhahran. I glance back at the picture on the wall, willing Dad to shake his head and explain why it wasn't his group.

The TV screen shifts to an image of the night sky. It's cloudy, and a few lights from the city below reflect upward. It could have been Syracuse. It could have been anywhere. The camera begins focusing on the tiniest blip. It's an insignificant gray image, which might be only static, but the camera pans toward the ground below, remaining centered on the blip. Bright lights glisten, reflecting off the tall buildings. It seems like a peaceful evening until a siren wails. Not like a fire whistle that increases and decreases in pitch and intensity. A constant high-pitched whine. The kind of sound that even thousands of miles away instills panic.

I picture the people running from the sound of that siren, unable to see the dropping object. The blip descends, and I imagine Dad sprinting for safety, searching for a building, a doorway, or a shelter.

The siren stops, or at least I stop listening. A fireball erupts on the TV screen, reaching high into the air. Orange and yellow collide with the night sky, which retreats only for a moment before turning most of the city black. Only a dull flicker of orange remains on the screen.

There's a stillness on the TV and in our living room. My eyes focus on the images, afraid to keep watching and scared to twist away. I close the short gap between B. She's breathing heavy through her nose. Her mouth clenches tight. Maybe she thinks if she opens it, she'll scream again. My hand, still probing, grazes her wedding ring, and she recoils.

The scene twists from a skyline view to a building enveloped by flames that kick high into the night sky. In a frantic tone, a voice over the burning wreckage says, "The whole thing's gone. I mean, anyone in there is wounded or dead."

Wounded or dead. Not injured, or most got out in time. *Didn't they hear the siren? Couldn't they hear it? Were they sleeping?* I look away from the TV at B. *Is that what she's thinking too?*

"How many were inside?" says an unknown female voice while flames rip into the night.

"One hundred thirty, maybe. There were a bunch for sure from my unit that are gone."

Which unit? Tell me the unit. Just tell me that it wasn't from the Fourth Quartermaster. B remains motionless.

"That was a survivor." Images flood the screen like waves, pounding into my head. A parade of ambulances rush the injured toward a hospital. Sirens pleading for help. Footage of the wreckage, lit by spotlights, shows soldiers and townspeople frantically combing through the debris. Cement and dust spread everywhere as the building's twisting metal frame tries desperately to retain some form. Soldiers scramble over the wreckage, heaving pieces of rubble, searching. But for what? Belongings? Their fellow soldiers? The images come like punches from Jackson VanPatten, my stomach reeling from a blow to the gut, Jackson's elbow smashing my back.

B screams, her hands reaching up to shield her face while her feet stomp the ground in protest; the footage pans to a large blood stain on the cement. The red blood billows out like an obscene cloud, accompanied by shards of glass and what might be a canteen. It is too much. Too many images. All at once. An explosion, burning, the mangled wreckage. The lines on B's face grow deeper, turning into a never-ending crevasse.

Now, the image of a man, a soldier, or a Saudi, lying on a gurney breathing heavily. The screen shifts again to a soldier wrapped in a blanket. Then, just as quickly, it's over. That story is finished, and the following report about the progress of the ground war begins.

"Why did you stop?" I plead toward the TV, both regretting that there isn't more footage and thankful at the same time. There are too many images. Too many pictures all brought in at once. We both sit silent. *America at War* fills the screen as the news changes to a commercial.

CHAPTER NINE

B'S HANDS CLASP tight around her stomach while her shoulders hunch forward. Her vacant eyes stare at the same thirty minutes of cycling footage. Only the shallow movement of her chest suggests that she's alive.

I'm no better. Our legs almost touch, but I can't move my limp hands to reach her. I'm staring at the TV but only picture the crimson mark on the cement. I imagine the bloodstain becoming wider until all I can see is red. My tongue swells, filling my mouth and choking off my words.

This is why B worried. I focused on the Tomahawk missiles striking Saddam's army and the Patriot missiles intercepting SCUDs. There weren't body counts or images of soldiers exhausted from fighting. This wasn't Vietnam. It was a game, just like the videos at Mo's house. The good mutants were heroes and won. There weren't casualties. There wasn't destruction. B was right. A war is no game.

A ringing sound repeats, and my limp arms tuck in tight, remembering the warning siren on the TV. I think about pulling B to the floor, afraid of an incoming missile. She's so far away from our living room she can't hear the noise, lost in the shadows that have left her eyes blank and empty.

Stumbling, I break through the fog, heading toward the ringing phone. B springs off the couch, shoving me away and hurtling toward the kitchen like she's on fire. I blink back the confusion of B's quick movements and sway, using my hands to steady myself.

B claws at the phone, frantically pulling it off the wall. I hang suspended between the TV on one side and B, gasping a "Hello" on the other. She sighs like a deflating balloon heading toward the hall, but like a dog on a leash, the taunt cord prevents her escape. Spaghetti noodles crack and crunch beneath her feet like dried leaves as she leans into the wall.

She exhales loudly. "Yeah, it's where he's stationed." The words tumble out like crumbling pavement, forming a pile of rubble at her feet.

"I don't know." B clutches herself, her voice rising hot, and the coils of the phone line straighten.

This woman isn't my mother. Not right now. She isn't calm and quiet. I don't know what to say or how to act. I want to hug her. I want her to hug me. But I'm suspended. My head recoils between B's conversation and the TV like two rackets slamming a tennis ball across the net.

"Our chief military correspondent," announces Tom Brokaw, who knocks me back toward B.

"I know, Mom, I'm trying." B smashes me toward the TV.

"What we know right now is that Saddam Hussein—"

B sighs heavily. "No, stay home."

B ends the call, the volley stops, and I sink deep into the couch cushions. If Dad never comes home, B will fold deeper into herself, and I'll be alone. I want B to return to the couch, but she bends, grasping at the broken spaghetti from the floor. Our eyes connect, and I plead with her to sit beside me. But she looks away, returning to her task.

I can't sit here. I won't sit here, and I bounce from the couch to gather a small bouquet.

"Two peas in a pod," B says as she softly carries a handful toward the trash. Is this who my family is now—just the two of us?

"I'll pick up the rest."

Her words are a punishment. I want to be with her. I need to be with her, not sent away to another room. My lip trembles.

"Just give me a minute," she assures me. "I'll make some dinner."

I stare at Dad's lounge chair. The dark edges of the TV stretch toward the front door, and the shadow of the table lamp extends into the kitchen. I cuddle into the chair, pressing my face tightly into the fabric. There is a faint scent of Old Spice aftershave and a whiff of smoke. I imagine his trim mustache forming a dark line above his mouth, and my gaze floats to the family pictures on the wall. There aren't many, but the largest frame shows Mom and Dad each clutching me tight in front of the oak tree in the yard. We had moved into the house only two weeks earlier. My father couldn't get a job as a history teacher when he finished school, so he took the civil service exam. B had two months to set up the house and the nursery, but I arrived five weeks early; the house was in disarray, and the only spot for a picture was outside.

I pick at my sandwich, pulling off the crust. B does the same, pulling the food apart, like our unraveling family. "Who called?" knowing the answer but unable to stand the silence. It's like we're at the ocean, and B is underwater. Her edges are fuzzy, and her arms and legs sway gently back and forth as imaginary waves crash into her.

"Grandma." She softly swallows a crumb. "You should go write your letter."

I can't write my letter. If I leave, B will lock herself in her room. B's sharp voice stops my shaking head. "Write your letter."

Fighting back the tears, I carry my plate to the counter and slowly creep toward my room. Shadows leap from the edges of the living room, like wild animals ready to pounce. In the kitchen, B's head hangs in her hands.

In my room, my hand twitches as the pen scratches the paper. I can't form any words, all my pen can form are the jagged teeth of a saw blade. After a third attempt, I chuck the paper across the room.

Creeping downstairs, I wail, "B?"

There's no answer. The light next to Dad's recliner casts a long shadow in the room. Slumping into the chair and curling sideways, I press my nose into the fabric, closing my eyes beneath the pictures, thinking it's who we are, hoping it's not who we *were*.

CHAPTER TEN

SUNLIGHT POURS THROUGH the rattling porch window. My neck, still stiff from sleeping in the chair, refuses to straighten, and the blanket from my room, which I hadn't brought downstairs, twists around my legs, pinning me in place.

"Just open the door," a voice on the porch urges.

Freeing myself and using the blanket like a cape, a heavy yawn stretches my mouth wide, and the memories of last night return—the explosion, the siren, the bloodstain. Flinging the door open, several feet of fresh snow coat the lawn, and Grandma and Grandpa stand covered in fresh flakes. Lurching forward, I wrap my arms tight around each of them. They don't flinch, and Grandma rubs my back in short, circling motions that feel warm despite the cold draft. She escorts me inside, my fingers digging into her jacket, as Grandpa closes the door with a click.

Grandma must see the tearstains and the crinkled skin of my cheek that was pressed against the chair's fabric all night. She squeezes me tighter before leaning back. Her graying curls point in every direction from underneath her wool hat.

"What can I do?" She doesn't pretend that I don't know what happened. That I don't know whether Dad is alive. That B isn't awake, and her bedroom door is locked. That I've been alone all night.

"I . . . I'm hungry."

Grandma opens a bag, releasing the smell of cinnamon, and hands me a still-warm pan.

"Your mother's sleeping?" Her voice is sharp but not scolding. Her hands rest on her hips. She doesn't wait for an answer. She shakes her head, muttering, "Ever since she was a little girl. Runs and hides."

Grunting, Grandma marches toward the bedroom with the tenacity of a drill sergeant.

Grandpa pulls a knife from the drawer. "I owe you one, kid." He cuts himself a large square. "Grandma said I needed to wait for you to eat."

He hands me a plate, already chewing on his first bite.

I pull the larger clumps of cinnamon crumble off the top, popping one in my mouth and letting it dissolve.

When Grandma emerges with B, she suggests that Grandpa and I construct a fort in the snow. He's wearing jeans and a sweater, not exactly clothes for outside, but he tells me to change and meet him at the door.

I prop the bedroom door open, slowly putting on wool socks as I hear B recap what I already know. There are still no injury or death reports.

"As long as they don't pull up in a car, right now, no news is good news." Grandma's voice cracks like she hiccups mid-sentence. "But you can't be hiding in your room like a little schoolgirl," Grandma chides.

"Mm-hmm."

"Ethan needs you. He has questions. He will have questions. You still haven't talked to him about what Dr. Taylor said, have you?"

I'm bent over, my left leg in my pants, my right dangling out. I don't breathe. Downstairs, a chair scrapes against the kitchen floor.

"He doesn't think about that anymore. That was months ago."

"But you haven't talked with him? He's different, Phoebe."

My hand leans against the bed and prevents me from falling. I'm short and have two different colored eyes. Jackson VanPatten told me that I'm different from day one. Grandma never has.

"I know, but I don't know what it means," B answers. "No one does. Not even Dr. Taylor. The thought that he was once a set of twins and that one of them died—"

There's a long pause before, in a quieter voice, B says, "Did the one die because of me, or were they fighting and—" B's voice trails off.

I think about Mo and Aia struggling for control. Aia blocking the TV while Mo plays Nintendo. Mo kicking Aia under the table.

I'm embroiled in my thoughts when Grandpa yells, "You ready?"

***

At the door, he buttons his jacket tight to his chin. He follows behind me, dragging a shovel, snow sticking to his knees, and we dig a pit. Well, I do most of the shoveling. Grandpa stands and watches.

"Grandpa." Plumes of my breath puff away in heavy pants along with the shovelfuls of snow. "What does 'no news is good news' mean?"

His gaze moves from the road, his breath forming a small cloud before melting away. Clearing his throat, he looks me in the eye. "Do you also want to know what happens if a uniformed officer pulls up in a car?"

My shovelful of snow stops mid-air. The wet snow gets heavier, and my shaking arms drop. Grandpa takes several steps along the path. He puts a hand on my shoulder and squeezes tightly under my winter coat. "I know a lot is going on. And I know your mother is having a hard time." He sighs, and I'm not sure if he will yell at me for snooping or answer my questions.

"But if you have questions, need to talk to someone, or are worried about your mom, you can call me. Do you understand?"

I nod solemnly, but I'm not sure if he will answer.

"'No news is good news' means that if you haven't heard anything, that's good because it's usually bad news that comes first."

His hand grips my jacket, tightening his lips. "And if a uniformed officer arrives at your door," his voice catches, and he glances to the sky. I follow his gaze and find the sun shining brightly down. "They usually don't have good news."

We haven't ever had these conversations. Most of the time, Grandpa sits on the couch, out of the way, while B and Grandma chat.

"What else?"

From behind him, the curtain of the front window shifts. I don't think Grandma notices that I'm watching her, and as she moves aside, B's mouth tries hard to curl upward but can't lift the weight. B's face dives into Grandma's chest, and the curtain returns.

***

We abandon our snow fort, or snow pit, for hot chocolate. Grandpa wears a pair of Dad's pants and socks, and the two of us drop marshmallows into the steaming mugs, watching them dissolve.

When the phone rings, B pounces toward the kitchen, but her face slumps after she says, "Hello." She hands me the receiver. "It's for you."

I nearly burn my throat, swallowing down a large gulp of hot chocolate. Apart from family on my birthday, I'm not sure anyone has ever called the house before asking to talk to me.

"Only five minutes, okay?" B says, handing me the receiver.

I clutch the receiver, bringing the cold plastic to my ear, "Hello?"

"Curly? Are you okay?" Mo pauses, and from the crunch on the other end of the phone, he must be in the middle of an afternoon

Dorito snack.

"I mean, you weren't at school today." Mo pauses, and the crunching abruptly stops. "Is your dad okay?"

"I don't know. There was a missile." My throat tightens.

"It's gonna be okay, Curly. You'll see."

CHAPTER ELEVEN

IT TAKES TWO days for the sun to eat into the snow. The mounds shrink, leaving several piles like sentries at the driveway's edge. When cars rumble down the road, B rushes to the window and shifts the curtain with a shaking hand, but no cars stop in the driveway. When the phone rings, B clutches hopelessly at the receiver, but it's only Grandma.

Nineteen soldiers have been confirmed dead. An Army official contacted those families. But who is unaccounted for or injured still isn't known. The news only discusses the aftermath of the war, primarily the oil fires set by the defeated Iraqi army. The missile attack on the US Army base has been forgotten. Except for our family, the world has moved on, and B tells me to get ready for school.

I want to push back but don't have the energy.

**

Mo must see my flat expression at school and talks to fill the quiet.

"So yesterday," Mo says as he removes his jacket as we head to our desks, "I was going to play *X-Men*, and the Nintendo wouldn't turn on. I'm pushing the buttons and nothing. Dad notices the cord that connects to the TV is gone. I mean, it's completely gone. Not like pulled out or wriggled loose. So Dad yells for Aia because, clearly, who else could it be?"

In the corner, Mrs. Trayne tosses me a pitying glance. Mo's arms roam back and forth like he's searching for the cord before his hands rest on his hips, imitating his father. Mo tries to distract me, but everything he says is a reminder of how my world is different. I'm a short genetic freak whose father might be dead. No one in this school or even this country is as different as I am now.

"So, she comes downstairs all innocent," Mo continues, "and Dad lets her have it. He yells at her that it's not her place to take the cord and that the Nintendo is for the family. She starts bawling, and Dad doesn't fall for it. He keeps yelling at her until, finally, she hands it over."

I try to appear interested as he keeps talking about how he's hoping to get this new game called *Gyruss* for his birthday in a few months.

I remain in a haze for the entire day. Mo keeps me propped up and tries to convince me to take the bus home with him, but I decline.

In my room after school, after an hour, I still haven't completed the second math problem from my homework. When the front door clicks, I sprint down the stairs, praying for good news.

B shakes her head and softly says, "Still no news," and drags herself into the bedroom. Dejected, I return to mine. There's no point in turning on the TV. The war is over. Coalition Forces won. Finished. We have dinner in the kitchen. The two of us play with our casserole, leaving most of the food on the plate.

***

My reading light is on, which casts my shadow against the wall when B frantically thrashes me awake. Tears stream down her face. Rubbing my eyes, it's 3:32 a.m.

"I yelled for you!" B exclaims, bouncing on her toes. "I yelled Ethan three or four times, but you didn't wake."

I'm still not sure what's happening. "Your father!" she says, and now I'm awake.

"He's okay! He wasn't in the barracks. He was on guard duty when the missile hit. He's okay!" B screams in delight.

CHAPTER TWELVE

BY THE FOLLOWING week, B hums, her head bobbing to a beat while she cooks breakfast. She doesn't hand me a cereal bowl and, instead, greets me with a smile and a plate of French toast. She doesn't bury herself in her room after work, leaving me alone to read in mine. She asks for help making dinner, and instead of silently listening to the news, we sit in the kitchen talking about our day over baked chicken.

With the war over and the announcement of Dad's arrival within a few weeks, B's stress and worry have vanished. She has returned to me, the other pea in my pod. There's no more discussion about the war or my chimera diagnosis. They are like a cut. We've bandaged over the wounds, and they will heal. Those things are in the past. Those things are part of our lives that we won't revisit.

Even though B and I have returned to normal, how Dad will fit into our new routine is fuzzy. Our current schedule has replaced my memory of the day-to-day events that included him. It's like we moved forward, and Dad is stuck in last year. Before he left, I never read in my room after school or went to Mo's house for the afternoon. But just like when he misses a day working at the firehouse, Dad will slip like a brick back into the foundation of our lives.

Days before Dad arrives, B cleans the house, pulling six months of cobwebs from the corners of each room. We construct a bright yellow *WELCOME HOME* banner for the porch and invite Grandma and Grandpa for tacos, Dad's favorite.

I press my face to the glass at the airport, as each plane lands but taxis to another gate. Finally, a plane slowly rotates toward Gate 12, and a wave of bodies jostles tight against the windows. There's excitement as families wait for the soldiers to get off the plane.

When the jetway doors unlock, the airport erupts. Forcing my way back against the sea of people next to B, we bounce, trying to see over the crowd to locate Dad. I've grown an inch or two since he's been gone, but I'm not tall enough. There are hugs and tears, and families join together in locked arms toward the exit. I can see down the corridor toward the plane as the wave of passengers dwindles to a trickle. Then, the pilot, in a crisp uniform, strides out.

Did Dad miss the flight? B scans nervously through the crowd. Maybe we missed him? Maybe he was camouflaged behind some of the other passengers and went downstairs to baggage?

B's eyes go wide. She must see him. I sprint toward the jetway, following the direction of B's gaze. After four strides, I trip over my feet. Dad paces in short, slow steps. Creases line his face, and his trim mustache is haggard. He's in his uniform, but he no longer stands tall. When we meet, I want him to cling tightly to both of us. Instead, we hang onto him like ornaments on a sagging Christmas tree.

He's tired, that's all. We cancel dinner because of the long flight from Saudi Arabia. Grandma and Grandpa can visit another night.

***

Two weeks later, the banner hangs still on the porch. Dad sleeps odd hours, waking in the early morning and keeping the house dark because of a never-ending headache. "Just an adjustment period. He's been away for so long," B says. "Grandpa had an adjustment period when he returned from Korea."

I ask Dad if he wants to go to the movies.

"Not today. Ask tomorrow."

After two weeks, I stop asking.

Over dinner, he tells stories from Saudi Arabia instead of his outrageous fire calls; I ask what happened during the airstrikes, the ground war, or the SCUD missile attack? B leans close to him or massages his shoulders, and he shrugs. "Not much to say. We were either on guard duty, standing in the hot sun, or playing cards. Playing anything to pass the time."

***

Near the end of the school year, after lunch, Mo asks, "How's having your dad back?" I want to tell him that it's great. He's home and working again at the firehouse, but the odd hours make it even harder for him to sleep. The broken Lego on my bookshelf reminds me of Dad's sleepless nights.

The sun casts my shadow onto the ground next to Mo's. They're nearly touching and almost equal since I've grown another two inches. I appreciate my shadow. Most of the time, shadows are dark or sometimes evil. Mine is a silhouette that casts only an outline without any of my detailed features. My shadow looks the same as Mo's and the same as any of the kids in class. It's normal.

"Good," my silhouette takes another step forward.

"Good? Your father was in a war, an Iraqi missile hit his unit, and he's back, and things are only good?" Mo shakes his head. "My sandwich was good."

"I just thought things would be back to normal." There's that word again. But the edges of *normal* are fuzzy. "Lately, he's been tired. Which, I guess, happens after being away for so long. The time change messes things up." I think about telling Mo how Dad and B are arguing again. It's only happened twice, about things I couldn't overhear, but I'm almost missing the quiet. When they argue, I shut my door and read.

"Did he have any stories?" Mo's question pulls me from my thoughts.

"He said it wasn't that big of a deal. He mostly complained about the heat and the food. He said the missile attack was terrible, but he wasn't in the barracks."

"Did you tell him about what happened?"

Mo's innocent question causes me to quickly take a puff from my inhaler and then another.

"You okay?"

I nod, waiting for the chalky medicine to calm my nerves. "What do you mean?" The words stick in my throat, afraid that B told Mrs. A., and she explained to Mo that I'm some genetic freak.

"I mean," Mo answers, "all the stuff he missed. How we're friends, about your asthma attack, and how Jackson doesn't bother you anymore."

I'm relieved that he doesn't know. My mouth opens to tell him about who I am. What I am, but just as quickly, I snap it shut.

"Yeah, he knows about all that stuff."

PART TWO

September 1992

"I'm no hero."

— Spencer Rivers

CHAPTER THIRTEEN

MY HAIR HAS a mind of its own. Squeezing gel into my palm, I force the slimy substance against the curls that cowlick on my left side. For a moment, I've won. The hair, heavy with the weight of the gel, remains tamped down. But, like a rising flag, the errant curls shed their temporary position, reaching toward the sky, and I slam the package of gel into the garbage. The left side of my body is going to do what it wants.

There's a crash from downstairs. B could have inadvertently dropped the milk or slammed one of the cabinet doors. It could also have been something else. Something urging me quickly downstairs.

"Where's my father?" I have untethered the word *Dad* from my vocabulary. Dad implies affection; father is biology, something I can't escape. My question, drawn out and slow, is not out of curiosity, but for security.

I've learned how to watch and how to listen. From my room, I focus on the sound of heavy footsteps. Like he can't lift each leg effectively, and the weight of his boot slaps against the linoleum floor. If he's tired, he's irritable, and if he's irritable, he can get angry. When darkness envelopes our house, not just the kitchen or a bedroom, but the entire house, there's trouble. When the lights are off and the shades are drawn, it's a sure sign that his headache is back, so I stay quiet and disappear. Each year, his boots slap a little louder. The house gets a little darker. B and I tread a little more cautiously.

***

I nearly gag from the smell of burned coffee. The pot brewed around 3:30 a.m. was forgotten on the burner again. The curtains conceal the single kitchen window over the sink, letting only a sliver of light slide between them at the center. Like most mornings, I expect to see my father hunched over in the corner seat of the kitchen table, his fingers interlocking, and his hands pressed tightly against the top and sides of his face like a visor. His two or sometimes three days of graying porcupine stubble and unkempt mustache signal us to stay away. Right now, his seat is empty. The room is dark and quiet. If he isn't here, he was.

"He just stepped out," B says. There's a wobble in her voice that sounds like she's trying to talk underwater, forcing the words out. The hitch is worrisome, the hesitation that something isn't right.

I can barely remember when her voice would rise octave over octave as she got excited or happy. Lately, her voice hasn't gone above an alto.

Interrupting my routine and pressing B for answers will force her to hide. Instead, I've learned to work the edges of the problem, one step at a time.

"What are you looking at?"

She doesn't hear me. We're only three feet apart, but entire rooms full of space lay between us. She continues to focus on the narrow gap between the curtains. I assume she's staring at either my father, the shed in the back where he goes after breakfast, or maybe both. Since it's just the two of us, I flick the switch for the overhead light. There's no reason to eat in the dark with him gone. The shadows vanish to the edges of the room, filling the once dreary kitchen with light. For an instant, maybe less than an instant, this is normal.

B vaults and clings tight to the countertop for support. She starts to rotate, but her hands anchor her body which boomerangs back, and her gaze again cements on the gap between the curtains. Her scrubs are unwrinkled, and her hair is in a tight ponytail. On the counter, her lunch sits in a brown bag next to a mug. It's 7:30 a.m. If she doesn't leave soon, she'll be late.

"Are you going to work?" forcing a sidelong glance at B while pulling the Cheerios box from the cupboard. With him gone, I pour a bowl, not caring about the clang of the spoon or the noise as each tiny O drops into the dish.

"Huh. Of course. I'm okay," B answers, still standing at the sink. Her hand gently rubs part of her face, and the moment of normalcy evaporates.

"Beeee," drawing out the syllable like I'm the adult and she's the child hiding something.

"It's nothing. Really." She insists and slowly twists. Her hand hovers over her chin but can't camouflage the strawberry-sized welt. The mark looks angry, extending up her jaw toward her ear. The swelling creates a speed bump on her ordinarily tight jawline, and by tonight, the reds will blend into dark blues and purples.

The air instantly exits my lungs. This time, no matter how much makeup she uses, this bruise will raise questions from everyone she passes. This is a bruise that makes a thousand accusations at once.

All the puzzle pieces assemble—the crash, the absence of my father in the corner, but the lights still off, and B lost in some far-off place.

She tries to curl her lips upward, but the movement of her facial muscles twists her mouth into a grimace. "It's nothing," she repeats and swallows, maybe trying to believe her statement. That, of course, a giant red mark on her face appears on everyone. I wonder if B kept the lights off because she's afraid he's coming back, or so that she won't have to look in the mirror as she leaves.

I leap to my feet, dropping my spoon into the bowl with a clatter, splattering droplets of milk onto the table and closing the gap of space between us. Up close, her chin has tiny scratches that accompany the bruise.

"What happened?" Of course, I know the answer but not the lie she's about to tell.

"It was an accident, really." She shakes her head. She laughs, trying to appear careless. B is many things—a good mother and a great nurse. But she's no actress.

"I was trying to get the grapefruit bowl, and I whacked my chin against the cupboard door." Her voice falters, lacking practice. The repetition of the story, which she'll say in the car, will be more fluid by the time she's at work. The lie will lack a hitch when she's at the supermarket two days from now. By the weekend, after telling her story with increasing conviction, it will replace the truth when she sees Grandma and Grandpa.

"Just clumsy. It looks worse than it is," B lies. Her hand gingerly presses against the side of her face, and her body tenses in response.

It's my silence and inaction that's making her nervous. We both know that though her story is believable, it's fiction.

I should ask, Where's the grapefruit? But she'll tell me she threw it out and already emptied the garbage. If I go outside to check, she'll bury herself in her room or leave for work.

This time, I'm not standing still. I won't let my father keep doing this to us. I feel the courage building inside. "I'm calling Grandpa."

B's head jerks violently in my direction. It's what I threatened last time when she had a bruise on her arm that separated into four lines, one for each of my father's fingers. He wasn't in the room when

I came down the stairs that time either, but the back door slammed. That was two months ago. It's what I wanted to threaten a year ago when she was sobbing inside her bedroom, and the remnants of a beer bottle lay scattered across the living room floor. This time, before I can think, my hand wraps tight around the phone, ready to pull it off the wall. Grandpa will help. Grandpa will take care of this. All I have to do is call.

B's hand gently rests over mine. Her touch is light, and I can still pull the phone from the wall, but she takes a sharp breath. "Please, Ethan," she pauses, "not right now."

I can't stop staring at her chin and the red strawberry poking toward me. If not now, when? My father did this to her—*my father*. The yelling and the arguments were one thing. My father had always yelled at B for one reason or another. Those arguments about everything and nothing happened all the time.

Arguments about money, work, or parts of the house falling apart seem older than I am. I can remember him always being tired and not sleeping. I've held onto the fractured Lego in my bookcase as tightly as I've held onto that memory.

"Please." B exhales. Her green eyes catch mine, or maybe just my right eye, my B eye. Her gaze locks me in place. I want to say, "*Why? Why shouldn't I call for help?*"

B's answer to everything rings in my head. It's who we are. In that instant, my resolve shatters because if it's who we are and who he is, it's part of who I am.

I haven't spoke about my diagnosis for a while. It was something that I wanted to talk about but never did. B was stressed about my father in the middle of a war. My chimera diagnosis wasn't a priority. Eventually, Dr. Taylor switched my allergy medication and gave me a different inhaler. There wasn't much reason to talk about who or what I am. But at times, Dr. Taylor's words hammer in my head. Half of me is like my father, and the other half like B. Split down the middle. Separate halves.

***

A month after my father returned home, Dr. Taylor phoned the house asking if the family wanted to be part of a study. I was upstairs reading and could hear B talking. "I know this is important, but I'm just not sure. You know what happened the first time with all the needles."

I, of course, still hadn't forgotten Nurse Suzy, whose friendly personality was a diversion before an all-out assault.

The kitchen door latched closed. It was almost dinner, and my father was probably coming inside for a beer. "Who are you talking to?"

"Ethan's allergist wants Ethan to be part of a study."

I pictured B cradling the phone away from her mouth.

"For his allergies?" my father asked, his chair scraping against the floor.

"No, no. A genetics thing," B answered. "I told him we're not interested."

She explained my diagnosis. How the doctor thought I had two different sets of DNA. I kept waiting for my father's questions. Instead, he opened the fridge to get another beer. At dinner, he kept staring at me like I had a tumor on my forehead or was sprouting wings. He wasn't mad. He looked puzzled. Maybe he was wondering how he could be the father of a freak, or maybe he was forming a list of his traits on my left side.

"You told him," I said to B the next day.

"It's not that big a deal, Ethan," she answered. From that point forward, I was no longer a normal kid to him. I was different. Days later, he told me to paint part of the house. When my arm started to tire, he told me to brush with my left since it was stronger. Then he would subtly add comments like, "You don't always have to be like your mother. Well, maybe only half of you." Or "Why are you reading so goddamn much? Let my half get a chance." He thought he was being funny, trying to separate my two sides into a his and hers pile of clothes or toys.

Looking at B, with that giant bruise on her face, I remember that half of me is an angry and dangerous man. Half of me comes from a husband who beats his wife. Half of me comes from a father who bullies his son. A man who once took an encyclopedia volume outside with a lighter, threatening to burn it if I slammed the door again. A man who once tripped the breaker in the basement, turning off all the electricity, ensuring complete darkness after we accidentally turned on the lights too many times.

Half of me has a calm temperament. Half of me wants to ignore a problem and pretend everything is fine. Half comes from someone who takes the abuse and tries to smooth things over. Half of me comes from someone who spends the day caring for the sick as a nurse.

"It was an accident. Really, it was." B's voice, soft and even, pulls me out of my thoughts. She's pleading with me that this will work itself out. She will work this out; there is no reason to get Grandpa involved. Except that's what she said last time.

I want to stand firm. I want to do the right thing. I want us to be normal. I want to be normal. But my conviction and resolve crack with B's constant touch and my realization that I want B's half to have control of me. Because if her half isn't in control, then . . .

I shudder and release my grip. This is all wrong, and my hand drops impotently to the side. "Let me get you some ice."

B wraps her arms around me before I put a few ice cubes in a bag wrapped with a towel.

"My boy," she says, placing the ice against her tender chin.

Defeated, I return to my cereal bowl. I'm pretending. Pretending that I don't see what's going on. I know what happened, or at least I can imagine. My father was in the corner, the lights off and shades drawn because that's how he likes the house.

This morning, B probably didn't see him in the shadows, and

God forbid she turned on the lights in the kitchen so she could see. Or maybe she shut the refrigerator door a little too loud. Not so loud that I heard it from my bedroom, but piercing enough to aggravate his headache, making his blue eyes glass over and turn gray. Maybe he roared for his whiskey, Jack Daniels. Perhaps he had already put enough whiskey in his coffee and just finished the mug in a single gulp. Either way, he lashed out, and B took the abuse. When it was over, and my father realized he was responsible, he didn't stay and try to clean up the mess. He didn't get her a bandage or even apologize. He ran like a coward.

After five minutes, B opens a kitchen drawer, pulling out a box of bandages. She rifles through the contents, like someone searching through a stack of coupons, before selecting something large enough to conceal the welt. The bandage masks the injury but creates a chinstrap across the bottom of her face. She looks worse.

She kisses me on top of my head. "You heading to Mo's this morning?"

I've been through this enough to know what she's saying. "Probably." I shrug.

"You should. You only have a few more days before school starts again. I can give you a ride?"

"It's nearly 8 a.m. I'm not sure they're awake, and you're already late."

"Well, I still think you should go." And there are so many things B is saying. That she needs me to go, that I need to go.

"I'll pack a bag after breakfast."

B's face relaxes.

"When will you be home?" We've developed this language. The code that only the two of us understand.

"Four-thirty." she says softly, nodding in agreement.

***

Turning off the lights and leaving the kitchen the way I found it, I wander to the corner of the living room. Several columns of pictures are above my father's recliner, lined up like soldiers in an army. The images record the passage of time, but there's something about them. There's not a single cameo. Not a single impromptu photo of me riding my bike or the three of us at a park. Everything on this wall is scripted.

The backdoor clicks shut. My father won't come upstairs, but my exit is the problem. Sprinting upstairs, I don't have enough time to pack all my things. The second-floor window is too high, and I reject the plan to jump.

Shouldering the backpack that only holds a shirt, I tiptoe down the hall and the stairs. The house is dark, which will provide some cover. I skip over the seventh and ninth steps, so he won't hear them creak, clamp my mouth shut, and inch toward the door. I don't sneak into my house at night after breaking curfew. I need to escape during the day.

My father mutters, "Daniels," and a cabinet opens, probably the one above the fridge where he keeps his whiskey. I want to steal a water bottle but decide against it even though the summer heat is squelching. I clasp the door, hop on my bike, and pedal away.

CHAPTER FOURTEEN

THE EARLY SEPTEMBER sun feels like mid-July. The sky is a clear blue, and there isn't a cloud to shade the heat, which seems to rise from the asphalt in waves. Riding past Henderson's farm, fields of drying cornstalks droop heavy from the hot air.

I already regret not taking water. It would be faster to take Route 173, the main street. But I promised B I'd stick to Howlett Hill and Cherington Drive, the backroads with less traffic. "You're thirteen, not invincible," she said.

After the twenty-minute ride to Mo's house, sweat drips onto his driveway in steady streams, the drops marking a trail from where I left my bike toward the front door.

Snap!

I spin, expecting to see my father barking about leaving the house without letting him know. Of course, that doesn't make any sense. Although he knows where Mo lives, he's never been here.

Next door, the neighbor and his son throw the baseball. "Great pitch," the father says, standing from a squat. He's about forty, clean shaven, and probably doesn't smell of alcohol. He's a postcard for the All-American dad. "Just try and step directly to me next time." The son, maybe nine or ten, goes into a windup, and his pitch snaps into the glove. "That's it."

My feet lock in place, I'm unable to stop gawking. This is how a typical family lives. They probably had breakfast together, the dad drinking coffee and reading the paper while his son ate waffles. The dad lowered the paper and said, "Let's go outside and practice your pitching," and the son ran for his glove.

Last summer, my bike ran over a nail, and I asked my father how to fix a flat.

"Figure it out," he grumbled, heading back to the solitude of his shed.

I did figure it out. I carried my bike four miles, and at the hardware store, the owner showed me how to take off the tire and change the tube.

The back-and-forth sounds of the ball hitting the glove turn silent, and the neighbors return my blank stare. I raise a hand in an awkward wave and rush through the front door, away from their questioning expression.

There are several rules in the Alsoufi household. I'm not sure if the first only applies to me, but if the front door is unlocked, I'm allowed to walk in. My backpack clings to the sweat stains on my shirt, and I take off my shoes to follow the second rule.

Once I'd forgotten and labored through the punishment of vacuuming the entire first floor, Mo's ears flushed red with embarrassment. He kept apologizing. What he didn't understand was that it felt good. Not to vacuum—that was annoying—but receiving a punishment equitable to the crime. There had been no screaming or threat of violence, only Mrs. A. handing me the vacuum from the closet.

Mrs. A. pokes her head out from the kitchen. Her face is warm and inviting like she's been expecting me all morning. "He's upstairs," she says. This family is normal. Mrs. A. didn't wake up scared or worried. She didn't tread lightly around the house, concerned that Mr. A. might become violent. Mr. A. is at work and will return later tonight, tired maybe, but not bitter. He won't take out his day on anyone or yell for his liquor like an old friend.

"Thanks," I say and head toward Mo's room, pausing momentarily in front of the family pictures. Photos of Mo and Aia line the stairway. In each image, they stare away from the camera. There's a picture of Mo playing basketball last year, dribbling toward the hoop for a layup, or Aia playing tennis, the racket moving in a blur at her side. For the Alsoufi family, nothing is scripted.

My heavy footsteps announce my arrival, and Mo yells from the hall.

"Curly?"

Mo's room is to the left of the stairs next to the guest bedroom his grandparents sometimes use. To the right are two rooms, one is his parents, and the other is Aia's, whose door opens a crack.

I drop my backpack and slump into Mo's bright orange beanbag chair. Mo, like most of the city, is obsessed with Syracuse University. His room for the past year has been a shrine to the Syracuse Orange basketball team. Wrinkled posters of Derrick Coleman and Coach Jim Boeheim flank either side of his bed.

"You're here early." Mo's focus remains on the screen, trying in vain to destroy the enemy in *Mortal Kombat*. Blood splatters across his player's face.

I look away, thinking of my father's uppercut connecting with B's chin. Images of her erupting welt come haunting back. "B's at work."

The opposing ninja delivers a spinning kick, knocking Mo's player to the ground. *Game Over* floods across the screen.

Mo sighs, unfazed by the violence, and tosses the controller to the side. I swallow, still thinking of B.

"I said, what do you want to do today?" Mo asks. "You spaced out there for a minute."

Pretending to clear the cobwebs, I wobble my head. "I don't know. We've only got a few days before school."

Mo grins, and I'm in trouble. There's something about that grin. Not devilish or troublesome. Conspiratorial. His grins come with ideas, *most* of which are harmless.

"You know that apartment complex up the street?" His eyebrows flicker.

The gray two-story buildings were more like a neighborhood than an apartment complex. "Yeah," I say, knowing it's Mo's favorite place to ride his bike but wondering what he's thinking.

"Well, I want to go swimming, and they have a pool. We know that Mr. Jensen lives at 124. He's that new guy my dad works with, remember? I say that we pretend to be his nephews." Mo steps back, expecting me to punch holes in his plan.

"We don't look like brothers." Mo's skin is the color of caramel and has at least thirty pounds on my string pole body.

"Oh, we're not brothers. We're cousins." He stands smiling, enjoying the victory over round one.

"I don't have my suit or a towel."

Mo starts his victory lap, given the strength of my second objection. "You can borrow one of mine." He pauses for a second in case there's any further rebuttal and says, "C'mon, it'll be fun."

Creeping toward the stairs, Aia pops her head around the corner. "Where are you going?"

"Bike ride," Mo takes another step, pulling my arm forward.

"Then why do you have towels?" Aia's arms cross.

We freeze halfway down the next step.

Mo can sweet-talk his way out of almost everything, but Aia is the one person who can call him out. He looks at me, failing to explain why we need towels on a bike ride. Mrs. A. is still in the kitchen, just a short distance away. Any louder and she'll hear.

"We're going to that new apartment complex to swim," I whisper. Mo shakes his head, suggesting that he didn't know what to say, but the truth wasn't it.

"I'll come," Aia answers, and Mo shoots me a glance. "Gimme a minute. We can stop for sandwiches." Aia's door closes. She emerges minutes later ready to go, wearing a pair of green shorts and a T-shirt.

At this point, she's either going with us or telling Mrs. A.

Stuffing towels in my backpack, we tell Mrs. A. we're heading out for a ride, which technically isn't lying, Mo reminds me as we pedal away.

***

The apartment complex is only a few miles from Mo's house, but we're drenched in sweat when we arrive. Casually, maybe too casually, we parade toward the lifeguard, who leans back on a folding chair. Mo is almost swaggering, his shoulders moving up and down and back and forth. Aia fires me a look.

"You guys don't live here," says the lifeguard, leaning back in his white folding chair.

"We're staying with our uncle for a few days, and he said we could use the pool," Mo says confidently.

The lifeguard lowers his sunglasses onto his nose. Apart from the dark glasses, he appears nothing like a lifeguard. He seems a year or two older than us, but weighs probably as much as me. If someone were drowning, he could call 911 and hope one of the other pool-goers had the strength to pull the victim from the water.

"You look like you've been riding awhile," the lifeguard says, eyeing the noticeable sweat stains on our shirts.

"Yup. We all went for a ride to get good and hot before the swim." Mo's voice remains confident and unfazed by the inquisition.

"What's the tenant's name?" The lifeguard tilts his head suspiciously.

"Uncle Peter."

Mo is so much better at this. I would have said Mr. Jensen, which would have been a dead giveaway.

"Did he fill out the waiver?" asks the lifeguard.

Our pool oasis is getting pulled away because of some paperwork. On cue, Mo stands proud. "Of course. He handed it into the office on Friday." Mo points to the building next to the pool, the windows dark.

The lifeguard nods toward the clipboard. "Just be sure to sign in and out, okay?"

"Sure thing!" Mo pushes out his chest, and we follow our leader onto the majestic palace of the pool deck.

We toss our towels on two chairs and jump in, our eyes stinging from the chlorine. The water is cool, and we take turns cannonballing. Aia finds a lounge chair in the corner, periodically wading in and out of the water before returning to read a magazine. We eat the subs from the convenience store we bought on our way, and it's late afternoon when Mo announces he's going to the bathroom. Left alone, I towel off and sit in one of the chairs next to Aia.

She's reclining, her sunglasses shielding her eyes, and her ankles crossed. Her purple bikini top has shifted, exposing the tan lines on her chest. I want to look away but don't. "I'm glad you came." Despite what Mo kept muttering, she hadn't been in the way.

She tilts her head and pulls the sunglasses from her eyes. She's staring at me with such intensity that I think there must be something behind me or something on my face.

She smiles slightly. "I've always wondered. Why are your eyes different colors?"

I expect to feel the warmth rising in my chest and cheeks. Her question reaches the core of who I am. I'm not sure how to answer.

"It's not a bad thing." She shrugs, trying to reassure me. "Just different." Her words, which would be a slash to the gut if they came from someone else or were said differently, seem harmless. She leans back in her chair and repositions her glasses, missing the implications of her statement.

The day's heat is still in full bloom in the late afternoon when Mo returns and folds his towel. "We should probably think about heading home soon. Mom will be wondering where we went."

I scramble to find a clock on the side of the building by the pool. "What time is it?" My stomach knots, afraid of the answer.

"Almost 5 p.m." Mo tosses his towel in his backpack.

A dread descends over me like a wave. "We need to go now." I move with the urgency of an oncoming tornado. I can't leave B alone with my father. I have to get home.

Mo looks at Aia and shrugs. "Okay."

I gather my towel, stuffing it into my bag. The lifeguard, who must be nearing the end of his shift and eager for us to go, has a sour expression as I sprint past without signing out. Mo and Aia trail behind and quickly scribble down our exit times.

"Why do we have to leave so quickly?" Aia hurries next to her brother.

"I'll tell you later," says Mo as he straddles his bike. "Just speed up."

The three of us ride like Olympic cyclists. I split off at the turn for my road, forgetting to say goodbye.

When I reach my driveway, I'm out of breath. B's Buick sits next to my father's truck. They are alone together, just like this morning. I streak into the house, hurdling onto the porch, racing through the door, forgetting about the noise of my entrance. Looking, listening. There are voices from the kitchen, and I hurl my bag to the ground and lunge past the couch. B sits at the table with my father in the corner. He has a beer open and is cleanly shaven, no longer with the menacing gray stubble.

"You're just in time for dinner," he says, wearing one of his SFD blue shirts with the number twenty-four. "Your mom and I were wondering if you'd make it." My shirt clings to my back, and I heave into the chair and look at B, who hands me a plate with chicken and a spoonful of rice. We are posing again—all three of us.

CHAPTER FIFTEEN

B REMOVED HER CHINSTRAP two days later, opting for a heavy layer of makeup that ruefully disguised the bruise. By the weekend, the discoloration was barely visible, and the swelling was only a blemish on her chin. My father even noticed. "That mark on your chin where you hit the cabinet is looking better," he said one night. In the pause that followed, I wanted B to correct him, needed her to correct him. She turned away, rewriting the truth.

There was still a subtle mark. When the lights were on, and she tilted her head just right, there was a blemish on her chin. At night, alone in front of the bathroom mirror, I hoped that B still grazed her hand across her chin and held it there for an extra second, remembering what happened.

When I was three, or maybe four, I galloped around the living room at Grandpa's house like a horse, pretending I was one of the cowboys on *Bonanza* chasing the bad guys. I'd nearly caught up to the imaginary thieves when I tripped on the rug and fell sideways.

My outstretched hand hit the potbelly woodstove in the corner.

I screamed so loud that Grandpa cried. The doctor said it could have been worse after wrapping my blistered hand with a bandage. I don't remember much of the story. Not *Bonanza*, galloping around like a cowboy, or even the burn. Despite my memory lapse, there's a pinprick scar on my hand. I can't feel it and can barely see it, but it's there. Grandpa reminds me of the story each time I pass the stove, and reflexively, the thumb of my other hand grazes that scar.

***

When we arrive at Grandma's for dinner, Grandpa hugs B, and I hope that the light is perfect, and he'll hesitate before letting go. Maybe focus on what seems like a smudge and gently use a finger to turn her head to the side for a better inspection. If Grandpa can figure this out on his own, I won't betray B. Unfortunately, they embrace, and B wanders into the kitchen toward the strong smell of sauce.

"How was the first day of school?" asks Grandpa in an easy tone as we move to the couch. He leans back. His arms loosely cross over his flannel shirt, glancing between me and the football game.

My eyes travel away from the TV and toward the pictures of the USS *Antietam* and Grandpa from the Korean War.

"Wow!" Grandpa shouts, moving toward the edge of the couch. "Did you see that?"

The replay shows a player catching the ball and slamming onto the turf. The player who made the tackle quickly stands, slapping hands with his teammate. The player who caught the ball gets to his knees.

I see the impact, just like I imagine the crash of my father's fist hitting B. My muscles flinch and I inadvertently whisper, "No."

Grandpa's bushy white eyebrows arch into his forehead and slowly lower as the line between his eyes furrows. He's confused, but he's also concerned.

In that moment, I want to tell him about B and ask him to protect us from my father.

Grandpa's head angles to the side, his green eyes roving up and down, searching. "So, tell me about school," he says, but a little more softly. "You're in eighth grade."

His question breaks my resolve, and I chicken out. "It's okay."

"Just okay?" He leans back, his eyes still trained on me.

Why wasn't he this inquisitive when he embraced B? "Yeah, just okay." My gaze focuses on the VCR just above the TV, pretending to watch the game.

Time expires, and the announcer says, "And we're going to overtime!"

"Overtime?"

Grandpa focuses back on the game. "Sure. Rarely is there a tie. One side has to win."

Swallowing his statement like a bitter pill, I think about B's genetics and my father's. Left versus right. B stirs Grandma's tomato sauce in the kitchen, with no mention of her disappearing bruise. I fumble with the cap of my inhaler, prying it free for a quick puff. My breathing slows, but my thoughts still race a thousand miles an hour.

"How's your father?" Grandpa says as if right on cue.

I keep my breaths even and slow, like his question hasn't created a panic inside my chest, and shrug. I can't remember the last time Grandpa asked about my father. My father usually works overnight at the fire station, so he isn't at dinner. Though a few months ago, Grandpa muttered that my father wasn't good enough for B.

Grandma saves me by yelling, "Dinner's ready."

I spring off the couch toward the table. In the kitchen, four empty plates surround a serving platter filled with braciole and pasta. I usually dissect the dish, unrolling the beef and separating the components. The peppers and carrots I eat outright, then mix the spinach with the red sauce, and finally, cut the meat into small squares to eat with my pasta, like ravioli. Today, I dig into the braciole with my fork and stuff my mouth with several bites, so I won't have a chance to talk.

B chats about work and the new doctor who had just joined the practice, Dr. Bedford. "Dr. Bedford's got a different perspective than the other doctors. He has some ideas on how the office can be more efficient and several new medications that the old dinosaurs haven't used."

"Wow, Ethan," Grandma says after B finished her story. "I've never seen you eat so fast. You must be growing." Grandma likes nothing better than an empty dinner plate.

Swallowing my last large bite, I ask, "May I be excused?" and stand before anyone has a chance to decline my request.

Flipping between channels on the TV, most of the conversation from the other room is loud enough to hear. Grandpa asks if I'm okay, and B reassures him it's a new school year and I'm a teenager.

"How's Spencer?" Grandpa asks, and I lower the volume just a notch. "He's fine," B says, not a moment of hesitation in her voice. The answer hasn't changed, but there used to be a pause. An instant where maybe she thought about answering differently, and Grandpa recounted coming back after Korea, it took a couple of months before he returned to normal. A few of his friends were shell-shocked and shuffled around in a daze after the extreme combat.

"Spencer was not involved in hand-to-hand combat. He can't blame that," Grandpa would say with ease. "All those laser-guided missiles. No one was fighting anyway. It was a giant video game." Grandma changed the subject, talking about a new recipe for carrot cake that she had found. I wondered if Grandpa was wrong and if the war altered my father. That night, I read about shell shock in my encyclopedia, learning that it was a term for soldiers who sometimes had trouble sleeping after years of fighting in the trenches after World War I.

My father certainly had trouble sleeping, but he had trouble sleeping before the war. I reread his letters, which I've kept in the pencil case on my bookshelf. He didn't write about digging trenches and daily shellings. His letters were about games of Trivial Pursuit and brushing the sand out of the Christmas tree. Of course, there was the missile attack, but he wasn't in the building. He was at the edge of camp on guard duty. If any soldiers were shell-shocked, it would probably be Iraq's army.

***

The conversation from the kitchen gets quiet, and coffee replaces the meal before we drive home in silence.

If B's happy that I ate and left the table without a chance to say anything to Grandpa, she doesn't act like it. Deep lines on her brow are visible from the headlights of the oncoming cars. She looks like she's trying to solve the most complex problem in the world.

A few years ago, I got a Rubik's Cube. It came solved in the box. Each side was the same color. Most people either stick the puzzle on a shelf, pretending that they solved it, or instantly mess up all the colors and try to put the puzzle back together. I worked on the cube, altering one square at a time, and then learned how to solve the problem. Then I learned how to fix a row, then two rows, then an entire side. It's only in this way that I could understand. A problem that large needs to be broken into steps. Mixing it up at once creates an unsolvable mess.

I'm not sure B can solve my father's problem in steps, but I wonder if someone else can, one square at a time. I think back to her story about the new doctor. "Do you think he would ever talk to that new doctor?"

"Who?" B's eyebrows raise and furrow as the high beams from an oncoming car light her face.

"My father," I say, looking back down at my hands.

"Why would he need to talk to a—" She pauses, and I wait for her to continue, but she stops speaking. Minutes pass, and maybe she's still thinking about my idea, running the suggestion through her mind. The silence between us stretches until we reach our driveway.

The house is pitch black, and all the curtains are drawn. My father is working at the firehouse, but the remnants of how he left our home persist. In the kitchen, there is a note on the table.

I hope you had a nice dinner. I'll probably have to stay late tomorrow morning.
Spence

I crumple the paper and toss it. He doesn't care, not about us.

I want to talk with B. We've barely spoken since that morning a week ago. I can't tell if she's mad at me or upset that I threatened to call Grandpa. After spending a few minutes in my room, I head back downstairs. It's quiet. I expect to see her on the couch reading a magazine or watching TV. The lights are still off, and I momentarily freeze, afraid that maybe he didn't go to work and he's in the house somewhere.

Taking a cautious step forward, I peek into the kitchen, but it's empty. I'm about to knock on B's door but stop before my knuckles reach the wood. From inside, she's crying softly, and I impotently drop my arm.

CHAPTER SIXTEEN

SEPTEMBER ROLLS INTO October. B's bruise vanishes, and she and my father move on. I can't. They can ignore the situation, pretending it never happened or won't happen again. Each morning, I wait for the replay of my father's violence and wonder how and when his half will influence my actions.

This morning, I found another trait separating my two sides. I'd always focused on what was in front of me—my eyes, hair, and thumbs. Even my toes are different. My second toe is longer than my big toe on the right but not on the left.

Over breakfast, I drop my spoon, peering underneath the tablecloth and reaching blindly on the floor for the cool metal utensil. "They're the same." The chipped yellow nail polish on B's second toe is a beacon that extends beyond her big toe.

B lowers the article she's reading. "What's the same?" She gulps her coffee, folding the paper neatly in half.

"The second toe on my right foot is longer than my big toe." I extend my bare foot for evidence.

B lifts her leg and wiggles her second toe. "You found one Dr. Taylor missed, huh?"

It's said so casually. She doesn't understand the implications. It's another trait that separates my two sides. Black versus white. Good versus evil, and there are no ties. One side has to win.

"Yeah." I rise from the table to get ready for school. I pack my lunch, but images of my two different thumbs dance in my mind. At my locker, changing books for math, I can only picture that everything I see is through two different colored eyes. Running a hand through my hair while half listening to the teacher discuss the Pythagorean theorem, my fingers slide through the curlier strands on the left. The only information about who I am comes from scouring my body. That isn't getting me anywhere, and my encyclopedias aren't any help.

"Curly," Mo shouts, jolting me from my seat. Half the chairs in the room are empty.

"You not getting enough sleep or something?" Mo pulls me by the arm.

"Headache." I rub my eyes, trying to squash the intense pain. It sounds innocent—a headache. People get them when they're stressed or don't get enough rest. I've had headaches before, but this isn't just a dull pain. The pounding in the back of my skull wraps around my head like a vise.

My father gets headaches and buries himself in the shadows of a corner, disturbed by the faintest sound. Right now, I would love a quiet, dark room. Instead, the boisterous commotion from the hall constricts the vise around my head with every pulse of my heart.

Is this the first piece of evidence that his side is taking control? Is his half stronger? By next month, I'll need my hand as a visor to block the light. By next year, I'll be pacing the house at night, my feet slapping against the floor. The pounding in my head gets louder as if answering my question. Yes!

"Here." Mo thrusts several white pills from his open palm.

I swallow the medicine, wishing I had a glass of water.

In the hall, I fall out of step and behind Mo and Susan Rhinehardt. Susan sits on Mo's other side during math, and her locker is next to mine. While changing our books, they talk about the football game on Friday and how she'll be there if he wants to meet up.

Several lockers down, Jackson VanPatten pumps his fists. He's only in eighth grade but already wears a giant-sized class ring, the red stone center blinking like a snake's eye.

Jackson hovers over a seventh grader who must have gotten in his way, barking, "Who's your master?"

As I glance toward the poor kid in the fetal position, my eyes catch the bright hallway light firing arrows into my brain. My eyes dart back to my Nikes.

"Jackson! Jackson!" the crowd chants. Every syllable from the group echoes in my brain, and the vise tightens. Changing my books, I keep my head low, sprinting toward English.

Two steps away from the noise, a hand grips my shoulder. My book drops, and my fingers curl into my palm.

I need this noise to stop. I need to get away.

My fist raises, cocked and ready to pummel. Today, I'm punching first and asking questions later. I don't care if Jackson is bigger or how many of his friends are with him. Spinning, I see skin the color of caramel and drop my hand.

Worry spreads over Mo's face. His hands raise in surrender, and his body lurches backward, knocking into the wall. "Curly!" He focuses on my fists, balled at my sides.

I want to say that I'm sorry and didn't mean it. I want to tell him I thought he was someone else. My mouth is ready to explain, but my brain knows better. He's my friend, my only friend, but he won't understand what's going on. The Alsoufi household mails Happy New Year cards with a picture of all four wearing matching sweaters. His parents hold hands while watching TV. The family plays board games on Saturday nights. Mr. A. can talk without yelling. Mo and

Aia wake up each morning unafraid.

"Are you pissed I'm talking to Susan?" Mo breaks the silence.

"No." My head shakes. There's no way he can understand my problem, but there's also no possible way to explain it to him.

"It's your dad." Mo's whisper interrupts my thoughts. He didn't ask a question. He gave the answer.

John Schmidt passes behind and doesn't stop or turn his head. Judy Halloway moves in the opposite direction, focusing on her nails.

"My mom had a doctor's appointment a few weeks ago. She said there was a bruise on your mom's chin layered with makeup. At least, that's what I overheard while washing the dishes after dinner. She wanted to say something, but Dad convinced her that it wasn't any of their business."

There is a minuscule victory in that someone else noticed. That someone looked at B and was worried. But just like me, Mrs. A. didn't say anything. Just like me, Mrs. A. moved on.

"Does he hit you?" Mo's unblinking stare focuses directly into my eyes.

"No." I meet his gaze. My head wobbles from side to side.

Only after repeating my answer with more conviction does Mo break his focus, muttering, "It's not right." He walks with me to English in the wrong direction of his social studies class.

"Sis," Mo barks as Aia rounds the corner. "Take care of Curly for me," and Mo darts down the hall from where we came.

The initial intensity in Aia's eyes softens after Mo rounds the corner.

I slide into a seat in the second row, Aia joining me on my left. I wait for her to question what Mo meant, but Mr. Jones, our English teacher, rants about the themes from *Of Mice and Men*. He rambles that each character has dreams but is powerless to achieve them. George and Lennie want a farm but don't have the money. Curley's wife wants to be a movie star but is stuck on the farm. At the mention of the name Curley, Aia looks over and winks.

Staring into space, the aspirin calms the pulsing in my head. Mr. Jones is close, but he has it wrong. Each character isn't powerless. It's who they are. George is smart, but not strong enough to make it as a farmer. Lennie is strong, but his intellectual disability will always limit him. Curley is a mean son of a bitch who will never gain the respect of the people who work for him, so he'll never be successful like his father. Curley's wife is just manipulative. Sure, maybe they all have dreams, yet none will reach fruition, but not because of their circumstance. It's who they are, the fabric of their very being. It's like a blind person wanting to be a pilot or someone who's mute becoming a motivational speaker. Dreams or not, their expectations are outside of reality. Each character isn't powerless because of their circumstance. Their circumstance reflects who they are.

The bell rings, and Mr. Jones yells over our rush toward the door, "I'd like a three-page report on examples of how each character has an unachievable dream."

I walk Aia to her locker, her dark hair pulled over one shoulder.

"You're taking the bus home with us today?" She clutches her jacket.

"Maybe on Wednesday."

She and Mo exchange a worried glance. My father isn't working tonight, and I don't want B alone with him.

***

I run ahead, catching the bus to the high school, hoping for answers. Answers about who I am and what it means to be a chimera—someone who is split.

I assume there aren't any books about this sort of thing, but maybe there's something on the internet. I'd looked through Volume C of my encyclopedia and the entry for chimera. There was only the genetic definition and a mythological legend involving a creature that was half goat and half lion.

My back leans against the library's double doors as they swing shut with a clap. There's no one else here, only a woman in a faded blue dress standing behind a circular counter in the room's center.

"Can I help you?"

Her nametag, Mrs. Kraskowitz, is pinned to her dress.

"Can I please use the computer?" Next to the double doors are two computers and an orange sign that hangs on the wall above them. *Research Computers Only.*

"For what?" The wrinkled creases on her face remain slack.

"Research."

A single thick gray eyebrow rises above the other.

I'll need to divulge more to get what I want. "I'd like to learn about genetics."

She nods and notes the time.

I won't learn all the answers in thirty minutes, but it's a start.

Halfway through my time block, I've gotten nowhere. There is random information about DNA, dominant genes, and experiments that use peas and fruit flies. There's nothing about how genetics affect who a person becomes. Certainly nothing about chimeras.

My eyes grow weary scrolling through lines and lines of text, skimming for anything I can use.

"Finding what you need?" Mrs. Kraskowitz leans over my shoulder, and I catch a whiff of mothballs.

I fight the urge to conceal the screen. I don't want her asking questions.

"You might want to try looking through this." She hands me a heavy green and blue volume. "It's a few years old. We get some of the older reference books from SU, but you can make three photocopies of the pages that might interest you."

After she leaves, I find a few early pages on heredity. There isn't enough time to figure out what any of the words mean. Pushing the open book against the photocopier plate, I make three copies, grab my bounty from the machine, and scramble from the library like

I've robbed a bank.

At home, the driveway is empty. I won't need to worry about the windows rattling as I shut the door. I won't anchor to the wall, sliding around the room's edge. I won't listen to him inquire about my day like he's interested, offer a snack, or joke about my two halves.

Leaning back in my desk chair, the two back legs wobble and squeak from a loose screw as I read the first page. I need the dictionary for every fourth word. After an hour of still working through two paragraphs, I put the pages in the bottom desk drawer.

I clearly won't be handed the keys to unlock who I am today and instead focus on my essay for Mr. Jones.

Out the window, rows and rows of the pale-yellow stalks from Henderson's cornfield are ready for harvest. Exactly what Lennie and George wanted. As my eyes wander back toward our house, they focus on the shed in the back where my father often goes.

Once, when B was working, my father got a phone call from the firehouse. He wasn't scheduled that day, but several firefighters were sick. I told the chief that my father was in the shed. I thought that would end the conversation, but the chief didn't know what that meant and asked me to get him. I thought about just hanging up the phone but carefully strode to the shed. Even in the middle of the afternoon, the door was shut. After tapping on the door, there was a rustle and a murmur of activity. I knocked louder.

The doors flew apart. I nearly tripped over my feet, leaping backward. My father was red-faced. "What?" he barked. His breath smelled of whiskey. On the workbench, there was a half-empty bottle of Jack Daniels.

"The *Chie . . . chief*," I stuttered, taking another slow step backward, my heart pounding, afraid to turn my back and break into an all-out sprint.

"What, chef?" His voice came out in two hard gasps.

"Chief," I whined while protecting my face with my hands. "At the firehouse. He asked if you could come into work."

My father's Adam's apple bobbed, and he chewed his lip. "Tell him I don't feel well," and he headed back into the shed and locked the door.

Somehow, that shed is part of my father's identity. It's a piece of who he is.

***

Creeping through the house and down the stairs, I freeze as the seventh step creaks. There's no reason to sneak around. He isn't here. Still, I open the front door to check the driveway.

The gray paint of the shed chips off the clapboard sides, and the once-white trim is now brown. A single window faces the woods, and a broom handle between the handgrips keeps the two barn-style doors shut. My hands shudder as I slowly pull the broom handle, and the right door creaks open. I spin around, expecting to find him behind me, but there is only a gentle breeze. My fingers curl against the damp wood door. Inside, it looks like a cave. A blue tarp screens the window facing the woods, and though I need more light, I wait for my eyes to adjust. Everything is in shadows. How can he see anything with the doors shut?

My eyes acclimate, and my surroundings come into focus. Ahead, a pile of garden tools leans against a lawn mower shoved to the side. On the other wall, debris covers a workbench. Hammers and screwdrivers, saws and wrenches, some of which are so rusted they probably don't even work. Next to the workbench is a large garbage pail filled with glass. They're fragments from his whiskey bottles that he won't place with the garbage.

Above the workbench is an empty pegboard, hooks hanging askew, and a picture. The photo is out of place. The edges curl, bending toward me, and I untack it from the wall, moving closer to the door for better light. Four men and one woman in desert fatigues stand in front of a Jeep surrounded by sand. The men wear helmets, making it hard to see their faces, but the one standing in the middle looks like my father. The woman has her helmet off, and her long blonde hair blows sideways in the wind. They're all smiling and posing, just like we did for our family pictures. I flip the image over, and there's a date, *December 29, 1990,* and several names written in blue script. *Samantha Shepard.*

The picture rips from my hands.

"What the hell are you doing?" my father barks. He's breathing heavy, a snarl in his voice. "What are you doing in the shed?"

I stumble backward. "I needed—" The shed's contents scramble through my mind. "A screwdriver?"

"Why?" his teeth clench, and his hand grips the picture tight.

"The leg on my chair is loose."

My father brushes past me, shoving me aside. "Phillips or flat?"

I have no idea what he means, but answer, "Flat." My father slams the handle of a screwdriver into my hand so hard it stings.

CHAPTER SEVENTEEN

"**J**ULIE SCEMPER," MO leans on the elevated counter in his kitchen, trying to convince me to attend the eighth-grade dance.

He has a date. I don't.

He fixes on my narrow gaze and nods. Julie Scemper, in my English class, is probably the prettiest girl in our grade and is out of my league. Not that I have a league.

"What about Margaret?" Mo flings a chip from a bowl on the counter into his mouth. He crunches down hard, proud of his winning idea.

"Margaret Rucker? The girl who laughed at me after Jackson tripped me in sixth grade?" Mo's expression sours, and he finishes chewing, still thinking while tapping his finger against his chin. "Okay, okay, I got it. Alyssa Eager," he opens both hands like he's offering me a name from the heavens.

Alyssa Eager is six feet tall, meaning my head will land next to her armpit. That's a problem because she refuses to wear deodorant.

"No chance. Picture that."

Mo opens his mouth about to object, but nods again. "You're too picky. You don't quite have all the suave I do." He skips off the stool, gyrating his hips back and forth. "What do you think of my new moves?"

His arms and legs twitch like he's getting electrocuted. Aia strolls past and sticks a finger in her mouth like she's about to puke.

"I think she's right," I say, pointing my thumb at Aia.

She peers into the fridge and closes the doors empty-handed.

Mo continues working on his dance moves. "You guys don't know talent." He halts, his arms and shoulders pointed to the sky, frozen in a bizarre pose. "We'll have to find you someone. The dance is in a week." The imaginary tune in his head returns, and his arms and legs begin convulsing again.

I don't want to go to the dance and am fortunate enough that no one will be interested in accompanying me. My face resembles a pepperoni pizza, but mainly on the right side. B had acne as a teenager.

Mrs. A. returns with the food and sets it on the counter, and like a fly to honey, Mo hovers around the box, cradling a paper plate. Mrs. A. swats his hand. "You have a guest," she admonishes, and Mo steps back.

"Did you come up with a date for the dance, Ethan?" She pulls a bottle of cola from the fridge.

Stuffing a piece of pizza in my mouth and shaking my head, I hope my silence will change the subject.

"He's being a little too picky. He's not so brutally handsome." Mo raises an eyebrow like he's posing for the camera.

"Aia, you're not going with anyone. Maybe you could go with Ethan?" Mrs. A. pulls her slice of pizza from the box.

I nearly choke, but don't let out a sound. Mo's head shakes and then stops and tilts for a second. I can't see Aia's expression. It's probably the sour expression when she's looking at Mo, but a small part of me hopes it isn't. Mo's pizza remains suspended in the air. I crane my neck, trying to see Aia's face.

I can't read it. It's not repulsion, anger, or even embarrassment. At the very least, it isn't the sour face. Aia coughs and clears her throat. "I doubt Ethan wants to go with me." She says it like she's interested.

Mrs. A. doesn't give up.

"Why not?" she shrugs. "You're not going with anyone. He's not going with anyone. You both need someone to go with. The dance is in a week, and I'm driving you all back and forth anyway."

Her logic is so crisp.

Mo seems to weigh the idea, his pizza still suspended.

"Well, Ethan?" Mrs. A. folds her hands on the table. "Why don't you ask her?"

Three pairs of eyes beat down on me. Clearing my throat, I wipe my sweaty, greasy hands along my jeans. "Umm, Aia—"

Aia sighs, and I have a date for the dance.

By Sunday, I'm a disaster. It's true, Aia and I get along, but I have no idea what to do at a dance. Trying to read while Grandpa watches TV is no good. My body shifts and twists on the couch, thinking about this nightmare I've gotten railroaded into.

When Grandpa finally caves and questions what's wrong, I confess.

Without a word, he checks his watch, grabs his hat and the keys to the car, and says, "Let's go."

I look to B for direction, but she only shrugs. I'm afraid Grandpa will lecture me, but he remains quiet, the only noise coming from the light jazz on the radio. He drives to Macy's, where he insists on selecting a blue suit, white shirt, and pale blue tie.

It isn't necessary. I have a shirt and tie at home, but he continues whistling while paying the bill.

We're silent on the way home, but I can't stop grinning, thankful that I won't have to wear my '70s yellow shirt and maroon tie.

Grandpa's stomach growls loud for Grandma's chicken parm, and I wonder why he isn't driving faster. When he pulls into a grocery store parking lot and turns off the engine, my shoulders slump, dreading the speech.

"This girl," he asks. "You like her?"

My eyes squint, predicting his next question. I don't dislike Aia, and Grandpa doesn't understand that my pickings are slim. Plus, Mrs. A. railroaded me into this date.

"Yeah," I say, looking out at the row of cars.

"So, you'll treat her with respect." It wasn't a question, and I wonder what he's thinking. Is he talking about my left half? I've watched him catalog the differences between my left and right. He tries to be subtle, but his eyes linger too long on my hair. Is he worried my father's side lurks, waiting to exert control, and I'll treat Aia like my father treats B? My heart pounds, and I feel for the safety of my inhaler.

"Of course," I say, trying to stop the conversation. Grandpa looks serious, and lines crease his brow; his eyes focus entirely on me. Is this how a father is supposed to act? Is this a rite of passage? Maybe years earlier, Grandpa's father took him aside to explain how to treat a woman.

"I promise," I repeat, so he'll stop staring at me or my left half.

"That's what I want to hear."

The night of the dance, pulling the suit from the protective wrapper, I fumble several times before learning how to tie a Windsor knot, thanks to a diagram inside my encyclopedia. The plan is that Mrs. A. will pick me up from the house and drop me off at the end of the night. I plan to slip outside and wait in the dark for my ride.

At the bottom of the stairs, B leans against the banister with the camera. Worse, my father is leaning back in his chair. He has never complained that my best friend is Iranian. I've never even overheard him comment. But I've never been on a date with an Iranian.

"I'll be outside." I try to sound casual.

"Not so fast." My father stands from his chair. He strolls forward, and I gag from the smell of whiskey on his breath. His hand reaches out, straightening my tie so it's centered. Satisfied with his work, he takes a twenty from his wallet and tucks it into my shirt pocket. "Just in case you need to buy something for your date. Take care of her." He leans closer and whispers, "Don't worry, I won't embarrass you. Just let your mother take a picture." He places a hand on my shoulder and squeezes. "Have fun tonight," he says and returns to his chair.

After B takes my picture alone by the front door, I escape to the end of the driveway. Kicking at the stones with my shoes, I'm unable to find the words to describe my father's sendoff. *Normal?* A father giving his son some cash and asking him to take a picture.

Minivan headlights dot the horizon, and Mrs. A. pulls into the driveway. "You don't want any pictures inside with Aia?"

"No, Mom said the house was a mess," I lie and shut the rolling side door.

***

At the dance, the cafeteria is barely recognizable. The long cafeteria tables are folded and wrapped in black paper, with scattered rectangles of yellow to appear like the windows of far-off apartment buildings. Silver stars of different sizes hang from the ceiling and shimmer along with the disco ball at the center of the room. Music blares so loud that when I lean toward Aia, I shout in her ear.

"A drink?" I yell. Mo is already on the dance floor, his arms flailing. I can't tell if Susan, his date, is laughing with or at him.

The green rhinestones on Aia's dress sparkle in the strobe lights, and she gets on her tiptoes and leans in close. Her perfume smells sweet, and her chest is nearly touching mine.

"Lead the way," she says, and I pull her through the mob of bodies.

We sip our drinks while staying tight to the wall. I don't know how to dance, but what if Aia does? It's one thing if we both can't dance, but I don't want to disappoint her if she can. The music changes, and the mirror ball in the center reflects hundreds of spinning lights. Couples pair off on the floor, each moving slowly.

Aia clasps my hand and tugs me forward, nearly spilling my drink all over my shirt. "Let's figure this out," she says, and before I can object, the two of us are swaying with the beat. I put one hand in hers, but I'm not sure if the other should go on her shoulder or her back, or hell, maybe in my pocket.

"Relax, Ethan." She pulls me close, and my other hand wraps around her back. I'm unsure if she is leading, if I am leading, or if we are just in this sway together. But the two of us rock side to side.

"It's not such a bad thing, right?" Aia quips.

Pulling back an inch, even in the dim light, she must see my face relax and says, "Dancing with me. It's not so bad, is it?"

"No." It's actually nice. Her hair smells like raspberries, and I'm honestly having a hard time thinking that she's Mo's twin sister, the girl who blocked the screen when we were playing *X-Men*.

She rests her head on my shoulder and my muscles contract.

"Relax," she whispers, and I close my eyes, pressing her a little tighter to my chest.

CHAPTER EIGHTEEN

MORNINGS ARE SUPPOSED to indicate a new beginning. By late October, it's still dark at 6:30 a.m., and Monday doesn't feel fresh but rather more of an extension of the night before, which won't relinquish its grasp.

After B and I came home from Sunday dinner at Grandma and Grandpa's, we were surprised to see my father's truck in the driveway. After turning on the living room lights, a piercing scream echoed through the house. Even in the brief seconds of light, I saw my father in his chair, a glass of whiskey by his side, his body coiled and tense.

B flipped the switch, but it was too late.

"Didn't you see my truck in the driveway?" His snarl snapped at us like a viper.

"I'm *sa-sa*-sorry," B stuttered in a whisper, pushing me up the stairs.

I listened for a crash. A scream. Something, anything that would cause me to spring from my desk chair. B has always told me to stay away, probably to protect me from seeing him strike her. Would he stop if I lurched off the stairs and stood between them? I could raise my fists like a boxer. He would destroy me, but maybe B would be safe for the day.

***

I'm still wearing yesterday's clothes when my alarm startles me awake. In the absolute and total darkness, my heart pounding, I listen for an extension of the day before, or more specifically, the quiet. It sounds like an oxymoron—listening for the silence. What's even more unbelievable is differentiating quiet into types. There's quiet devoid of any noise. Not the sound of a footstep, a door closing, or a mug placed on the counter. It's a vacuum where every possible decibel is accounted for and squashed. It's in that quiet and darkness that B and I tiptoe alongside the edge of a cliff. Our hands press against the rocky surface, and our feet shuffle from side to side. One misstep and it's a long tumble down.

I don't know why my father can't or won't sleep. Even coming off the night shift, he's always awake in the early morning, lurking in the corner of the kitchen or pacing around the house. His bare feet slap against the kitchen linoleum. One year for Christmas, B gave him slippers so we wouldn't have to listen to him marching around the house in the dark. He wore them for a week before complaining his feet were sweaty. He's the only one allowed to produce a sound.

After several minutes, there's an occasional footstep and the click of the fridge closing. It's a peaceful quiet. I won't have to worry about buttering a piece of toast and the scraping noise of the knife on the crusty bread creating too much clatter.

Downstairs, the kitchen lights are on, and B softly hums to herself. She has moved on from the night before, forgetting the images that still cling to my memory. Her hair swishes in a ponytail to the beat of the song in her head. Right now, for only the briefest of moments, we are normal. We are happy.

"Thanks for the Cheerios," I say, raising my heaping spoon like I'm toasting with a glass of champagne.

"I'll be late today. There are a bunch of appointments," B apologizes.

I understand what she means, swallowing the information along with the cereal and devising a plan. Where to go and what to do. I could go to Mo's, but I'll stay at the library today and take the afterschool bus home.

***

At school, I twirl the combination to my locker. Behind me, kids rush past, trying to make it to class before the first bell. Over my shoulder, Julie Scemper laughs while tightly clutching Jonny's arm. Clasping my math book, I'm about to look for Mo when a hand shoves me forward. As I twist, my arm crashes into the edge of the locker door. A jolt of pain bolts through me like an electric shock while my opposite hand tries to protect my already injured arm. Jackson VanPatten swaggers confidently away with his friend Mikey by his side, the two laughing. He turns and points his finger and thumb like he has a pretend gun firing a round. The gun recoils, and my eyes fix on his class ring, the size of a brass knuckle.

I hate him. My teeth clench and my fingers curl into two fists. It doesn't happen as often, but Jackson takes every opportunity to shove me down, destroy my homework, or toss an insult.

My fists raise to my chest, shaking. My legs are ready to sprint after Jackson so that my trembling fists can punch him to the floor. I imagine my knuckles striking him over and over while he begs for mercy for today and for a few weeks ago when he knocked my English report out of my hand and stood over me when I tried to pull it from underneath his sneaker.

My breathing gets heavier, and I reach for my inhaler. The

chalky medicine makes me forget about the throbbing in my arm. For a second, I am calm and accept what happened because I won't act violently like my father. B's half is in control. Her half. It's who she is. *Let Jackson VanPatten walk away.* It's what B would do.

Mo approaches from the other direction. He sees my arm and glances down the hall. "Where is he?" Mo jumps, searching for the top of Jackson's blond hair or SU football jacket.

"Don't worry about it." I shut my locker door, walking to class, my arm throbbing with every step.

We're a minute late for class, but Mr. Stevens doesn't seem to pay attention, already explaining the quadratic equation.

I wish that my identity was solvable. I've tried. I've read through the pages of the genetics books and found a reference to a chimera, but there wasn't any information about the heredity from two different sets of DNA, and there's nothing to explain what being a chimera means.

I think for a moment about my Rubik's Cube and jolt upright, causing Mr. Stevens to stop working. He refocuses on the board after realizing I'm not a continued disturbance. There's an answer, a way to determine who I am. I need to divide this into smaller and smaller parts, and I understand how.

After school, I rush onto the bus, forgetting about the library and thinking about how to tell B. How do I convince her of my plan? I'm so focused on finally solving my lifelong problem that I'm halfway in the house before I realize my father's truck is sitting dead center in the driveway. The house is in complete darkness. Shutting the door, it clicks with a loud thud. Much louder than I intended.

"Damn it! Not so loud," my father barks.

I blink several times, needing my eyes to adjust. He might be in the kitchen or the hall. Sticking my hands out in front for guidance, I just need to locate the stairs and get to my room.

"Ethan."

There's an odor of Jack Daniels, and I feel him in front. His white T-shirt glows in the shadows. He takes two steps closer, and I swear his breath is eighty-proof, but he doesn't slur or stumble. Somehow, he doesn't act like the drunks on TV who can't walk a straight line. A stranger would have no idea that he just downed half a glass of whiskey.

When he returned from the Gulf, he had all these rules. Like he couldn't have a beer before dinner, and he couldn't have a drink if he had to go to work later. He wouldn't have a whiskey until after dinner. Somewhere along the way, the rules started bending, becoming more of a suggestion. He could drink in the morning, as long as he didn't have to go to work later, or drink before dinner if he'd just returned from work. It didn't matter if he came home from work at 9 a.m. or 5 p.m. Then the difference between a beer and whiskey blurred, erasing the rules altogether.

"How was school?" His voice is gruff. I'm not sure I can escape when he's so close.

"Fine." I slide my backpack to my other arm, inadvertently lifting my shirt sleeve. I'm not self-conscious and don't care. What I need is to go upstairs. My father is inches in front of me, and even in the dark, the angry tomato left by Jackson's shove stares out.

He sees my arm and barks, "What the hell happened?"

I don't know if it's because he's a fireman or a former soldier, but he instantly yanks my sleeve.

"Have you been fighting?" His teeth gnash, and I wonder what makes him think I would know how to fight. I'm barely a hundred pounds. If I were some secret boxing champ, I would have the worst physique in history.

"Na-no," I stammer. "Some kid just shoved me into a locker." I don't mention Jackson VanPatten. B knows Jackson's father, so it's possible my father does, too. He steps back, still looking at my arm. "Did you punch him back?"

The aggression is gone, and his voice is now more matter of fact. "He's bigger than me." Clutching the railing to go upstairs, he snares my other arm, pulling me toward the backyard. "Outside," he says. There's little room for negotiation, but I still try.

"I have to get my homework done," I lie.

"This will only take a few minutes." He jerks me again toward the back of the house.

The cool October air chills my skin, and my father stops and turns against the setting sun.

"Hit me." He opens both palms.

There have been times when I've wanted to strike him, but this isn't one of them. I don't want to play this game.

"No." I keep my tone flat, my arms limp at my sides.

He slaps the side of my face. Not hard, but just enough to know that I'm playing this his way or losing. "C'mon," he says, "You're my son. You've got this in you."

I know what he's saying. He doesn't mention the fact that I'm a chimera. But somehow, he knows it's a way to get under my skin. I just don't think he understands why. He doesn't know that this, right now, is what I'm afraid of. That he might awaken his side. His half. His genetics inside me.

"You've got half of me in you." He smirks. "Now fight me."

I hate him and raise my fists and punch at his palm.

He shakes his head and lowers his voice in resigned disgust. "All right," he says, "first lesson."

I don't want a lesson. I don't want him to teach me how to fight. This isn't something I want to learn. But I can't run, and I'm listening as much as I want to block out his words.

"You're right-handed, so this is your jab," and he punches using his left hand. "And this is your cross." He strikes with his right. "You keep your thumb outside, never curled under your fingers, or you might break it. When you punch, you twist like this," he says, twisting his forearm as his fist strikes. "It gives you more power." All I can picture is B's bruised chin and how my father twisted his arm so that he could have more power. I want to puke.

"Now, you try." He raises his palms back into the air.

I squint, facing the sun behind him. "I don't want to."

"Fight, goddammit. Be a man." His voice is rough, and he raises his hand to slap me again, but this time I duck. This isn't ending until I do what he wants, so I raise my fists, my thumb out, and jab with my left fist, twisting my forearm with a punch that slaps loudly into his palm.

"There you go. Again, with the left." He's enjoying this, like some kind of father-son bonding experience. If only someone were here to take a picture.

I strike with my left and then my right. I want to escape but keep punching, my fists slapping my father's palms. My knuckles are red, and his palms look angry. But each time, he raises his hands for another round.

B leans out the back door, a grocery bag in her hand, the sky a dark blue. "What are you doing?"

"Teaching him to fight."

B's face goes ashen. "You . . ." she pauses. "Can—" she stops again.

Staring at her, I pluck one of her words out of the air like it's a lifeline. "Do you need help with dinner?"

Life re-introduces into her. "Yes!"

I speed to her side, hook the bag of groceries, and head into the kitchen.

"Can you make a salad?" B asks, and I pull the vegetables from the bag.

Cutting the lettuce with a knife, my father stomps into the kitchen. I'd thought he'd left or returned to the shed. There's conviction in his step, and I grip the knife tighter.

"He needs to learn to defend himself," my father roars. "The bullies of this world will roll over him if he doesn't."

I want to laugh because my father can't see the irony. Maybe he should teach B how to punch back.

"I just don't think he needs to learn how to fight." B spins from the stove where she's browning hamburger. This time, she isn't speaking in her typical soft tones.

"He's almost fourteen. He needs to learn to be a man. Defend himself. Hell, when I was thirteen . . ." his voice trails off as B turns off the stove and heads toward her room.

"Goddammit, Phoebe. Don't you walk away from me." He hurries after her and pounds on the bedroom door. "You can't keep walking away. Locking me out."

My father slams the front door, and his truck rumbles out of the driveway. The knife quakes so violently that it clatters on the cutting board.

I wait five minutes. Five minutes in case he returns and for B to have a peaceful quiet before going to her door. I don't try to creep. I don't want to surprise her, and despite the sobs, this time, I knock lightly at first, and then a little louder. "It's just me." My nose inches away from the yellow pine door. "I won't use what he taught me. I promise." Soft footsteps move toward the door. B wraps her arms tight around me like I might be a balloon trying to float away.

CHAPTER NINETEEN

"**E**THAN."

Mr. Jones stares from the corner of the classroom. His legs outstretch on the desk, a newspaper on his lap. His long gray beard and rotund belly suggest the appearance of a younger Santa until he speaks; his voice is coarse after too many cigarette breaks.

Jerking upright from a slouch, I pull away from Aia and our quiet conversation.

"Is your father named Spencer?" Mr. Jones shifts in his seat.

Behind me, Julie Scemper is talking about a sale at The Gap. Two hands slap together in a high-five from the other side of the room. The class isn't paying attention to Mr. Jones—yet.

I swallow the cold dread that makes the frigid November temperature from this morning's bus stop seem like a tropical sauna. The inevitable catastrophe of my father. What or who did he destroy? The bell will ring any minute, and Mr. Jones will describe what my father has done in front of the class. Aia doesn't seem alarmed, but she doesn't understand. My father wasn't home after working last night. Sometimes, it's because of paperwork or an accident just before he leaves. This morning, I enjoyed my breakfast with the lights on. I'm about to discover why.

"Ethan?" Mr. Jones coughs.

"Yes." I want to bury my head into my desk. Maybe my father was in an accident driving home because he was drunk. Maybe he was in a fight. Maybe Mr. Jones saw him at the bar, and they talked. How Mr. Jones knows my father can't be good.

"Your father's a hero," he says flatly.

I must have misheard. Last week, Grandpa called my father a lazy drunk. Grandma tried to correct him and said Spencer was misguided. My father is many things but not a hero.

I blink several times, my jaw hanging slack.

Mr. Jones repeats, "He's a hero," enunciating each word. "Front page." Mr. Jones offers a baton of folded newspaper.

It's a trick. That's the only explanation. My hand reaches for the paper. On the front page, directly below the big blue letters of the *Post Standard*, is the headline, *Local Syracuse Hero*. There are two pictures beneath the title. They're grainy, pixelated, and hard to see. On the left, a firefighter surges toward the camera away from a house fire with a victim. A helmet obscures the firefighter's face and any other details. Except on the helmet is the number *24*—my father's number.

Two paramedics lean over the victim in the second photo. The camera doesn't focus on the victim's legs, which stretch past the paramedics applying aid. It's focused on the firefighter in the background whose helmet, numbered 24, is on the ground facing the camera. The fireman is on his knees. His hands hang limp at his sides, and his face gazes toward the night sky like he's praying.

This isn't possible. It's just not possible. This man hits B, the man I tiptoe around and avoid. The same person that B and I are afraid of cannot also be a hero. The person whose traits make up my left half. Beneath the pictures is the caption:

Spencer Rivers, a firefighter with the Syracuse Fire Department, heroically pulled an unnamed Syracuse University student from a house fire last night, handing the victim to paramedics and praying for the victim's wellbeing.

Reading the caption three times, I'm hunting for the mistake. Aia tugs my sleeve, pulling me away from the paper. "What is it?"

"He pulled someone from a fire." My words don't seem right. Hearing my statement aloud sounds backward or part of some foreign language.

"Impressive." Aia beams. She doesn't understand. My father isn't a hero. He's an angry, bitter man who strikes out at his family. I stay silent and read:

During last night's bitter cold, a neglected meal in an oven resulted in a fire at 358 University Avenue. The three-story house consisted of several apartments, and although most residents made it out safely, an unnamed Syracuse University student was missing. Spencer Rivers, a veteran of Operation Desert Storm and a longtime Syracuse fireman at Station One, found the victim on the second floor and pulled him to safety. The victim, taken to the SUNY Upstate Medical University burn unit, is now listed in stable condition and expected to make a full recovery.

When asked how it feels to save a life, the national and now local hero, Spencer Rivers only commented, "I'm no hero."

Chief Mackey, a longtime Syracuse fireman at Station One, said, "Spence is one of the best. He served our country during the war and now does it for our community. We're lucky to have such a strong and humble man within our city."

This isn't possible. I'm pulled away from my thoughts. Mr. Jones said something, but I have no idea what.

"I said you must be very proud," Mr. Jones repeats, standing beside me, his arms crossed, waiting for my reply. There are no words.

From the row behind, Julie Scemper leans over. "Is that your dad?" Julie hasn't said hello in two months. But the word *dad* seems strange, a term I haven't used in years.

"I guess." Looking at the newspaper, the newsprint goes in and out of focus.

Mr. Jones shakes his head and walks away. "Teenagers," he mutters.

"That's so cool." Julie leans over to her other side. "Ethan's dad is a hero."

Mr. Jones starts teaching, but I can't ignore the newspaper. I'm searching for what everyone else missed. The fact that makes this all fit. This is not my father. Rereading the story over and over, scrutinizing the picture, tilting it in the light, I am looking for a different angle that might show that it's another firefighter. This is an unsolvable Rubik's Cube.

When the class bell rings to let us go, I'm still clutching the paper tight.

Aia nudges me when we reach my locker. "You gonna get your books?"

She doesn't understand. She doesn't know, and I can't explain it to her. I can't explain that what's in the newspaper can't be real. That the man I fear is also a hero.

"Curly," Mo shouts, running behind as Aia ducks away to meet some friends about an afterschool project.

I'm still clutching the paper like a baton, staring into the distance.

"You clipping coupons?" He pulls the baton from my hand, scrutinizing the front page. "Pretty cool."

It is not pretty cool. My jaw stiffens, and my teeth clamp down hard. I am a volcano that erupts. "No!"

Several lingering students glance in our direction. Mo steps backward.

In a heaving breath, my energy spent, I mutter, "You don't understand!"

"Of course I do." Mo taps the folded paper against a locker. "It turns out your father isn't such an asshole all the time."

But that's who my father is. He's a husband who beats his wife and a father who keeps his son at a distance.

"C'mon," Mo says and pulls me down the hall.

The cafeteria is almost empty, except for the few workers cleaning after lunch. We find a table away from a group of seniors at the other end of the room.

"Listen," Mo says. "I know why you're always over at my house. I get it. It's not right that he hits your mom. But my father can get pretty mean too." Mo sits straight and raises his hands before I can utter a syllable. "Not nearly as bad as yours. There's no comparison. I'm not saying that. I'm saying that Dad can get mad, and it gets ugly. You never see that, just like I never see what happens in your house." He looks around to ensure we're both alone and leans in closer. "I'm saying there are always two sides, you know? It's not black and white. He can't be all bad."

Mo doesn't know about my two sides. "You don't understand," I say quietly.

"All right, fine," Mo shakes his head. "Let's say, for the moment, he's all bad. A complete and total hundred-percent ass. What does it matter to you? It's not who you are. You're not like him."

"I'm not like you." I can't believe I'm about to say this.

"No kidding, Curly," Mo slouches.

"I'm serious." My words are a whisper, and Mo leans in to listen. I don't want to tell him, but at the same time, he needs to know. He needs to understand why this is such a big deal. "I'm a chimera. A genetic freak." The words, once out, can't be pulled back.

Mo looks at me, the corner of his mouth arching upward in

contemplation. "What the hell are you talking about?"

"You and Aia are twins. But imagine if you fused into one person. Not like the conjoined twins in the news. Not like the ones we read about in history last year, the ones who were in the circus." I can't believe I'm still talking. "I'm made of two different sets of DNA. Two different identities in one body."

"Curly, you're making this shit up." He shakes his head several times, but my expression makes him stop. "You're serious?"

Nodding, Mo looks at me quizzically.

"I was supposed to be a set of twins, just like you and Aia. Except something happened, and one of the twins died, and we fused. The one twin is like my father. The other is like B. The allergy doctor put it all together."

"Wait, the allergy guy? The one that poked you?"

"Yeah. You know about my eyes. Haven't you ever wondered why they're different colors?"

I put my hands, and more importantly, my thumbs, underneath the table.

Mo scrutinizes my face. I can tell he can see the discrepancies as his head shifts to the right and then to the left. He sees that my acne is worse on the right, my hair is curlier on the left, and my different colored eyes. It's subtle until he starts pulling the veil away. Then, he can't stop cataloging the differences, maybe finding some I didn't know were there.

"Okay, fine," Mo smacks the table with his palm, and the lunch ladies glance in our direction before returning to their task. "So, you're different. I'm different. There aren't many Iranians."

"It's not the same." My gaze travels to the floor. "Fine, you're Iranian. You and Aia are the only Iranians at school. But you know who and what you are. You know that you're Iranian. I don't know who I am. I don't know which side controls my personality."

I take a long breath. "Something isn't right. That's all I'm saying. My father is *not* a hero. That's not who he is. His half makes up part of me, and nothing ends in a tie. Someone has to win."

"What are you talking about?"

Under the table, my hands clasp as if I were praying. "I'm split. One side lines up with my father and the other with B. So who will I become? The aggressor or the victim? It's just the way it is. Genetics can't end in a tie. Nothing ends in a tie. One of the sides has to be in control. One side has to be dominant. Only I don't know which."

"How do you know about the genetics stuff?"

A cracked piece of taco shell on the floor goes in and out of focus while I look away from my friend. I haven't told Mo about my library research and why I'm going to the high school so often. "I've been printing off pages from a genetics book." There's regret in my admission. All the things I've kept from him.

"Wait, is that why you've been at the library?" Mo shakes his head, but he's not upset.

"I'm trying to learn how my genetics control who I am and what I'll become."

A large, wrinkled hand clasps Mo's shoulder. It's the assistant principal. "What are you both doing here?"

Mo straightens in his seat. "Sorry, sir, just,"

An authoritative voice booms, "Move on, or I'll see you in detention."

Mo leans over to whisper in my ear as we exit the lunchroom, "We'll get you some answers, Curly. Don't worry. It'll all make sense, I'm sure of it."

***

At home, I tiptoe past my father's truck as if creeping toward a lion. I know who my father is. What my father is. A newspaper story doesn't change that. Clutching the porch railing to swing myself up, to avoid the teetering creak from the two front steps, I twist the handle and apply the slightest pressure to the door that opens silently. I expect darkness and shadows, but the kitchen shade is up, and the hall lights are on.

Carefully closing the door, my hand twists the handle so it won't click. I won't make that mistake again. My foot nudges against the first step of the stairs, and I'm safe.

"Ethan, is that you?"

Who else does he think it could be? No one ever visits our house. Part of me wants to dart up the stairs and bury myself in my room.

"Ethan?" my father repeats.

After a few deep breaths, I feel my pocket for the security of my inhaler. "Yeah."

The back door is ajar, and my father walks in. "I was just working on the mower. How was school?"

This is not my father.

"Okay." I'm looking for the trap. My father dries his hands with a towel and steps closer. I nearly plug my nose to avoid the smell pouring off him. It's not whiskey, it's smoke.

I want to go upstairs. Ask if I can go. But some part of me needs to see how my father acts. "Was there a fire last night?"

"Yeah." He nods, offering nothing else. He's still drying his hands, the dark grease streaking the white towel.

"You made the paper." Studying his face and his eyes, I'm looking for a spark of regret where the paper has a piece of misinformation. The moment my father might recognize that the article is wrong and takes a quick breath or darts his eyes away. Something. Anything.

"Front page," I say, staring at him with an intensity I think might make him burn. He gawks back with the same concentration. His eyes don't travel, his hands don't fidget.

"That's only because of the chief. There was a photography student there, and she snapped a few pictures. The newspaper ran with it. I wouldn't say anything. You know? All the guys helped. I was just the one who stumbled upon the kid. But Mackey gave the paper all this info about me being a veteran and a longtime member of Station One. He thinks it's gonna be hard for the mayor to cut the budget in the spring if the public remembers the publicity from the fall." He shrugs. "It's no big deal."

There's no pride, but there's no denial, either.

The front door bangs with the violent force of an oncoming tornado. B's bag flops against her hip. She drops it by the door in a single step, surges toward my father, and wraps her arms around him. He catches her embrace, though a little off guard.

"Honey." B shudders.

One event, and B calls him Honey? She hasn't used that name in forever. He makes the paper, and we are a happy family. Suddenly, we're all smiles.

"Everyone at the office was talking about you. How you saved that kid." B's voice climbs with each sentence.

My father grins and tells how he and Bobby were sent in with a line to locate the source. After they were inside, Mackey radioed that there was a victim. He and Bobby found the fire on the second floor, but my father found a door everyone else missed, went inside, found the victim, and ran like hell to get him out.

B is mesmerized by every word. By the time he's finished, she's crying. I'm trying to be skeptical, wanting to put holes in his story, searching for something that doesn't add up. B looks happy. Truly happy, like she hasn't been in years, and I can't—I won't—take that away from her. In these minutes, we are a normal family.

"We should go out tonight," B says emphatically, and not long afterward the three of us pile into the Buick and head down the road to Ronni's Diner. It's not that busy. The booths are only half filled. When I spill ketchup all over my shirt, there's no arguing. There are no fists that bang on the table. When it's time to pay, the waitress doesn't offer the bill.

"Not tonight, Mr. Rivers. Not too often we have the front-page news eating here." She points to a stack of newspapers with my father's photo. She thinks we are a happy cookie-cutter family that wears matching sweaters for our Christmas cards. That we wake up, skipping toward breakfast, giving each other hugs. What she doesn't realize is that normal is only skin deep.

It's not until we get home that my father finally takes a shower after B gently reminds him that he still smells like smoke. On the local news, I'm hoping for a story about the fire, but by the time the weather comes on, I turn it off, reminded of when I tried to catch a glimpse of my father when he was in Saudi Arabia.

The pictures on the wall don't help me to connect my father, the man who can both beat his wife and force us under periodic veils of silence and darkness, with the man who can also be a hero. It's like mixing black and white and refusing to allow the colors to form gray. Either it's black or white.

I'm about to head upstairs when my father leaves the bathroom in a towel. "Holy shit," I mutter and take a step backward. My father shields his chest with his hands and darts into the bedroom. Red splotches snake around the front and back of my father's chest. Red, angry, irregularly shaped circles with a golden crust look like abstract art or a Rorschach plot. I can't move. I can't get past this sight. I'd never seen him with that rash before.

He emerges from the bedroom, a blue SFD shirt concealing his chest and back, and after several minutes, heads straight into the kitchen. He pulls down his bottle of whiskey and pours himself two inches into a tumbler, which he tosses back before replacing it with another three.

"That's from the fire, isn't it?" I'm shaky and afraid that talking about it will set him off. That mentioning what's on his chest will force him over the edge and ruin B's temporary happiness.

He swirls his drink, the amber liquid nearly reaching the rim of the glass, before he nods. "Yeah. The fire."

I feel sorry for him, for the first time. There's a physical mark from his service, and the protection of lives comes at a cost.

"I'm sorry," and I mean it.

"It happens." He downs the rest of his drink. "I'm going outside," and he heads toward the shed.

CHAPTER TWENTY

TWO WEEKS LATER, Grandma and Grandpa came to our house for my birthday, and all five of us had dinner. Rather than staying in separate rooms, Grandpa talked with my father for an hour about the SU basketball season. When Grandpa left, he shook my father's hand. "Hope to see you at our house next Sunday."

It's incredible. One event has shifted everyone's perspective. I want to believe in this new version of my father. That he pulled someone from a fire, and it altered his outlook. I've heard that a near-death experience will force a person to re-evaluate their life; maybe saving a life has the same impact. I could ignore the past and move forward. It would be so easy. Then I picture a bruise on B's chin.

I know which version of my father is real.

For a month, there's less yelling. I don't hear my father pacing the living room at 3 a.m. The lamps in the house remain lit most nights. It's not until the day of the mayor's Christmas party that my father appears on edge.

Mr. Henderson's tractor backfires, and my father scrambles into the kitchen. "Daniels, Daniels!" he screams, crashing toward the cabinets. His eyes are a dull gray, and my fears cement in place. As I plan an escape route, he pours several inches of Jack Daniels into a mug and leaves for the shed, never acknowledging my presence.

B is in her room choosing a dress for the party. I want to tell her the monster is back, that he was yelling for his whiskey again, his eyes glassy and gray. She's been fooled just like everyone else. I know who he is. I know what he can do. I've known all along. Instead, I retreat to my room to read.

Hours later, I hear him talking downstairs.

"Yeah, I feel good. I'm not sure how good I'll feel in a suit at the mayor's house."

Picturing the two of them getting ready, B glides around the room, palming her earrings while my father fixes his tie. They're costumes, just like in the wedding picture.

"I'm just so proud of you," B's voice cracks. "I mean, for so long." There's a broken sob and a long pause. "I'm just so happy."

Her voice trails off. Why can't she smell the whiskey? Why can't she see who he really is?

"I owe you some better jewelry, for taking care of things when I was gone, for being so strong."

"I don't need jewelry," B answers. "As long as I have you back. That's all I need."

I want to scream. *This is fake. This is a charade. He is fooling you!* But I focus on the words on the page, refusing to take this happiness away from B.

"Ethan," B says, "ready to go?" She turns to my father. "I'll be right back. Just don't have too many."

"It's my first beer of the day." He raises the half-empty bottle in a salute.

I'm spending the night at Mo's. I want to tell B in the car. I want to say that his eyes glassed over and that it might be his first beer, but it was certainly not his first drink.

But her voice scales several notes higher, "Jim Boeheim, the SU basketball coach, is supposed to be at the party."

I can't force myself to do it. Not only because I'm afraid that I'll ruin her blind happiness, but also she won't believe me.

***

Darting from B's car, I scurry up the stairs to Mo's room without a hello to Mr. and Mrs. A. on the couch. I'm in the middle of explaining how bad things are, that my father has fooled everyone, and that he's not a hero when Aia opens the door.

"I didn't say you could come in," Mo snaps. "This is my room."

Aia glides forward and sits next to me. Our legs touch, and she looks square at Mo. "I didn't ask." She turns to me. "What's wrong with your father?"

I focus on my socks and away from her gaze. She reaches over, setting her fingers on my arm. It's the simplest gesture, but I've never forgotten waiting for the bus, her purple gloves resting on my arm. There's a warmth from her touch, or maybe just the memory.

I fracture, spilling words onto my lap. "My father is a bad man."

Aia glances at Mo before returning to me, her hand still resting on my arm. "Are you okay?"

I'm not. I'm not okay. "My father drinks too much and always wants the house dark. Like complete darkness. If B or I bother him, he gets angry." I know I'm saying too much, and an avalanche of emotions tumbles out. I shouldn't say this in front of Mo, especially not in front of Aia. But I can't stop. "Really angry. And when he gets angry, he starts to hit. Everyone thinks that after he rescued that SU student, he's a hero and that maybe he's different. But he's not. I know he's not." The words tumble out of my trembling mouth.

"Does he hit you?" Her soothing voice battles against the concentration in her eyes.

I swallow. I could stop right now. Tell her that I misspoke. That I didn't mean it. My jaw trembles, and her green eyes look deep into mine. "Just B. But I can't protect her. She won't let me. She keeps pushing me out of the room. And worse, I'm afraid I might turn into him."

"You're nothing like your father." Her voice is stern, her rebuttal sharp.

"You don't understand." The words are hot. My eyes meet Mo's. I realize that he's kept our secret.

"I'm different." I blurt out.

"We all are."

Aia doesn't understand. "No, I am different. I'm a *chimera*. I'm like two different people fused into one. It's why I have different colored eyes and my hair is straighter on one side. I'm two different people bound together. Half like my father and half like my mother, and I don't know who's in control. I don't know how to figure out who is in control."

Mo and Aia share a glance and then concentrate back on me. "Why does it have to be just one in control? How can you figure that out?" Aia asks.

"Nothing ends in a tie. Someone has to win." I echo the lines from Grandpa. "I have so many questions," I say, concealing my tears.

Aia snags a pad of paper and a pen from Mo's desk. "Okay, let's make a list," her pen to paper, she sits next to me, even closer this time.

"What makes one gene dominant or recessive?" I know certain genes are dominant or recessive, but I can't figure out what makes them that way or how that might influence my two sets of DNA.

Aia scribbles the question down and writes a number two. Our eyes meet, and she nods for me to move forward.

"How often does a chimera occur?"

We have eleven questions, some about chimeras and some related to genetics. They're some of the same questions I've had since the beginning of the year.

"We meet at the library tomorrow after school, and we'll find the answers," Aia says confidently, and I want to believe her.

CHAPTER TWENTY-ONE

MY FATHER AND B made it home safe after the mayor's party, and it felt like we dodged a bullet. B's only comment about the night was that the food was good, but they didn't know anyone, so they left after about an hour. But since that afternoon, I have watched my father, waiting for another example to show B that he isn't a hero.

I've spent each day in the library after school. Mo and I searched for pages in textbooks about chimeras.

During the second week, when Mo is at the table with us, Aia asks to show me something in the back.

In the corner of the library, between two musty stacks of books, Aia's dark hair hangs onto her left shoulder, and she searches my two eyes. Not between them, but both at once. "I need to know."

My foot taps, curious why we left the table, and worried someone might look at our papers.

Aia leans in and kisses me, just a peck on my lips, and steps backward.

I blink, my mouth hanging open. She's Mo's sister, who blocked the TV when we played Nintendo or who pushed her way into what we were doing. Her head hangs slack.

She's the person whose purple gloved fingers were a source of comfort. The person who's helping me now. I pull her back, just like when we danced together.

We walk back to our table hand in hand. Her warm fingers intertwine with mine.

Mo glances up from his book and laughs. "It's about time the two of you figured it out."

From our time in the library, we found a list of dominant genes but couldn't determine what makes a gene dominant. Some genes were associated with different diseases, but none were associated with personality.

We read about a famous set of conjoined twins, the Siamese twins Chang and Eng joined at the chest. They came to America in the 1800s as a sideshow and became wealthy. Each married a sister, and every three days, they rotated which wife spent the night. Very rational. What's truly astonishing is that the twins fathered twenty-one children. The duo alternated between who was in charge and whose actions dictated the pair. I don't have the luxury of outlining a schedule for who will be in control of me.

I need to understand more about my specific genetics. The library isn't enough. Talking with Aia, I remembered another source of information, an idea devised months ago in math class.

***

I wait until after Christmas, the two-week break, when I'm huddled in my room alone or over at Mo's house. In early January, I clear my throat to tug B away from her magazine. "I'm willing to do Dr. Taylor's study." My arms hang loose, but my fingers keep moving like I'm playing piano. I try not to sound or look awkward.

B eyes me from above *Good Housekeeping*, uncrosses her legs, and sits upright. "Dr. Taylor's study? Really?" She lowers the magazine to her lap. "Why the change?"

Dr. Taylor asked, and then pleaded, for a full genetic workup of our family, which he said would increase the medical community's understanding of chimeras. It wouldn't improve my treatment, so we refused. It only sounded like an opportunity for Dr. Taylor to stick me with needles and then boast about his clinical acumen. But maybe a few needle pokes will get me answers to my questions.

Keep cool. No need to make B suspicious. "I might learn something. We're studying this in school," I lie. "It's sort of like a special science experiment." Pulling my hands behind my back, I clasp them tight so B can't see me fidget. "But there's something else."

B's eyes narrow.

"Dr. Taylor needs all of us to take the test." My request hangs in the air. B's narrow eyes relax, and she groans.

"We need his DNA." Getting my father to Dr. Taylor's office will require pleading and some luck.

B shrugs and burrows back into her magazine. "I'll talk to him. It'll be okay."

She says it so convincingly. I'd prepared for more questions. I'd thought she'd ask why I was willing to get poked by needles or maybe in which class we discussed genetics. If I wasn't awkward before, I am now and charge toward the stairs without another word.

***

It takes a week for Dr. Taylor's office to arrange an appointment on a Saturday afternoon so that I won't miss school. My father needed to skip watching part of the SU game on TV, which might have been a deal breaker, but since the team was losing, he didn't object. We take separate cars so my father can head to work after the appointment. The medical building appears deserted. The lobby, usually bright, is dimly lit, and the doors are locked. My father grunts, thinking this has been a waste of time, but within seconds, Dr. Taylor rounds the corner.

He wears a light blue sweater and a nice pair of shoes. "Good afternoon, good afternoon." His hand ushers us to the elevator, where he shepherds us to his office.

We bustle through the dark office, past the empty reception desk, and into a patient room, where a woman in a plaid skirt sits in the corner. She has short blonde hair and gold-rimmed glasses so thick her eyes look fuzzy.

"Ms. H., one of my associates, will perform the tests." As Dr. Taylor introduces us, I notice a cart of tubes and vials. I scrutinize the contents, not for needles, but for the names of the solutions on the bottles. There's *TRIzol, RNAse*-free water, and *phenol-chloroform*, the chemicals I've read about from the books in the library.

"Essentially," Dr. Taylor says, "I'm going to give you a paternity test." My mind races to an afternoon talk show. There isn't much of a question about who my father is.

"I'll analyze DNA from Ethan's left and right sides and compare it to the DNA of both of you." He turns to my parents and nods. "I won't examine the entire sequence of DNA, just several short segments. Since Ethan is a chimera, I expect there will be distinct differences in those short DNA segments between his left and right side."

Genetics are the blueprints of life, and I want to know how much my father dominates my genetics on the left. This little experiment is the best way to determine my father's control.

Ms. H. stands and extends a welcoming hand. "Who's first?"

Dr. Taylor opens his mouth to say something like, "I'll be in my office if you need anything," when I clear my throat. "I'm not giving a sample."

"But your mom said—" Dr. Taylor's voice trails off as he pleats the front of his fluffy sweater.

"I have several questions first." My arms cross, and Dr. Taylor glances at the ceiling.

"Okay, Ethan, what questions do you have?" he asks sarcastically.

"You'll be comparing the DNA from my left and right side to the DNA of my parents, right?"

Dr. Taylor's smile tightens. "That's what we discussed."

"How will you be analyzing the sample? PCR or HLA?" From my research, PCR is more accurate and can yield more information. The HLA test will only examine my white blood cells and won't examine the DNA differences. If they're unwilling to perform PCR experiments, I want to find someone who will.

The room goes quiet. B glances at my father, whose mouth hangs ajar. Dr. Taylor's eyes dart to each of my parents and then back at me. The only person who seems unfazed is Ms. H.

"Uh—" Dr. Taylor stutters but is saved by Ms. H., "PCR. It's much more accurate."

"Did he learn that in school?" my father whispers as B shakes her head.

"Okay, if that's it?" Dr. Taylor spins on his heel, maybe initially surprised but over the astonishment of my question.

He makes about a quarter rotation before I interrupt. "It's not."

He spins back, his eyes closed. "Of course it isn't," he mutters.

"How many products are you testing?" Dr. Taylor's facial expression tightens.

Ms. H. saves him again. "We plan to run ten different bands."

"And you'll separate the bands on a gel and take a picture?" The gel is Jell-O like where DNA products separate according to size. The bands are the short DNA segments.

I've read all about this procedure. After binding with a radiographic probe, heavier bands travel only a short distance, and the smaller fragments move farther away. The series of white dashes, or bands, are photographed. Bands inherited from my father will match up identically with mine.

Hopefully, I can identify a reasonable number of DNA fragments from my father that aligns with each side, even though I might not physically notice any differences. That will show that genetically, I'm much more of a mixed bag. Yes, there are two sets of DNA, but not with one dominant and the other recessive. A mutt.

Dr. Taylor needs me, and I propose the most important question. "May I have a copy of the results? Not the report, but the pictures of the gel."

"I'm not sure," Dr. Taylor answers, but Ms. H. interrupts, "Sure. Do you want us to mail it to you?"

"Yes." I stick out my arm, ready for the needle, while giving her my address.

***

My arm is sore from the needle poke, and my tongue travels to several rough spots along the sides of my mouth, where Mrs. H. used a toothbrush to get tissue samples from my left and right sides. The tissue samples from my mouth will establish that there are DNA differences between my left and right side.

B is very quiet on the car ride back, and I catch her glancing at me several times. We are nearly home before she asks, "Where did you learn all that genetics stuff?"

"The library." I can't look her in the eyes.

"Why?" Her one-word question is drawn out.

My mouth opens and then snaps shut. B doesn't see the problem. She doesn't understand that my two halves can't mutually coexist like Chang and Eng. Just like there's no harmony between B and my father, there is no harmony between my left and right side. She doesn't see it, and maybe she can't. She notices the physical differences and moves past the consequences because she's my mother. She accepts me for who I am, just like Grandma accepts B for always hiding whenever there's a problem.

"I don't know who I am." I blurt. "I'm two separate halves. The one like you is fine, but there's one like my father." My chest heaves. "The one like my father . . . what if it's dangerous? What if it's violent? What if his half starts to take control?"

"Ethan," B says, an apology in her tone. "You're not like your father."

We pull into the driveway, and she turns off the car. I look her straight in the eye for the first time during our trip home. "It's who I am. I just don't know who I am." I open the door to the car and head to my room. Downstairs, B does the same.

CHAPTER TWENTY-TWO

FOR TWO WEEKS, I feel like I'm on a talk show awaiting the results of a paternity test. Countless scenarios race through my head. Maybe Ms. H. forgot her promise. What if she messed up the experiment? Two weeks and two days later, a thick yellow manila envelope sits in the mailbox.

Who I am is right here. My trembling hands clutch the packet, like a student hoping for a college acceptance. Yellow papers, along with several photographs, slide out.

I read everything twice and tell B I'm not hungry, staying in my room with the pages strewn across my desk. Downstairs, B sits on the couch watching *Wheel of Fortune* while I stare at the glowing white dashes representing the different DNA fragments. The little white blocks gaze back at me like all-knowing eyes.

These markers are only a tiny percentage of my overall DNA. As if my hair color, eyes, or hell, even my thumb isn't enough evidence of my genetic freakishness, in proverbial black and white is all the evidence I need. From the genetic material on my left side, all ten segments align with my father. And on the right, it's only five.

On a piece of stationery, there's a detailed description of the experimental steps and interpretation of the results. Ms. H. doesn't understand why so few of my father's DNA segments line up with mine on the right side. They only tested 10 segments, so maybe if they tested more, there might be different results. But I understand. My DNA aligns perfectly with his on my left side, but not on my right. There's now biological and genetic proof that my father controls my left side. Downstairs, the front door shuts, and heavy boots pound against the floor. There's no complaining about the loud TV or the bright living room lights. There's also no cordial hello.

"Did that asshole VanPatten come to your office today?" my father barks. He's angry, but it doesn't sound directed at B. He steps into the kitchen and a cabinet opens. I imagine him pouring Jack Daniels over ice.

"How did you know?" B answers, her voice curious.

"There was an accident on Salina Street yesterday."

My father's boots return to the living room, and I wonder when he started and stopped working. It's well past when he should have gotten home from any shift. Peering around the corner of my door, I can see B's straight blonde hair resting on the back of the couch.

"Nothing major, just a fender bender. A semi hit a car from behind. It was low speed. We took the guy out of the car on a backboard as a precaution. He wasn't complaining about anything, but you know it was the safe thing to do."

"Right," B puts down her magazine.

"But as we're loading him in the ambulance, this fucking blue Mercedes pulls up. A bald guy in a suit tries to get to the victim, and hand him a business card. Asking Bobby if he thinks the driver is at fault. Trying to get Bobby to say that the semi probably wasn't inspected recently or some horse shit." My father sinks into his chair and lets out an exhaustive moan, and his glass clinks against the side table.

"The guy on the stretcher takes the card, and I hear VanPatten, like on the TV, 'I can get you all the money you deserve.'" My father's voice imitates the commercial on TV. "And then he says, 'Especially since your back hurts.' The guy wasn't even complaining about his back. We were only taking the guy to the hospital as a precaution."

My father swirls the ice cubes around in his glass. "Anyway, I had to go in the ambulance, which is another story entirely because of some dispatch fuckup. But I'm in the back with the guy, and five minutes into the ride, he complains that his back and neck are hurting. The pain is excruciating, and I'm shaking my head. But what can we do? So we have to hit the sirens because now it's a fucking emergency, and we divert to the trauma center. And I'm pissed. Like that piece of shit lawyer will cost that semi driver his job."

"How did you know he came to see Dr. Carter today?" B shifts her weight, and the couch groans.

"Oh, yeah." The sound of the ice swirling against his glass returns for just a moment. "So I'm filling out the last of the paperwork in the emergency room, which I haven't done in like four years, so it takes me forever because they changed the form, and now there's this new triplicate version, and I had to write down the guy's PCP, and guess who should strut in?"

"VanPatten."

"Yup. He strolls in, asking for the guy's name. He says he's his lawyer, which he isn't. The guy hadn't called anyone, so I walked up to VanPatten and told him to fuck off. And do you know what he says to me?"

"What?" B shifts toward the edge of the couch.

"He tells me that he's trying to help victims just like I am, and that if I knew what was best I'd get out of his way."

"What did you do?"

"I was going to clock him right there, but Randy pulled me away before I had a chance."

"Just like his son." B shakes her head.

"What do you mean?"

"His son, Jackson, is in Ethan's class. He's the school bully, always causing trouble and never getting caught."

"It's in the DNA." My father gulps the remainder of his drink, and I stare at the blot in front of me.

CHAPTER TWENTY-THREE

THE MORNING STARTS peacefully. From my room, the soft sounds of the news and a pan clanking against the stove echo through the house. Outside, a pair of headlights highlight the blanket of white stretching across our lawn and onto Mr. Henderson's field.

Throwing on thick jeans and a white Spalding sweatshirt, the front door slams shut, shaking the house. The peaceful quiet dissipates. It's barely 7 a.m. He shouldn't be home now.

"Why, after I work all night, can I not get some peace and quiet?" It isn't a plea or desperate request. There's anger in his voice.

"I didn't think—" B's voice trails off. I can picture it. She's rushing around the house, pulling the shades and turning off the lights. The house is going dark, one light and one window at a time. In minutes, the first floor will be darker inside than out.

Creeping, one step at a time, I head downstairs.

"Jesus, Spencer, this isn't normal. This just isn't normal." B's deep alto voice is full of urgency.

I take a puff from my inhaler. It doesn't help. I'm still breathing hard. Is she confronting him? Why? Why now? That's not what B does. She placates his actions. She softens the blow. She doesn't add gunpowder to a lit fuse.

The hall light is still on, and crouching on the stairs, I can see both of them in the kitchen. I think about my father's broken rules and the garbage pail full of broken bottles.

"My God, did you just drink half the bottle in a gulp?"

Does B really not know? She has to know.

"It's 7 a.m.!" B shouts, and I take another step and peer over the railing. My father is gripping his Jack Daniels like a baby would their bottle. This is my father. Right here. Right now. Not the pictures of the hero on the front page of the newspaper. The angry drunk who hopefully will head out to the shed and leave us alone.

"It's my medicine," he barks, taking another swig from the bottle. There's no smoke in the air, but maybe there was a fire last night? Something that caused him to lose sleep, and the headache this morning is more intense, and that's why his anger is boiling.

Crouching on the steps, I'm unsure whether to interfere but certain that I can't return to my room. B seems to reassess and ambles toward him like he's a feral animal, her hands outstretched. His back is to me, and even in the dull light from the hall, I lock onto B's eyes, and she gives the subtlest of shakes for me to stay away. I freeze. B is good at defusing him, good at settling him down. She's told me before that I should let her calm him down. She's nearly in front of him and places her hand on his forearm. She will put him back to where he's manageable.

I stare at my parent's wedding photo. The two pressed cheek to cheek, and I think of the mayor's party when my father was drunk, and I said nothing.

B's soft voice is almost a whisper. "I think we need to get you some help. Maybe doctor—"

My father shoves her hard, and B nearly trips as she steps back to regain her balance. The sight of this assault ignites something inside of me. I will not let him do this. I will not let him hurt her again. I clench my left fist.

"I. Don't. Need. Any. Help," my father growls in staccato syllables. I picture his teeth gnashing together. He pulls the bottle back to his lips, and B stumbles toward him again. Maybe she's going to try a different approach. Maybe she thinks my father won't react a second time and that the hero the city has seen and recognized for the past three months will return. But that's not who my father is.

He shoves her more forcefully this time, and she falls to the floor on her back. He marches toward her. I know that march. That's the same way Jackson VanPatten charges at me.

I lurch off the last four steps. The house quakes, and the bottle of whiskey plummets from my father's hand, shattering on the floor. Glass and amber liquid spread over the white linoleum like an oil spill.

He twists, and his eyes are as gray as storm clouds. There is no light. "Daniels," he roars. His face is pale, and his fingers curl into one another, coiling into a fist. I ready myself. He looks from side to side and steps toward me, glass crunching under his boots. He takes another step forward, and there's another crunch. I can't tell how fast or slow this is happening. I only know he's coming toward me, and I'm surging toward him.

His upper body convulses in erratic, jerky movements, but his legs are as steady as oaks. His jaw is set, and his gaze remains square on me.

I never see B standing from the floor. Her hand grips his shoulder, spinning him around. His face and body swivel away. What is she doing? What is she thinking? What is he thinking?

The cracking sound of my father's fist colliding with B's cheek answers all three questions. A deafening thunderclap resonates throughout the house. I put my hands over my ears, but I can still hear. I shut my eyes, but I can still see. She is falling. Her head thuds against the kitchen counter, bouncing like a ball against a bat, and she crumples to the floor. She doesn't move, and from here, I can't tell if she's breathing.

Every instinct tells me to run. *Run away!* But to where? Henderson's farm is nearly half a mile away. I can't leave her alone with him for that long. Every muscle inside my body surges toward my mother. Every fiber energizes me to her side. I take two steps, slip on the whiskey, and land on the glass with outstretched hands.

My hands sting from the cuts and then burn from the whiskey. I try to speak, but only a croak escapes. Then another croak. The sounds are barely audible. My hands are covered in blood, and I nearly puke. My throat clenches tight, and I can't gulp the air down. My blood is on the floor, B's blood is on the floor, while my father looms tall over us.

"Why?" I finally muster. The shredded agony in my voice cracks into my father's head, and he looks at me now with blue eyes. He's shaking. Not just his upper body like before, but all of him is convulsing so violently that soon I think he'll join us on the floor. But that isn't who my father is; I know it even before he does.

I wriggle on my side, inching toward B. The blood from her head has colored her hair black in the dim light. The glass presses into my side, and I find the strength for only one word. "Mama."

I want her to answer. But she doesn't. She doesn't move. Have I witnessed my father killing my mother? I see him streaking out the front door, which swings ajar, letting in the faint light and the bitter cold.

Crawling to the wall, I topple over, cutting my hands. The second time, I clutch the receiver. Blood smears over the phone, and the green glow of the numbers goes dark with each button I press.

A voice answers. It is soft and welcoming. Happy. "Grandpa," and I don't even know if he hears me. I can't even tell if I'm saying the words loud enough because it's getting harder and harder to breathe. It's the worst asthma attack I've ever had. I'm trying to gulp the air into my lungs.

"Ethan?" The cheer in Grandpa's voice falls away.

"I think he killed Mom," and then everything goes black.

CHAPTER TWENTY-FOUR

THE ROOM'S EDGES come into focus. I blink, and everything is white, and I wonder for a moment if I'm dead. If I'm dead, I shouldn't have pain. The last thing I remember is the blood. The blood on my hands. The blood on the floor. The blood on B. There's a massive void between that moment and now, and I have no idea when now is—an hour, a day, maybe even a year later.

I catalog my surroundings. There are bright rainbows and fluffy clouds on the wall. The too white sheets feel as starched as a dress-shirt collar. Raising my hands in front of my face, they're wrapped in bandages that resemble paddles just like when the stove burned me in Grandpa's living room. Between slow, short breaths, I trace several wires connecting my skin to a monitor above my head, and I turn my neck to see the numbers on the screen.

I must be in a hospital room, but where is B? To the side of my bed is an empty chair. I make it my mission to find where she is. I swing my legs to prop myself upright, and the wires disconnect from my skin. A series of percussive pings chime from the flashing monitor above my head.

"You trying to escape?" A man in scrubs stands at the doorway. He has dark hair, glasses, and the most prominent Adam's apple I've ever seen. I stare at it for a moment, longer than I should. He hurries next to me, which is good because the room and my head spin. Guiding me back into bed, he secures the sheets around my legs and raises the back of the bed so that I can sit.

"B?" I murmur.

His head tilts to the side before I change my question. "Where's my mom?"

His cheery expression goes tight like he still hasn't understood the question. My paddles anchor to his arm, and I lean forward to see his nametag. Nurse Kevin tries to look away. He swallows, and his Adam's apple bobs.

"She's in the neuro ICU," he whispers, "but I don't know more than that."

My paddles drop. My eyes shut tight, and a single tear forms at the corner and hangs tight to my eye. *She's alive.*

"And Spencer?" Kevin's eyes jolt back to my face. "You're safe from him." Kevin walks toward the door. "Let me get your grandfather. He wanted to be here when you woke."

I lean back into bed, trying to piece together the emptiness of the void in time that I've lost. I can remember the crack of B's jaw and the thud of her head hitting the counter. It is a syncopated rhythm that seems to get louder and louder. Only when my gauzy hands bind tight to my ears is there quiet. Stillness.

"Ethan." Grandpa shifts toward the bed, and his voice cracks. Somehow, there's both agony and relief in the way he calls my name.

"How is B?" He rubs his face. After I called him, he dialed 911 and raced to the house. When he arrived, the ambulance and police were already taking us to the hospital.

B came to the hospital and needed emergency surgery to relieve blood collected around her brain, and right now, she's very sick.

He uses words like *subdural hematoma* and *intra-cerebral pressure*. Words I don't understand. I had cuts on my hands and a bad asthma attack when I arrived. They gave me medicine to relax, and I probably wouldn't remember much.

"And Spencer?" hoping he isn't sitting next to B as we speak.

Grandpa's jaw hardens, and his eyebrows narrow. "Your father," Grandpa's teeth gnash, "was arrested several hours ago. He tried to flee and then fought several officers at a bar. And will likely go to prison."

I want Spencer and everything he's touched put far away. I think of my room, where the pencil box sits on the shelf. I'll bury it. Bury his letters. Bury everything.

PART THREE

September 1995

"The son of a snake is, most probably, a snake."

— Mr. VanPatten

CHAPTER TWENTY-FIVE

A CROSS MY DESK, paper piles together in haphazard stacks. There's a brochure for Syracuse University underneath my biology book and below my math homework. My junior year started a week ago, and I feel underwater. SU is the only school I want to attend when I apply next year. Mo and I have a plan. We'll room together. Aia isn't sure, but Syracuse is high on her list. Maintaining my good grades is my only shot at an academic scholarship. But my grades may not matter if the admissions counselor who reads my application remembers my father.

It's been two years since Spencer went to prison for assault and domestic abuse. That's certainly enough time for a community to forget about a husband beating his wife. But his name burns deeper into everyone's memory when he made the paper's front page, first as a hero and then as a villain. Since I have to put Spencer's name on my application, I'm unsure if I'll get an interview.

B was hospitalized for a month after the assault and spent another month in rehab. She had been in a coma for two weeks while the swelling around her brain improved. When the doctors finally removed her breathing tube, I clutched her hand and the edge of her bed. I wanted to wrap myself around her but was afraid of the tape and tubing. I wanted her to say something, anything. When I asked her for the third time to speak, her mouth opened, but no sound came out. She was choking on the words. Eventually, she cried, heaving out several long sobs.

I stayed at Grandma and Grandpa's during B's rehab. At school, most teachers pitied my situation, but a few kept their distance. I assume they worried that the kid who witnessed abuse at home and was bullied at school might be a loaded weapon.

When B finished her rehab, I wanted to stay with Grandpa. It was safe there, far away from the memories of my father. B refused, and we returned home. I wanted to rebuild the kitchen, but we didn't have the money to remove the cabinets or the floor. I tried to take Spencer's chair to the curb, but B said there wasn't another to replace it.

We don't talk about Spencer. It's like he's away at war. We don't get any letters, but the house, our existence, is the same as the day before the assault. The lights are dim, maybe because that's how we are used to them now, or perhaps his grasp on us remains tight.

This morning, I focus on the imaginary line tracing my center. Even beneath my shirt, I can finger that thin strip of neutral territory where the left meets right and black meets white. After Spencer went to prison, I tried to ignore it, hoping his removal from my life would minimize his influence. But I can't alter my genetics or Spencer's fingerprint on my left side.

I've scoured for answers, hoping for signs that I won't become my father. I've found nothing to assure me his half won't take control. Dr. Taylor gave me several medical journals, but they weren't helpful. I went to SU for an afternoon to use the library but found nothing.

Mo has tried to convince me that I'm not different and, just like him, that half of my genetic material comes from each parent. He's right; my DNA is an assembly of the same random set of building blocks. But unlike Mo and Aia, I don't have an identity. Their physical and personality traits trace back to each parent. Aia has her father's eyes but her mother's nose and temperament. She doesn't think about it because she has a clear identity. She doesn't wake up each morning wondering if she'll need glasses like her father. But she might if she dreamed of becoming a pilot needing 20/20 vision. Each time she saw a Snellen eye chart, she might read the bottom line, proving that despite having the same eye color, she didn't have her father's astigmatism. Because if her vision failed, it would shift her mindset and maybe her career.

Traits can even be diluted or enhanced. Anger inherited from one parent can be tempered by the other. But my physical characteristics are at odds. Each morning, I look for signs of an ongoing conflict. Which side is winning? More and more, I'm not sure I have command over Spencer's half. I am Abel bound to Cain.

I've learned there's a rule that form follows function. The way something looks determines its purpose. It's evolution. The form evolves so that the cell or organism can better adapt. Here's the catch-22. I wasn't designed as two different people. I should have been a single person. But something happened, binding two twins and fusing them rather than keeping them separate. And the result is that I don't know who I am or who I take after.

***

I slip quietly down the stairs. Two years of working to develop a morning routine that's not predicated on fear, but I can't adapt how I move through the house. The living room light is on, but it's the only one.

In the kitchen, I still hear the crack, thud. Crack, thud. Two sounds I'll never get out of my head. Only seconds apart, they form a rhythm getting louder and louder. The crack of B's cheek after Spencer twisted his arm so that his punch would have more power—the thud of B's head against the counter. I shield my eyes with my hands but still see it. I can still hear it. The sound pulsates in my head like the rhythm of a beating drum, increasing in intensity until I cringe at the pain.

B scrambles eggs in a pan. Only the dim sliver of light sneaks between the curtains, and I'm thankful for the darkness that will keep my headache at bay. My eyes glance at the cabinet above the fridge and what remains there, but head to the coffee pot instead.

"If you drink too much of that, you'll stop growing."

She's trying to be funny. I'm no longer the two-eyed midget. Just shy of six feet, I'm the two-eyed freak whose father is in prison—hero to zero. But I wonder if she thinks that the coffee is another sign.

"Just tired." I grab a bowl and open the cereal box, careful not to make any noise.

"You didn't sleep?"

Even in the dark, her voice has an edge of concern. Maybe she's adding another trait and another symptom to Spencer's column. There can't be a tie. Someone has to win, and so far this morning, Spencer is up 2-0.

"Studying all night? Your math test isn't until next week."

Nodding, I think about the paper I read last night before working on my homework from my most recent library search, published in the *American Journal of Human Genetics*. Like all the rest, that paper focused only on how an organism can have two unique DNA strands.

"Don't stress out. You'll get into Syracuse next year." B pats my arm with assurance.

Mo has wanted to attend Syracuse since the men's basketball team made another run into the Final Four. For me, it's close to home. I can't leave B.

Grandma died almost a year ago of a stroke. One morning, Grandpa woke, and she was unable to speak, and half of her face drooped to the side. The doctors said they couldn't do much, and she died several days later. Alone without Grandma, Grandpa died a month later of a heart attack. For a year, it's just been the two of us. B and I, two peas in a pod.

"You have your bio lab today, right? That's exciting." B sits next to me at the table. For a moment, we stare at the empty seat in the corner, the continued reflex acknowledging that he's not here.

"Yeah, Dr. Meyers, a genetics professor at SU."

The guest appearances happen once a month in my AP bio class. Our teacher, Mr. Lane, arranged for a college professor to lecture on a specialized topic. I'd been looking forward to them since he told us the schedule on the first day of school. Last week, Mr. Lane announced our first guest, Dr. Meyers, an SU professor who might put in a good word for my application.

***

"Good morning, good morning!" Dr. Meyers said in a British accent during the first class yesterday. The man had personality, sort of a James Bond meets Bill Nye the science guy. He gave a twenty-minute lecture about the structure and function of DNA, emphasizing the importance of understanding the human genetic code and its significance in life and disease. For the second half of class, we headed into the lab space in the back of the room.

"We are going to plot your DNA." Dr. Meyers grinned as if he were part of some inside joke.

"Each of you will swab inside your mouth to collect DNA. We will then break it apart." He used a karate chop motion, gaining only mild enthusiasm from the students. "I thought that was quite good," he paused, smirking. "Anyway, we will cleave the DNA into small segments. Then, I'll take your experiments to my lab and amplify them with a polymerase chain reaction, or PCR, separate them using electrophoresis, and then run them on a gel with a radioactive probe. Tomorrow, we will discover how much you all have in common." He cleared his throat. "Well, at least genetically. You will find the kits with detailed instructions in front of you."

"Basically, we get to learn who I really am. Ninety-seven percent human, three percent donkey." Mo unpacked his kit, separating the different components into piles.

The group next to us snickered, but the group across gave a sharp gaze, already organizing their kits.

"Pre-med wannabes," he admonished.

"You want to go to medical school."

"Yeah, but I'll be pre-surg. Definitely cooler."

I shook my head, breaking apart the first package. I'd done this experiment already, remembering Dr. Taylor pleading for my DNA profile. Ms. H., scraping the inside of my mouth and waiting for the mail, hoping there would be an equal number of the tested genetic segments from Spencer on each side. My DNA was probably part of a case report on the back pages of some allergy and immunology journal. I was only happy they didn't publish my name. I certainly didn't need to see those bands again.

Around the room, students opened wide to scrape both sides of their mouths. I knew better, opening my mouth as wide as possible, I focused to keep the brush dead center. After moving the brush toward the right side, I faced the lab bench, scraping my cheek.

While removing the brush, a crash echoed behind me, and I twisted to the left. Tommy stood slack-jawed over a broken beaker of distilled water. The sour taste of plastic filled my mouth. The brush still in my hand went limp in the left side of my mouth.

I wanted to rip the brush out. Chuck it on the floor and stomp on it. But what would Dr. Myers say? What would the class say? The brush slid from my mouth like a wet noodle. I looked at the course, green bristles filled full of my DNA. With shaking hands, I put the brush in the appropriate tube and added the necessary reagents. It wasn't a firm scrape. I probably didn't go deep enough to get a sample from my left.

I handed my tube to Dr. Meyers, labeled with my name.

"Tomorrow, my young scientists, we will all go over the results together," Dr. Myers beamed.

"Together?" My stomach turned.

"Yes, indeed. A genetic exploration of each of you."

I took a few puffs from my inhaler before Mo gently nudged me out the door.

* * *

"You okay?" B asks, breaking me out of my memory from yesterday. She stares a little too long. This afternoon, I expect my genetic diagnosis on display. My bowl clatters in the sink, trying to scrub away the cereal.

"Just tired."

Her circumspect gaze tries to find the answer, but the sound of Mo's blue Ford rumbling on the driveway doesn't give her a chance.

"I gotta go."

"Be good."

I speed out the front door and slide into the back next to Aia. "Good morning," and I kiss her nose. It's the one part of her body she dislikes, the same nose as her mother's, and what I love most about her. It's long, pointed, and hooks outward before sloping down.

Aia and I have been together for two years. At first, it was okay because Mo was dating Susan Rhinehardt. When they broke up, it became awkward. I would call for Aia, and if Mo answered, he would reluctantly hand the phone to his sister. It took almost a year before he decided that if someone had to date Aia, it might as well be me.

The radio blares as we park across the street from the high

school. A jackhammer sounds in the distance, and the noises of the continued construction seem loudest in the morning. Last year, the parking lot was next to the school, but with all the heavy equipment, the lot moved across the street.

We pause at the crosswalk until the crossing guard, an older guy with a mustache and a USMC tattoo on his forearm, waves us forward. At this early hour, the cool air in late September sends a reminder that I'll soon need a jacket.

As we near school, two students pass, looking suspiciously back at us. Ducking my head, I still get the random glances. No one forgets when your father nearly kills your mother, especially since I was already the school freak. Mo rolls his eyes at the kids staring at us, muttering, "Yes, people, brown skin, must be a terrorist . . . be afraid, be very afraid." Somehow, Mo thinks the kids are looking at him, not me. The sounds of the jackhammer ramp up, drowning out any further comment.

"What's with that creepy guy?" Mo quickens his pace, pulling ahead of me.

Is he making a joke about the two students who were eyeing us? "Huh?" shrugging off their stares, Aia clings tight to my arm.

"The car back there. The black one in the corner of the lot."

I twist, and Aia swivels with me.

"Don't look," Mo says sharply as if we were on some secret mission and almost blew our cover.

"You told me to look?"

"No, I said, what's with the creepy guy?" Mo corrects. "For two weeks, a guy wearing a baseball hat in a beat-up black Pontiac has been watching us every Friday morning. There's no reason to wear a hat, especially with the windows up."

"You're paranoid," I say, shaking my head. "Probably a janitor." When I casually glance back, I don't see anyone or the secretive black car.

Our AP bio class is the last of the day, and I chew on my

thumbnail while taking a seat. In front, a projector displays the image of several short segments of DNA. Swallowing hard, I remember the blots from Ms. H. Soon, my diagnosis will be on display for the entire class. Dr. Meyers and Mr. Lane murmur in the front, periodically staring at me. Mo shrugs. I told him about my brush mishap yesterday, and true to form, Mo said not to worry.

"Ethan," Dr. Meyers approaches our desks. "May I have a word in the back?"

I slouch further into my seat with absolute dread before following Dr. Meyers to the lab. My hands sweat, and I wipe them on my jeans. It isn't until we're in the back that I realize Mo has followed me.

Dr. Meyers's eyebrows narrow. "I just want to talk to Ethan about his gel?" He looks at Mo, but like always, Mo stands close to my side.

"Ethan's gel probably appears a little different." Mo's palms open like he's carrying a watermelon. "Ethan is unique. He tried to take DNA from only one side of his mouth, but instead, he took it from his *two* different sides."

Dr. Meyer's eyes shift toward me, scanning up and down, focusing on my eyes. I can tell he's found the green on the right and the blue on the left. His head makes several subtle movements. Left then right. Right then left. He nods, lifting the curtain, and sees me for the first time. I hate it. I can imagine how my gel looks, probably with twice as many bands as Dr. Meyers would expect.

"Interesting," Dr. Meyers says and straightens. "Well, we should get started."

I want to disappear, but Mo nudges me back to class before I can plead with Dr. Meyers not to show my DNA.

"It'll be okay." Mo leads me to my chair, and I sink low into my seat as Dr. Meyers goes over the first two gels, showing the different bandwidths from one of the students. Miraculously, he doesn't name the classmate associated with each gel. He doesn't call them out, and, even more amazing, several minutes before the end of class, he turns on the lights, never showing my results. Never describing to the world what I am.

I remain still as the class claps, thanking Dr. Meyers for his time.

Dr. Meyers is packing his things, and the room empties before I approach. "Thank you," I say in nearly a whisper.

Dr. Meyers coils a cord into a tight circle. "How long have you known?"

My head swivels, confirming that we are still alone. "About four or five years."

"Impressive. Impressive indeed."

"It was first described in '46," I say, "but the more recent article by Hangano is making the diagnosis more recognizable."

Dr. Meyers steps back. "You read *Molecular Genetics*?"

"I want to go to SU to study genetics."

I let Dr. Meyers absorb my statement. "I know there are genes associated with different diseases like Huntington's, diabetes, or heart disease—" my voice trails off with the end of my list. "But are there genes or DNA differences associated with personality?"

I'm just tired of wondering, and he might know the answer. After all, he was decent enough not to expose me to the class.

"Are you asking if there is a type of DNA associated with people willing to help carry groceries for old ladies across the street and others associated with running a high school freshman up the flagpole by their underwear?"

It's precisely what I'm asking, but I feel stupid when Dr. Meyers puts it that way. "No." I shift my stance and transfer my book to the other hand. "I just don't know if genes are associated with behavior and personality."

As he thinks, Dr. Meyers taps his finger against the tip of his chin. "There are many things we don't know about the human genome. But per se, I'm unaware of any genomic personality differences." He pauses. "That being said," he taps his chin again, "I guess it wouldn't be too difficult to investigate. If you read *Molecular Genetics*, perhaps you know my research?"

"On schizophrenia?"

Dr. Meyers nods with enthusiasm. Dr. Meyers published his data on the genetics of schizophrenia using microarrays to look at the expression of nearly the entire known genome at once. It was like a fishing expedition. He was dropping a line in the water to see if anything bit. Dr. Meyers was lucky. He caught a whale and published his findings in *Nature*.

"Perhaps you could examine some of that data to identify if there are personality differences. Of course, there are multiple ways a schizophrenic patient can act."

He lowers his gaze, his chin resting upon his chest. "You said you're interested in applying to SU next year?"

"It's my number one choice."

Dr. Meyers nods with approval. "Well, if there's a genetics question you need assistance tackling as you peruse the scientific literature, I'd be happy to help." He pulls out his wallet and hands me his business card.

I thank him, and inside, fireworks glow hot and bright as I leave to meet Mo and Aia.

CHAPTER TWENTY-SIX

AFTER SCHOOL, WE sit at the kitchen island. Mo takes notes on the next biology chapter. Aia writes an essay, her pen scrolling on the page. They're working. I can't figure out how to solve for the derivative in a calculus problem, and my wheels are spinning; I'm struggling. The phone rings, and Mo pulls the receiver from the wall. Finally, something to distract me.

"Hello, hello. Alsoufi residence."

I think he might continue introducing his entire family, but his expression flattens. "It's your mother."

B never calls here, not even when Grandma had a stroke. Mo cradles the receiver like a racing baton, and I reluctantly touch the phone to my ear. "B is everything—" but I can't finish the sentence. I haven't heard her cry since she woke up in the hospital. Right now, she's sobbing.

"What's wrong?" The words are slow, like they're said through molasses. Aia puts down her pen.

"You're there!" B gasps. "I just needed to know that you were, and you weren't—" she says, her voice cutting off.

"What's going on?"

There's a long pause before B eventually continues. "This afternoon—" a staggered breath, like one from an elderly person gasping for air before death, interrupts her words. Seconds pass.

"There were two letters. One for me—" B breaks off again, and Mo's eyebrows arch in concern.

"From who?" I already know the answer. Maybe it's a sixth sense or a feeling. Who else would send letters through the mail? It was how Spencer communicated with us for nine months while he was in Saudi Arabia. He's been away for over two years, and we haven't heard a word. Not a note. Not a call.

"Throw out the letters," I say, relieving B from uttering his name. I don't know what he wants, and I don't care.

"You don't understand," B interrupts. "He didn't mail them."

I want to duck to the floor. Cling to the wall and cover the windows. Turn off the TV. He was there.

"They were taped to the door. Two envelopes, one with my name and one with yours."

My heart rate triples, and my hand probes my front pocket for the safety of my inhaler. I picture B on the kitchen floor. *Crack. Thud.* "Did you open yours?"

"No." Her single-word answer, a staccato note, passes fleetingly.

"I'm coming home." If Spencer is back and looking for a rekindling of our family, or maybe even revenge, I'll protect B. Shouldn't we have gotten a call, a letter, or something to tell us he was getting released?

"I'm coming home," I repeat.

"Okay," she replies meekly.

Mo's book is closed, and Aia's pen has been put away. Both are poised for action.

"We're coming with you," the twins say simultaneously.

"Spencer's out of prison," I blurt.

Mo's head bobs in understanding. The implication is that if Spencer's out, B might be in danger. I might be in danger. The three of us rush to the car. Within minutes, we're at my house.

Hurdling toward the front door like an Olympic sprinter, I leap toward the kitchen and don't realize how B might react until she gasps. "It's me," I yell, too late to avoid her panic.

She's clutching two envelopes, sitting at the kitchen table, shaking. No, convulsing, like the letters contain an electric current forcing her hands to squeeze them tight. Her vacant eyes return to the letters. She may be next to me, but her mind is far away.

"*B!*" Yelling her name doesn't pull her from her trance. I place a hand on her arm, halfway expecting to receive a charge. "I'm here, B."

She turns her head and tries to smile. Her upper lip curves into a cupid's bow, but her jaw is slack.

"Did you open yours?" I expect she has already read hers. "It hasn't been four years. Weren't we supposed to get some warning when he was released?" I thought the violent nature of his crime required some kind of notice. Maybe that was from an episode of *Law and Order*?

The envelopes in her hands appear ordinary, purchased from a drug store or a random supermarket. "Ethan" is scribbled across the center of one. "Phoebe" across the other.

I wonder what Spencer thought as he approached the front door. Was there nostalgia? Regret? Revenge? Had he watched, peering at B to see if she had moved on with her life?

"Are you going to open it?" Aia interrupts the silence.

I want to burn it. There was nothing he could write that I wanted to read. If he was sorry, so what? If he felt guilty, he should. B nearly died. In the hospital, each time Grandma talked with the neurosurgeon, her face aged a decade. Grandpa's anger left me wondering what he might do if Spencer wasn't in prison. The neurosurgeon's words still echo in my mind. *"Lucky we got to her so* quickly," and *"We have to wait and see."*

Without a word, B hands me my letter. I rotate it like it's part of a card trick, trying to assess the weight of the words inside.

"Just burn them." Mo steps from the wall, standing stiff. He remembers what Spencer did to us as clearly as I still do.

"They can't do that." Aia slides next to her brother. "They need to know what he wants. Maybe he just wants to talk."

B wobbles her head. "I don't know what to do." She places her letter on the table at the exact spot where Spencer used to sit in the corner and drink his coffee. Her hand pulls a few strands of hair back behind her ear but catches for a moment by the side of her head. Just for a second. Not long. Probably not long enough for Aia or Mo to realize. In that moment, I can see what she's doing. She remembers. Her hand searches for the divot on her head, where her skull bone was removed. That hidden spot, concealed by her blonde hair, is a reminder of what Spencer did to her and what he did to us.

"I need a nap." B pushes herself up from the table, heading toward her room. "You guys should get a bite at Ronni's."

I chew on the side of my mouth that's still raw from yesterday's biology lab.

"I don't need you here to protect me. Whatever Spencer wants, he's not coming back today. Let me take a nap, and when you get back, maybe we can decide what to do. God knows Mo is hungry."

"You know me, Mrs. Rivers. I'm always hungry." Mo bounces on his toes. "But maybe tonight we could get takeout."

"It's okay. Go to Ronni's. Ethan needs a cheeseburger. On me." She pulls several twenties from her purse before closing the door to her room and finishing the conversation. Her letter remains on the table, and I remember as a kid waiting for the opportunity to snoop and read what she wrote to Spencer. I shove my letter into my back pocket, trying to ignore its weight.

***

Over the years, Ronni's Diner has never changed. The black and white checkered floor remains shiny and vibrant. The red and white striped leather booths are still stiff and unweathered.

After our food arrives, Mo and Aia are silent, afraid to talk, or maybe waiting for me to begin.

"Look who it is," a voice booms from the door. Several patrons glance and then refocus on their plates. Jackson VanPatten strolls past with two of his goons.

"Buzz off, Jackson." Mo keeps his attention on a French fry layered in ketchup.

"Buzz off? What's that supposed to mean? Is that some terrorist code?"

"See if you can decipher this code." Mo raises both middle fingers.

"We better move out of their blast radius, boys." Jackson and his friends travel to the far corner of the diner.

"It's good to see nothing ever changes," I say, biting into my burger and leaning back. "I just want to know why Spencer would come back?" finally voicing my thoughts. "I just don't get it. He never wrote any letters from jail. Even Uncle Jack and Aunt JoJo don't send Christmas cards to our house anymore. They want to forget Spencer and what happened, and the easiest way is to cut out everything associated with him."

"Like I said, burn the freakin' letter," Mo answers. "It doesn't matter. You and your mom have moved on. There's nothing he can say or do to change that. If you ignore him, he'll probably go away. He has no reason to stick around here without the two of you."

Mo is right. There's nothing else here for Spencer other than us. His family is in Pennsylvania, though I couldn't imagine Uncle Jack or Aunt JoJo inviting him over for dinner.

"This is only going to dredge the pain." Mo finishes the last of his fries. He is right about that. One way or another, whatever is in the letters will resurrect painful memories.

"The thing is," I say and swallow hard, remembering how Grandma barked at B. "She's still married to him."

"No way." Aia shakes her head. "Why?" The single word asks nearly a thousand unanswerable questions.

"I don't know."

Grandma argued when I was in the other room, trying to convince B that she needed a divorce. "I don't care if you're Catholic. I'm Catholic, and as your mother, I say it's fine. It's more than fine. It's what needs to happen. If you don't, he'll return."

"It's not about being Catholic, Mom," B answered, which made sense because I'd never seen the inside of a church.

"Then what?" Grandma asked, exasperated. "Why would you stay married to the man who nearly killed you?"

"I don't know."

"If it's about the money, I'll give you the money. It would make me more than happy to give you the money. You certainly have grounds for divorce."

"It's not about the money." B's soft voice was downcast.

"Then please explain it to me. Explain it to me because I don't understand. You can't still love him. Not after what he did to you."

B stayed silent, and Grandma threw up her arms, muttering several choice phrases. B never said it, but I remember her letter to Spencer during the war. She worried that something would happen and he wouldn't return home. I remember her conversation in Grandma's kitchen. She'd accepted years ago that as long as Spencer came home alive, she would remain happy.

As I relive their conversations, there's a movement from the corner of my eye. *Crack!* A hand thrashes down onto Aia's head, causing her whole body to lurch forward and her hands to thud into the table. She winces in pain as a tear trickles from her left eye.

Jackson VanPatten wiggles the ring finger on his right hand like it has an itch. "You terrorists need to get the hell out of here," he says with a smirking grin.

Every muscle in my body tenses. I'm out of the booth in less than a second.

I grit my teeth and swing with a jab, twisting my fist like Spencer taught me. Boisterous conversations muffle the crunch of Jackson VanPatten's nose breaking. Customers lean against the counter, shouting to their neighbors above the noise. A family not ten feet away continues to enjoy their dessert, oblivious.

"Ethan," Jackson screams, and the bubble containing our violent chaos bursts. The diner turns eerily quiet. Chocolate ice cream threatens to drip from the spoons held by the children nearby, kids not much older than the three. At the counter, all heads jerk in our direction. Jackson stares down at his hands, watching drops of blood spill into his palms. Like an actor who needs to see the tear in his clothes and the blossoming circle of blood to register that he's been shot, Jackson can't believe I hit him.

"Ethan, I'm going to kill you," Jackson growls, stepping forward.

My jaw clenches so tight my teeth might crack. I ignore the throbbing pain in my knuckle. Jackson's hard eyes glance from me and then back to Aia.

My fist is in mid-air, jabbing him hard in the abdomen. A gasp quickly replaces his scream like the sucking sound after opening a jelly jar. His arms wave in a failing attempt to keep his balance. His body falls violently backward, his head striking hard against the table edge with a *crack* before his skull collides with such force against the floor that the thud reverberates loudly within my head. It is the sound of a hammer crashing down and breaking a piece of wood. The sound of breaking bone. I know that sound. I remember that sound.

No one speaks. No one breathes. Jackson lies crumpled on the floor. His legs cross precariously, and his left arm cradles his head while rivulets of dark blood spill into the seams of the linoleum tiles. On my shirt, Jackson VanPatten's blood has spattered onto the white fabric. My eyes widen, the color too red, too real. *What did I do?*

Mo still sits in the booth, his mouth ajar. Next to him, Aia, scans the crowd, searching nervously for the threat of retaliation. For the moment, it's too far off. Jackson's friends remain at the other end of the diner and only now stand. "Jack," one of them says, looking at the floor and then at me. The rest of the diners remain motionless.

And then the adrenaline fades. My vision clears; my hands and legs vibrate. My jaw loosens, and my teeth chatter like I'm freezing. I want to deny this, insist it wasn't me, that I never lifted a hand against him. Maybe this is a dream or some sort of nightmare. But the acrid taste of blood in my mouth from inadvertently biting my tongue suggests otherwise.

Jackson remains motionless on the floor. Towering over him, the apparent victor in this struggle, I'd almost convinced myself that my father's half didn't have a grasp on my personality or actions. Clearly, I'd been wrong.

The pad of feet approaches from behind the counter. The owner wags a Louisville Slugger. His roving eyes assess me like a feral animal.

Scanning the surrounding faces, what am I searching for? Praise that I've slayed Goliath? Or an escape? I lock onto the parents at the table next to ours, cradling their children. They stare at me as if I'm a monster.

"I am not my father!" No one is convinced.

"I don't care who you think you are, don't move!" the owner commands while a waitress behind the counter speaks into the phone. Jackson's two friends fix their eyes in my direction and stride calmly forward, their fists clenched at their sides. I could stand and accept my punishment. Take responsibility for my actions. Instead, just like my father, I run.

CHAPTER TWENTY-SEVEN

SHOVING THE SHIRT deep inside a garbage bag, the next morning, I'm hiding the evidence and gasp aloud, thinking of Spencer's garbage pail filled with the glass of empty whiskey bottles. The evidence he hid in the shed. More proof. More data that I'm acting like him and don't notice until afterward. I put his letter in my back pocket and hurl the garbage bag into the closet.

B's in the kitchen, but I head to the bathroom without a word. From the cabinet, I shake a few Tylenol into my palm and resist the urge to scream. If I'm not in a prison cell, I expect my room will be in total darkness within a month. That I'll unintentionally shout at Aia when she turns on the lights, and one day, I'll hit her.

I take a puff from my inhaler. I don't need it, but my asthma is unique to me. Something Spencer doesn't have. As the powdery residue fills my lungs, the tremor in my hands subsides. I'm home with B, and her half is still in control, at least some of the time.

In the kitchen, B stares at her letter, still unopened. It anchors her to the table like a ball and chain. A white robe cinches tight across her chest, and strands of her blond hair hang snarled on her shoulders.

Sliding into the chair beside her, I massage my temples, shading my eyes from the light. It's quiet, and the silence mixes with the Tylenol to provide some calm. The storm inside my head begins to fracture. The large hurricane divides into several smaller downpours. B still hasn't moved, and neither of us has said good morning. I need silence. She isn't playing chicken. She doesn't realize I'm in the room. It's been several years since she's acted this way. Her body present, but her mind thousands of miles away.

"You know—"

Her shoulders point toward the sky, nearly obliterating her neck, and then relax when she realizes it's me.

"When Spencer was in Saudi Arabia, I wasn't sure what you were thinking."

She offers a weak smile before returning her focus to Spencer's letter and empty chair.

"So, one night after I wrote my letter—"

B spins and sighs, "You read mine."

It's a small victory, but I've broken through. "You knew?" I was so stealthy. I even twisted away from her photo on the wall.

"The brownie smudge marks on the pages were my first clue." She grins for only a second before it slips off her face. "You were out late last night."

My face hardens, thinking about Jackson VanPatten crumpled on the floor, the consequences of throwing the first punch, and who I really am. Stretching my neck, I glance toward the counter. It's empty. The newspaper must still be in the mailbox.

I want to tell B, along with a hollow plea, that it was a one-time thing. It will never happen again. It was different because I was protecting Aia. But I wasn't. If I hadn't punched, Jackson would have walked away. I could have walked away. That's what B would have done. Jackson may have tapped Aia's head, but I threw the first punch.

"Just talking with Aia and Mo." My eyes land on B's letter, and I feel the crinkled envelope in my back pocket. Each is an echo of Spencer standing in the kitchen. We need to talk about Spencer. "Maybe I should read your letter. That way, whatever he wants, you won't have to learn about it alone."

B tilts her head, a reminder that it's always been the two of us, just two peas in a pod. She leans forward, sliding her letter across the table. The paper scraping across the table makes a *shhh* sound like someone telling a secret. I don't wait for her to lean back before my fingers wrap around the envelope.

I rip an opening and peer inside, expecting to see a chasm. A single sheet of paper slides out, and I unfold the stationery like an antiquities director wearing white cotton gloves and handling a relic.

Blue ink covers the page in tiny block letters, and the words shift in and out of focus. In my hands is what Spencer wants. What if there's something on this page I can't read aloud? B rips the letter from my hands, and the tiny letters blur.

"Read yours first." B's eyes dart across the room as if someone is watching.

My letter isn't as crisp. An evening in my back pocket has wrinkled the envelope and the letter inside. My eyes focus on the same blue letters filling the page, and I'm halfway through the first sentence when B asks, "Well?"

I read aloud:

> *Ethan,*
> *I want to write so many things and only hope that you will read this letter. It's hard to describe how sorry I am. I will never forgive myself. When I was home, I often mistreated both you and your mom. Hurting your mother was the single worst thing I have ever done in my life. I wish I could change the past. I wish I could change the way I acted. Of course, I can't do either, but if I could explain what happened to me,*

you might better understand.

I glance above the page. B's eyes fixate on every word. She's falling for this apology. She will let him back into our home, and he'll kill her this time. He'll claim he didn't know what he was doing. That he had a headache or was drinking. But she'll be dead. I want her to touch the side of her head. Touch the physical scar where the surgeons drilled a hole.

"Is that it?" B questions, and I reluctantly continue.

In prison, I met with a psychiatrist, Dr. Hearn. She told me about Gulf War Syndrome. It's a bunch of symptoms that many veterans have. No one is sure exactly why or what the best treatments are, but she started me on several medications to help my mood, headaches, and sleep. Sometimes, I have bad memories of my time in Saudi Arabia, which makes things worse. Dr. Hearn forced me to write a journal about my illness, which you might want to read.

I'm a lot better now. I understand you may not want to, and I get that, but I would like to see you. I miss you, think about you often, and wonder how you are doing. You are my son, and I love you more than you will ever know. Please think about this. Think about talking with me and let me explain what happened.

Dad

Tears form in the sides of B's eyes. I want to scream. The letter goes in and out of focus as it trembles in my hands. Does he think he can write a letter and go waltzing down the street to apologize? I want him to move away. Go to California, or farther, maybe to Russia. Somewhere where he can't hurt any of us again. I want B to feel the same way. I want her to touch the side of her head, but we flinch at the knock at the door.

CHAPTER TWENTY-EIGHT

MY STEPS ARE short and light, creeping toward the front of the house, dodging behind the couch like a spy. B stands behind me, gripping the kitchen table. Moving one of the floral curtains an inch and peering out onto the porch, I expect to see stubble and a pair of blue-gray eyes wanting forgiveness.

Mo and Aia carry a bag of bagels.

"What's wrong, Curly?" Mo pushes me aside, no doubt ready to dive into the bag. "You don't look so good."

Mo doesn't know about the contents of the letter, but he knows about Spencer's release. He was with me last night at the diner. He saw how I hit Jackson, just like Spencer taught me. Before I can answer, Mo is in the kitchen with B, his upbeat tone muffled by a mouth full of cinnamon raisin bagel.

Aia touches my arm, letting me know she's here. She saw what I did to Jackson. She knows which half of my personality was in control yesterday. Maybe she doesn't know about the headaches, my inability to sleep, or even that I've been on edge. But she must see who I'm becoming, and if history repeats itself, which it often does, it will put her on a path to injury.

My biceps flex, tense at her touch.

She nods to B in the kitchen. "You didn't tell her?"

Of course not! I pull the words back before they're out. "No," I whisper, afraid that B might overhear. "She's already so distant, thinking about Spencer. I can't tell her I've become a monster, too. Not now."

"You're not." Aia pushes against my chest.

She's so confident. But, she doesn't know about my symptoms lining up like dominoes.

"I phoned the hospital this morning," Aia smirks. "I said that I wanted to send flowers to my friend Jackson VanPatten."

My gaze bolts to the kitchen table. Mo is still eating. B stares at the wall.

My arms envelop Aia, hoping to contain any news she's about to tell. After a few seconds I blurt, "And?"

B and Mo turn from the kitchen and then resume their conversation.

"And he was released from the emergency room early this morning. He can't be that hurt."

My feet sink into the floor, my legs turn to jelly. I got away with this. There won't be a trial or jail time. Just as quickly, my relief pulls back like a blanket ripped away. Spencer got away with a lot before having to deal with the consequences. How many times did he hit B? How many times did he finish a bottle of Jack Daniels before noon?

"Did you open your letter?" Aia drags me from my thoughts.

"I read mine. We still haven't read B's. He's not angry. He's blaming some made-up diagnosis called Gulf War Syndrome. Like all the soldiers who went to the Middle East were damaged, and that's why he beat B. That's why he yelled and screamed at us. That's why he drank all the time. He won't take responsibility." I shake my head. "Even now, I wish he would acknowledge that he's violent. Stop blaming people and say that he's violent. Accept it. That's who he is."

Aia looks like she's trying to see inside my brain and dissect what I just said. But it's clear she disagrees and won't offer any indication that I'm right. I'm also violent. Jackson VanPatten wasn't beaten as severely as B. Jackson didn't need a craniotomy or a month in the hospital. Jackson didn't die. But he could have. And he could have because of my actions.

"It happened once," Aia echoes her answer from yesterday. "I don't care if your father used to say it. I don't care if you or your mother used to believe it. Your father doesn't have control over you. You were protecting me. You're not him."

Of course, he doesn't have control over me. I'm not his puppet. But it's the genetics from his side that worries me most, and B's voice echoes in my memory, *"It was just this time. It won't happen again."* Except it did. And again after that.

Knowing that I won't win this argument, I nod stoically. I could have protected Aia by getting out of the diner. That's what I would have done in the past. That's what B would do. But when Jackson smacked Aia's head, I threw the first punch. That's what Spencer would do.

Aia guides me into the kitchen, where Mo slows in the middle of his third bagel. "Your mom says you opened Pandora's Box, huh?"

He's trying to sound nonchalant, but he's bruised that we read my letter and agreed with Aia. "It's better to know what he wants, even though we don't want anything to do with him." Eying B, she stares down at her breakfast.

Mo swallows his last bite and leans back in his chair. "So that's what you've both decided. That you want nothing to do with him?"

Silence wraps around the four of us like a blanket, and the longer it stretches the tighter and more constricting it becomes. It's smothering, and the three of us are looking to B for release. B stares only at her garlic bagel.

"I don't know what I want right now." She pushes away from the table.

Mo blows out his cheeks with a deep exhale. "Huh?" His eyes follow B toward her room. He's never watched B crawl into her shell. He shakes his head, swiveling it back and forth like a spinning plate atop a pole. "How? Why? What?" The words stumble out of his mouth.

"I don't know." I try to decipher her admission. "There's something about a pact she made with God or life or something. I can remember overhearing her tell my grandparents that as long as he came back from the Gulf in one piece, she wouldn't ask for another thing for as long as she lives." Shaking my head, I say, "It's sort of like she sold her soul to get him back, and now it doesn't matter what he's done to her. She won't drive him away."

On the table, the envelope labeled *Phoebe* is empty. Lunging toward the envelope, I tear the sides apart like a steamed clam.

"Did she read it when you were here?" My eyes dart toward Mo. "Her letter from Spencer."

Mo shakes his head, and we all look toward B's bedroom door.

CHAPTER TWENTY-NINE

SURGING DOWN THE hall, the house quakes with each step until I reach the doorknob and twist, not bothering to knock. The handle won't budge. I want to scream. I know it won't be of any use. She's crawled back into her shell. Again.

After she was discharged from the hospital, I pleaded with B to talk with me. I begged her to explain why we couldn't stay with Grandpa. If we had to go home, could we at least remove the kitchen table, his chair, or Spencer's picture on the wall? She only sighed, lowering her head and walking away.

Even Mo noticed. One afternoon, he asked, "Why don't you get rid of his stuff?" I didn't have answers then and still don't.

"Okay, then, I get it," Mo pulls me back to the kitchen. "You popped Jackson last night, which I hope felt pretty good." His grin stretches cheek to cheek. "I mean, you really got him." Mo's mouth flattens after Aia and I aren't smiling along. "But you defended Aia. It's different. Stop worrying about who you are. You're Ethan, not your father."

Dropping the empty envelope, my thoughts race from Spencer to Jackson. "You know what I am. Even Dr. Meyers saw what I am. If that didn't prove that I'm two different people, two different sets of DNA, then I don't know what can."

Mo looks to Aia for support, but she stays silent. "Okay, let's say for a minute that you aren't a chimera."

"I am a chimera." Because if we are talking about what ifs and what thens, what if I could fly? Or what if I could deconstruct my genetic code, remove the left half, and replicate my right half into a whole person?

"I know, I know." He puts a hand up like he's trying to stop traffic. "Fine, then me. I'm not a chimera. Just like you, I'm the combination of my parents' DNA. No real difference."

"Yeah, but you're one person. Only one set of DNA. You're not worried that part of you is a girl like Aia."

Mo's eyes meet Aia's. He shudders.

"Listen, you know who you are. You have a physical identity and a genetic identity. So does Aia. My identity is—" I pause. "It's like having Superman attached to Lex Luthor. Half of me might act one way, only I don't know which half has control, and last night," I sigh, putting my hands on the table. "Last night, I found out that despite what I wanted to believe, his half has control, at least sometimes. His half can be violent. I can be violent. Don't you see?"

My hands are extended, trying to get them to understand. But it's like me trying to understand what it's like to be Iranian. I don't know what it's like to get stares from people convinced that because of their darker skin, they have a bomb. They can't understand that I have no idea which half of my DNA controls my personality. Yes, last night it was Jackson. He deserved it. But what about next time? What if I swing at Mo, Aia, or even B? Despite years of trying, I can't control Spencer's personality. It's like taking home a wolf. It's fluffy and cute when it's a pup, but deep inside it's a predator. The wolf will eventually bite no matter how much the owner cuddles and soothes the pup. Maybe it doesn't happen for years, but it will. Mo shrugs. "I guess," he says, but doesn't mean it.

"Imagine," I say, forcing him to understand. "You want to be a surgeon. You'll need steady hands." I look down at Mo's hands and realize they aren't as large as his father's. "Your hands are small, probably more like your mom's."

"Are you trying to tell me I have dainty hands?"

"No, but what if your mother's hands started to twitch? If she developed a tremor. Since your hands looked like hers, you might wonder if your hands might begin to tremble too and never have a career in surgery. There's nothing you can do about it. That's your DNA. Then one day, maybe when you were nervous, your hands began to quiver. From that day forward, you'd stare at your hands, the physical part of your mother, and think how yours might shake also."

Mo's fingers extend. His hands remain stationary.

"The problem is, it's the physical part that you'd focus on, and if it were part of your genetics, there would be no way around it." I think he might get it. He can't outrun genetics.

Aia interrupts Mo's concentration. "I need to get to work." They both work at the hardware store down the street from the high school. It was the deal they made with Mr. A. to get the car.

She strokes my right arm. "You want to come over to our place?"

"I need to stay here," I say, shaking my head. I need to wait for B to exit her room.

"I'll call after work?"

Alone, I drop onto the couch. I would love a distraction: TV, a magazine, my encyclopedias. I haven't read them in ages, but right now, it might feel good to lose myself in random facts, even if they aren't directly helpful.

The toilet flushes, and B rounds the corner. She gawks at the door, staring at it for over a minute. Is she leaving? Without a word, and with her body stiff, she opens the front door and returns to the kitchen.

"Close the door. It's fifty degrees outside!" She ignores me and quietly sits at the table, her hands folded on one another as if she's in prayer.

"Leave it. It's a little warm in here."

"Well, then, we can turn down the heat."

"It's fine. Where did Mo and Aia go?" she says, still looking at her hands, which she starts kneading.

"Home and work."

"You didn't go with them?" B swirls a new mug of coffee.

I push the empty envelope across the table like I'm plowing a road between the two of us—a connection. B gazes at the envelope, and I interrupt the silence since she refuses. "What did yours say?"

She squints at the envelope. "Mostly the same as yours. That he's sorry."

There's more than that. My chest caves because there's more than she's telling me. She's locking me out, and my frustration bubbles to the surface. I fight to remain calm. That's what B would do. That's who I want to be, but I'm slipping.

"Can I read it?" There's an edge to my question that I can't soften. It's not that I don't trust B, but she's holding back. I want to see the words for myself.

"I flushed it," she says. Like she has just emptied the trash of last night's takeout dinner and not destroyed Spencer's written intentions. It's like pouring gasoline on a fire. A whoosh of hot, crimson, and orange air reaches up to burn.

"You flushed it?" I need her to repeat it. Doesn't she understand that his letter to her has just as much to do with me?

"Mm-hm."

"What else did it say?" My teeth nearly crack they're biting down so hard.

"Nothing else." She stands, heading back to her room, back to her safe haven, where she won't have to talk with me. I jolt, blocking her path in the hallway, my arm outstretched against the wall.

"This isn't like you." Her words sting.

Making demands and forcing her to stay in the room are all things Spencer would do. But I don't care. "I need to know so I can help you."

Her head shakes. "I don't need any help. Why don't you head over to Mo's," her eyes dart between me and the front door. "I'm just going—"

"No!" I scream. "You need to tell me what is going on. What he said." My arm flexes. My hand curls into a fist. B's eyes widen at my balled-up hand, which she cradled as a child. The hand that so delicately folded inside of hers. A pea in a pod.

"Just tell me this," I plead, unflexing my fist. "And honestly tell me." I take a few breaths. "If he asked to move back in. I mean, if he came to the front door pleading to live with us, what would you say? You're still married. I have no idea why you never divorced him. But honestly, would you let him back in the house after he nearly killed you?" The last two words echo like a thundercloud.

B swallows and looks from me down to her hands. "It's who I am."

"B!" I yell. "It's who you *were*! He went to prison for nearly killing you. Are you telling me that after all of that, after everything that happened, you would let him back into your life? Like he was away on some vacation or work trip?"

"I'm still his wife." She looks at the floor, clutching her own hands for dear life. She meets my gaze. "He's still your father."

I take a step backward, using a hand to brace myself tight against the wall. "You don't have to remain his wife. *You owe him nothing!*" I scream, hoping my words smash through to her. *"Nothing!"*

"This isn't black and white," B says, "it's gray."

"I'm forced to be his son. There's nothing I can do about that. But I don't want him anywhere near you."

"Forced seems strong."

"I can't alter my genetics, B. I can't. If I could surgically remove his half," and shake my left hand as evidence, "I would. I would tear it off. But I can't."

"It's who you are." She looks into my eyes, and I can see a mixture of fear, worry, and hope that this will all go away, that by hiding everything will get better.

"Help me understand." My hands outstretch. "Help me understand why?"

She touches my cheek with her hand, wiping away a tear I didn't notice. "I can't explain it," she says softly, shifting past me.

"Can't or won't?" I ask.

"Both." She exhales. "I'm just going to take a quick nap. Why don't you go spend some time with your friends?"

The bedroom door locks, ending our conversation. There's no way I'm leaving home and abandoning her to the jackal that's my father. I head to the back of the house. With Spencer's letter in my pocket, I return to the burial ground of his past.

When B was in the hospital, I had taken the box of his letters and brought it to the corner of our property. I dug a hole, threw the box in, buried it, and stomped on the ground. I matted the disturbed soil so that it was nearly flat, trounced the dirt, and compacted it close to its original grade.

It didn't work. Two years later, that spot in the lawn is always bare, and the ground remains ever so slightly raised. Those mementos were poison. He is poison.

I reread Spencer's newest letter, still wondering how B could be so ignorant. He wasn't blaming the alcohol as his lawyers had done in court. He was blaming some disease. He still couldn't accept responsibility.

***

Across the field, Mr. Henderson is harvesting corn. The long, tall picker rips each stalk, pulling the ears off one by one. It will be late afternoon before he makes his way to our end of the field. I wish

Grandma and Grandpa were alive. Maybe Grandma could talk some sense into B, and Grandpa, no matter how old, would stand and defend all of us.

Turning back toward the house, a black car parks next to the driveway by the side of the road. The driver's side door opens, and a clean-shaven man wearing an SFD T-shirt and jeans steps out. The clothes are too big and hang off his limbs like a scarecrow. Walking around the front of the car, he gazes at the house as if trying to take it all in. Spencer is home.

CHAPTER THIRTY

I **WANT TO SIMULTANEOUSLY** run at him and sprint away. I'm hot with anger that he's here and yet numb. With my jaw set, I march toward the house, rigidly taking a step at a time.

Spencer hasn't noticed me. He's staring at the front door, which is ajar. I can't see B standing there or in the window, cautiously moving the drapes aside. Hopefully, she's in the bedroom and I can remove Spencer before she notices he's here.

Spencer mutters as he steps forward. His movements are a shuffle rather than purposeful strides. He used to dart across the room toward his target.

Twenty feet away, at the edge of the house, I lean against the siding for support. He's wearing glasses now. Black frames form a scaffold for his face, and he's thinner, gaunt even. The mustache that sometimes concealed his upper lip is gone, and his hair is almost entirely gray. Only a few renegade dark strands lay on top, combed over to the side. He's bent, and his back seems to arch a little more with each step forward, as if he's entering into a space too short for his height.

"What are you doing?" My voice booms across the porch. For the first time in my life, Spencer lurches away from me.

I remember the power he wielded over us and how we clung to the edges of the room. Today, the ominous bear looks haggard, stiff after waking from hibernation.

"I . . . I didn't think—" Spencer seizes the railing at the front step, and it rattles loosely under his weight. He's staring at the open front door. I can see straight into the kitchen through the storm window. B isn't there.

"What do you want?" I try not to sound angry, knowing I've failed. I want to be steady, maybe even apathetic.

Spencer clears his throat and glances back toward his car. The front bumper hangs askew, and several large scratches dent the passenger door. It's a Pontiac. It's a black, battered Pontiac. My mind crashes back to the high school parking lot. I assumed Mo was paranoid.

Spencer's been stalking me, and he's probably done the same with B. Standing in the woods, driving past at night. Waiting for her at work.

Spencer faces the car, maybe considering a retreat. If I've caught him off guard, he might leave us alone. He looks back at me, his back arching forward.

"Did you get my letter?" His words are forced but hopeful.

I nod, but only once, trying to keep my posture stoic. I bite my tongue and maintain a narrow gaze. He may look weaker, but he's still capable of violence. What he doesn't know is that so am I.

"Did you read it?"

I nod again and relax my jaw, or soon I'll be tasting blood.

"And I know your mom read hers."

Something about the way he says "Mom" catches me off guard. He knows something I don't. My upper hand falters. There's some relief when he says, "Mom" and not Phoeb, the name he affectionately called his wife. *Mom* indicates a lack of possession. When he nods at the front door, I realize B provided a signal by leaving the door ajar. She, physically and figuratively, will let him back into the house where he broke our family apart. My hands shake, and my heart races; energy and anger combine and surge.

"What do you want?" I snarl through clenched teeth.

Spencer tries to straighten his back, leaving the assistance of the railing, but remains bent. "I want to say that I'm . . . that I'm sorry."

"Great!" I sound like a defiant teenager, but I don't care. "Now you can go."

"I'd like to say—" he exhales.

I can see creases around his eyes. This is difficult for him, and I don't care.

"I'd like to say I'm sorry to Phoeb." His head hangs, but I'm not certain it's with shame.

I feel the tips of my fingers curl tight into two balls. "I'll let her know."

"Please, Ethan, I can imagine how hard this must be for you."

"Can you?" My teeth grind, bone on bone. Hot tears sting at the corners of my eyes, and I turn to wipe them away. I don't want him to see what he's done to us, what he's done to me. "Really, can you?" I repeat. "You can imagine what it was like holding B's hand in the hospital and having her unable to squeeze back because the doctors had to put her in a coma? *A coma!*" I scream. He can't see B lying in a hospital bed with a breathing tube. He can't see my hand clenched tightly in hers, wanting her to move, speak, or do anything. But she was still, and I was broken.

"They had to remove part of her skull because of how you hit her." I pause to let my words sink in before striking again. "You can imagine how hard it was for Grandpa to explain that if B died, I could stay with him since you were in jail. You can imagine," my voice cracks, "how I would walk into school, and teachers would look at me like I was a loaded weapon ready to explode because of what you did. And you can imagine, I wonder every day if I will end up the same way. Do the same thing. That your half, your genes, will someday cause me to beat my girlfriend and destroy my family? You can imagine all of that?"

Each statement snaps out with the crack of a whip, and he recoils. A slash against his back, a crack across his chest, and with each blow, Spencer gets smaller.

I think about Jackson lying on the diner floor and now Spencer shaking from my lashing. I am my father. Form follows function. The left side of my body is the form, and violence is the function. I feel my muscles tense, flex, and then burn, wanting to strike. Beat him for what he did to me. Beat him for making me.

"No," he says quietly. "I can't understand. I don't understand. I don't know how to pay for the past. I just want to try to explain."

"You don't get that opportunity." My cheeks burn red.

B grips the storm door, and we turn like two fighters returning to their corners. The door rattles so violently that the hinges screech like an intolerant baby. She wets her lips, wanting to say something, but remains silent. I wonder how much she's heard. How much she witnessed before interrupting.

"Phoeb." Spencer's face glows.

I expect B to ask, "Spencer, why don't you come inside?" or "Ethan, can you give us some time alone?"

Do not let him in, B. Don't let him back into your life.

B pulls a strand of hair behind her ear, her hand lingering for just a moment, an imperceptible second, at the scar. A wave of relief washes over me, and my jaw relaxes. She remembers.

"What do you want?" Her tone is even, and I think about rushing past Spencer to stand closer to B to show a unified front, but I'm confident now. I'm confident in B's ability to remember who he is and what he can do. The passage of time hasn't erased her memory.

Spencer clears his throat. "We're still married. That's gotta mean something."

B nods but offers no answers. The continuous squeaking of the front door is the only sound.

"I mean," Spencer continues, "maybe the two of us could talk a bit."

"No," I interrupt sternly. "So you can finish the job."

"Ethan, I was sick. Can't you understand that?" He looks like he's about to drop to his knees. "I was sick. The meds they put in me over there, the chemical warfare. Nobody knows what happened, but there are a lot of soldiers who are sick."

"Then why hasn't it been on the news? Have other fathers been sent to prison for nearly killing their wives? You destroyed our family."

"The government."

"The government now!" I explode. "That's who's to blame because, at your trial, it was the alcohol. That's what you blamed, or at least according to your lawyer. Now, it's the government. Why can't you ever accept the responsibility that it was you? *You!*" I scream again. "It's who *you* are."

A white Mercedes pulls into the driveway and cuts my verbal assault short. B and Spencer are thrown off guard, each with curiosity and apprehension.

The car door opens and there is an uneasy silence. The tinted windows shield the driver, and at first, we can only see the shoes, fine embossed stitched leather, the color of dark honey.

A man in a blue pinstripe suit stands. His head is completely bald compared to the photograph hanging in the elementary school lobby. The man locks eyes with B, then robotically with Spencer, and eventually with me before he snarls and walks quickly forward.

CHAPTER THIRTY-ONE

MR. VANPATTEN STRIDES forward like a raging bull, forming the third ring in this circus. Faint recognition passes over the faces of B and Spencer. "You're lucky I'm not coming here with the cops to toss your ass in jail," Mr. VanPatten shouts. His threat might as well have been a punch, but not at me. B sways and steps backward.

"What the hell are you talking about?" Spencer clenches his fists. His eyes, for now, are still blue and unglassed.

Mr. VanPatten sneers. "They don't know? Seriously?" He emits a garbled laugh, quickly cut short. "Your son," he takes the time to point to B and then Spencer, lingering on each for an extra second, "sent my son to the emergency room last night."

"There must be some kind of mistake." B steps off the porch to my side but stops two strides short, as if she's run into a wall, realizing she's also moving closer to Spencer. "Ethan?" she asks so many things in a single word.

I grit my teeth. My eyes squint, and it's the answer to her question.

B shakes her head. "No," she whispers.

I want to stand with her. I want to explain that it was only the first time. I was defending Aia. It will never happen again, and I'm not like my father. Instead, in a throaty voice, I say, "I'm sorry."

Tears stream down B's cheeks, and she takes two steps back as I step forward.

"You're sorry, you son of a bitch. You're sorry?" Mr. VanPatten echoes. "Jackson needed sixteen stitches, not to mention his broken nose. He could have died. *Died!*"

He screams the last word, but he doesn't need to. I know what could have happened. B knows what could have happened and how the chips could have fallen. I wouldn't be receiving an angry father but the police, a holding cell, and a prison term.

"Ethan beat your son unprovoked?" Spencer's arms hang stiff at his side.

"That's what I'm saying."

"Well, what is Ethan saying? Because I doubt my son would do anything like that."

"Your son," Mr. VanPatten interrupts with a laugh that bellows outward, "your son, you mean because you're such a model citizen." He chuckles loudly. "What was the line from the *Post Standard* again?" There's a pause as if he needs to probe his memory. I know he doesn't. Everyone remembers that headline. "I remember now," Mr. VanPatten grins. "Hero to Zero."

Two pictures of Spencer. The first of him kneeling in front of a fire on University Avenue after rescuing a Syracuse University student. The second was of him in handcuffs, his head slouched over to the side, his hair askew, and wearing a prison jumpsuit.

"The son of a snake is, most probably, a snake." Mr. VanPatten sneers. "I'm surprised they let you out of jail after almost turning your wife into a vegetable, because you were drinking, and she turned on the lights too bright in the kitchen or some shit? Isn't that what your lawyer was trying to sell? That was a great defense."

Spencer scuffs his feet, but he doesn't move. I can see his blue eyes, curly hair, and the rage inside him. I expect Spencer to yell for his whiskey, and then he and Mr. VanPatten will roll around in the dirt.

"Listen." Mr. VanPatten pulls his suit jacket taunt. "I haven't decided what I'm gonna do yet. I might press charges. I might not. I might sue the crap out of you to pay for Jackson's medical bills so that you lose your house."

There's a glint in VanPatten's eyes now. An air of superiority, that he has the upper hand and that we should genuflect to kiss the king's ring.

"I don't know what I'm gonna do, so maybe you should pay me some respect."

"I'm sorry." My apology is a whisper.

"You're just like your father." VanPatten stares down at me like I'm a vagrant. "A no-good piece of shit that hits people from behind. A coward."

My eyes open wide, and Spencer convulses like a seizure has overtaken his entire body. I've noticed that look before. I fully expect Spencer to pounce. Pounce on Mr. VanPatten. Pounce on me. Pounce on B in a spectacle of absolute carnage.

Mr. VanPatten gets into his car. He slams the door with such force that the snap echoes around the yard.

I know by Spencer's tense jaw, or his hands balled into tight fists, or because the sun just broke free of the clouds cloaking us in bright light, what he's going to do. He's going to splinter wide open. I take two steps back to protect B, but I don't have to because Spencer is running. At first, I think he's surging at VanPatten's Mercedes, whose tires spit gravel in a speedy retreat. But Spencer bypasses the driveway, heading straight for his own car. He flings himself inside, driving away in the opposite direction.

There's so much I want to say to B. That Spencer is still the same. She must see that now. He can write whatever he wants, but he's the same person who left our house for prison nearly two and a half years earlier. But I never get the chance.

"What did you do?" B pleads, with an anguish in her voice that tears me in two.

"I'm not like him." Trying to believe what I'm saying, her head wobbles side to side.

"It's not who you are," she says, broken.

I hear Mr. VanPatten. *"The son of a snake is, most probably, a snake."*

"Mama," and her head swivels, knowing that *Mama* is a word I haven't used in a long time. Not since I cried for her, screaming in her ear while she lay motionless on the kitchen floor. "He's the same, and so am I."

The look in B's eyes at that moment makes me freeze. I stop breathing. "This isn't about your father."

"What did he say?" I plead. "What did he say in his letter?" Trying to shift the focus to what Spencer wants.

B turns to leave, not even facing me.

"Damn it, when will you treat me like an adult, not your little kid, and talk to me?"

B smiles, caressing a hand across her teary cheek. "You'll always be my little kid." Like a turtle, she crawls back into her shell and shuts the front door.

CHAPTER THIRTY-TWO

THE OFF-WHITE FRONT door goes in and out of focus. Standing limp, I wait for B. Seconds turn to minutes, minutes to hours. There is no sound or movement in the kitchen. She doesn't open the front door, and I'm alone.

Mr. Henderson's tractor sounds in the distance, and I surrender, leaving the front porch for the edge of our property. The rows of corn stalks lean like soldiers fatigued after a battle. Their spines stand mostly straight, but the tassels and the tan husks hang limp—just like Spencer. It's not their weathered appearance that draws me close. It's their uniformity. No plant stands straighter or taller than the rest.

I've wandered into the mass before, hunting for the stray. The one in a million that stands unnoticed. Its husk might be a vibrant red or even orange. Something that stands out from the rest. But I've never found it and I'm not even sure it exists.

Stepping off the lawn, over the mound of raised dirt in the corner, I vanish. The rough husks scrape against my sleeve like clawing fingers, and I stagger through the narrow space between the rows before sitting in the dirt. Hiding.

When Dr. Taylor first diagnosed my genetic anomaly, I searched for answers in my encyclopedia. The only citation about a chimera was from an ancient Greek myth describing a fire-breathing monster killed after Bellerophon hurled a block of lead into its throat. The lead block melted when the chimera started breathing fire, choking and killing the beast. There is no lead for me to swallow, no Bellerophon to excise Spencer's half.

Maybe Spencer's genetic material has been dormant until now. Maybe Spencer's return has awakened that part.

I want to solve this problem one square at a time. Moving the red row into the green and then rotating, but this problem doesn't feel solvable. *How can I keep his DNA from affecting my personality? It's already there.* Pulling the inhaler from my pocket, I grip the cylinder tight and take a puff. My heart rate accelerates, and my breathing slows.

Something clicks in my head. A row on the Rubik's Cube rotates, and the yellow square completes the side. With the first step out of the corn, the bright light of September hits like a warm embrace. After each stride, my footing gets stronger, a path formed.

Shingles hang loose off the shed, and only paint splinters cling to the wood. I don't care what B wants; I need Spencer's fingerprint on this house erased, and the shed is the first place to start.

Yanking at the stick that holds the doors locked, I hurl it into the cornfield. The doors creak, revealing a tangled mess of rakes and shovels at the threshold. I almost slip, spinning on the blade of a shovel, before stumbling to the back. The blue tarp sealing the window keeps this shed Spencer's cave. My fingers curl in the space between the tarp and the window, and I yank. The staples anchor the tarp at the edge, but the tarp rips, and blades of light stream in, highlighting the floating dust. I wad the tarp into a ball, launching it onto the lawn. This building is now only a shed—not a dungeon.

Free from Spencer's grasp. To my right, my next target, the garbage pail filled with glass shards from countless bottles of booze. The splinters sparkle like diamonds even under the heavy coat of dust and dirt.

With fevered activity, I organize the shovels and rakes, leaning them against the far wall to create a path. The garbage pail is heavy, and it takes most of my strength to drag it across the lawn to the end of the driveway. Another part of Spencer is gone. Another piece of his grip on this household released.

On the workbench is a pile of rusted hand tools, and I return each to the pegboard, revealing a surface covered with paint stains. I see it only after all the tools are organized—a picture.

The edges of the photo, still curled, almost reach toward me. It's been retacked to the board since I examined it years ago, but the colors are still bright. Four men and one woman stand smiling. I put the photo and the letter in my back pocket, intending to toss both items into the trash.

Looking in the shed from the doorway, I've erased Spencer's fingerprint. His dungeon is destroyed. I tighten both doors with a rope before moving toward my next target.

***

The phone rings inside the house. I don't want a distraction, but pull it from the wall after the sixth ring.

"Curly," Mo asks, "what's up?"

I scan the house, cataloging Spencer's possessions. His easy chair, his pictures on the wall, and I lock eyes with his corner seat at the kitchen table. "I don't know," I say, still focusing on the room and trying to reconfigure the space in my mind.

"I'm coming over."

Before I can say no, that it might be better if he didn't, the line goes dead.

I drag the table out of the corner across the kitchen floor. The entire house vibrates as the legs move inches at a time. B runs to the kitchen, staring in bewilderment. The table is halfway across the kitchen in the way of everything—the sink, the fridge, even the doorway. "I'm moving the table," I announce as if it weren't obvious. Sweat drips from my brow, and my cheeks flush red, feeling as awkward as the table looks in the center of the kitchen.

"It only fits in the corner." There's almost an apology in B's voice. That she thought of it also, but the table is too big. The room is too small. She sighs, "Let me help you."

We slide into our seats and stare at the empty spot in the corner. Moving the table back feels like a defeat.

"You're not like your father," B whispers, but with enough conviction that even though my mouth opens for a retort, it closes just as quickly. I nod silently, and she seems to accept this as agreement.

"Promise me you won't see him." I try to switch the subject. If I have to accept so quickly, so does she. She left the door open for him as a sign, and I can't always be here. B takes a deep breath and glances toward the empty seat in the corner, and then around the kitchen. I wonder if she can see her blood, my blood, both mixing on the floor.

She flinches at the sound of a car door closing from the driveway.

"Mo said he was coming over."

Color returns to her face, her grip on the kitchen table relaxes, and she returns to her room.

On the porch, Mo points to the road and the green garbage pail. "Cleaning house? Because you could make my mother very happy if you went to ours next." A big-toothed grin plants on his face. "Any chance I can snag one of those bagels?" He raises a single brow.

I laugh so hard that I nearly start crying.

We wander to the woods. At the stream, I pluck a small piece of shale and flip it in the water. The stone doesn't skip. It sinks directly to the bottom.

"I miss anything?" Mo searches the shale for a stone of his own.

"He came." I toss another rock, intending for it to skip, but it sinks.

Mo stops chewing, opens his mouth, and his teeth are coated in poppy seeds. "And?"

"He has more excuses." I pitch another chunk, the edges sharp in my hand.

"But you got him to leave?"

"No. Jackson VanPatten's father came." I explain Jackson's father's threat and how Spencer ran off.

We fling piece after piece of layered shale into the water. The larger pieces make the biggest splash. The smaller ones, the sections we splinter apart, slide over the water's edge like a skier. I'm unsure if Mo doesn't know what to say or just doesn't want to say anything. I don't think he's ever been this quiet. After an hour, he leaves to pick up Aia from work. From the driveway, he hugs me tight like a brother might.

I head to my room and collapse onto the bed. The crinkle of paper in my back pocket is like a talisman, the picture and his letter. Part of me wants to toss both away, and burn them so that they're erased from my life forever. But like the pencil box in the yard, I'm not sure I can ever bury my past.

I tuck both in the desk when B yells downstairs, "Aia for you."

I pull at the phone cord anchored to the wall, stretching it as far as it will go into the living room.

"Hey," and I sound as exhausted as I feel.

"So what happened today?" Aia gets right to the point.

I tell her about B flushing the letter, opening the door, Spencer coming, how he tried to explain his behavior on a syndrome, and then Jackson's father pulling up in a Mercedes.

"So this is good, right?"

Befuddled, I'm at a loss for words. When Spencer pulled the SU student from the fire, Aia was impressed. This morning, after I told her about Spencer's letter, she disagreed that he was making more excuses. I snap.

"What the hell do you mean?" There is a long pause over the phone. I can picture Aia's eyes crossing, her face stern, and in the silence, regret the ferocity of my comment.

"What I meant," she finally answers in a weary tone, "is that there's a reason for how your father acted. That if the war made him sick, then all your worries about half of your personality being controlled by him are washed away."

It takes all my strength not to scream. That, of course, she'd believe him. She doesn't understand all of the excuses he used to make. This is only a new defense, a new place to put all his chips. I keep my reaction in check, "You believe that?"

"I don't know. I guess I'd have to look into it."

I feel betrayed. Choosing Spencer over me burns. She knows what he did. "Why don't you do that." I slam the phone on the cradle.

CHAPTER THIRTY-THREE

I SIT, KNEES TO chest, as sandwich crumbs collect in my lap, leaning against the book stacks. My eyes travel to the spines that form a rainbow of colors. For the past three days, I've been hiding in the library. Aia won't return my calls, and if she isn't talking to me, I'm sure Mo won't either.

They finally have put it together. My headaches, inability to sleep, lashing out at Jackson, and yelling at Aia prove I am my father. In the morning, after taking the early bus, knowing that Mo won't give me a ride, I leave school early to avoid him in AP bio. It's better this way. Safer for Aia, safer for Mo. But without them and with Jackson VanPatten's return to school, I'm vulnerable.

My eyes track to the author names: Lee, Leigh, Levine, and with disbelief L'Engle, the author of *A Wrinkle in Time*. The author gave me a place to belong when I was alone. The book has a musty smell, and flipping through the yellowed pages, the print is more gray than black. But it's all there. Good vs. evil. Right vs. wrong.

"Ethan," a voice growls.

The book jumps from my lap and flops open to my side. I stand and face Jackson. Mikey steps from around the corner on the other side. I'm trapped.

My eyes travel to the bruise on Jackson's cheek under his left eye, and his nose that now angles subtly to the left.

He grits his teeth and takes two steps closer.

I could raise my fists and go down fighting. But that's what Spencer would do, so my head lowers in surrender. The gold shines on Jackson's ring and the light glints off the central red jewel. The part of his brass knuckle that hit Aia will now strike me down.

I'm not afraid. My legs don't quiver. My lips don't tremble. Jackson stands toe-to-toe, breathing heavy like a runner after a race. My body remains bent. Nothing happens. Minutes seem to pass, and Jackson doesn't move, doesn't speak. How long does he intend to continue this stalemate? *Hit me. Knock me down. What are you waiting for?* It isn't until my head raises to look him in the eye that he speaks.

"I'm going to beat you to a bloody pulp." His fists flex tight like a boxer's.

"Just do it." I lower my head like a victim before an execution.

"Curly," Mo yells, striding toward me with Mrs. Kraskowitz.

"Mr. Rivers, are you eating in the library?" Mrs. Kraskowitz pulls her spectacles to her face.

"I'm sorry, I was just—"

"You're about to vacuum the entire library if you don't clean up your lunch." With her hands on her hips, she bulldozes her way past Mikey.

Mo flashes a smile.

"Mr. VanPatten," Mrs. Kraskowitz says, shifting her attention to Jackson, "do you intend to check out that book?"

Jackson's mouth, full of clenched teeth, stretches. He glances down at the book. "No."

"Then kindly put it back on the shelf, and all of you can be on your way."

Quietly, Jackson says, "This isn't over."

Mrs. Kraskowitz clears her throat. "The book, Jackson. Please put it back." He spins to return the book, giving us time to escape.

We sprint to my locker, periodically glancing to see if Jackson and his thugs follow, but the hall is empty.

"I thought I would need to fill out a missing person's report. Hunt through the library with a Curly sniffing dog." Mo grins. "Who knew I stumbled upon you when Jackson was about to stuff you into the shelves." Mo's grin is so broad that he must have known where I was the entire time. Fumbling with the combination lock, unable to meet his gaze, the dials twirl to the wrong numbers, forcing me to start again.

"I've missed you at lunch," Mo says. "Today, the cafeteria had a wonderful mac and cheese, but the cabernet wasn't to my liking. Perhaps, though," he says in a horrible French accent, "tomorrow, the sommelier will find a nice bottle of Mountain Dew."

I shut my locker door and put my bio book in my hand out of habit.

"Curly." Mo drops the accent and sounds serious for maybe the third time in his life. "No matter what happens, we're friends. Best friends, okay?"

Mo's eyes are bright green like his twin's. Just like my right eye.

"A lot is going on. I know that. So does Aia."

My head spins at her name. "I'm sorry," I say, unsure if I'm telling Mo or Aia or even asking Mo to tell Aia.

"Let's get to class." He tugs me down the hall before I have a chance to refuse.

**

While we wait for Mr. Lane to begin his lecture on photosynthesis, my mind wanders to Aia. How I spoke to her last, and if it's possible to apologize. After an hour of hearing chloroplast a hundred times, I ask, afraid of Mo's answer. "Will she talk with me again?"

"Probably." Mo shrugs. "She doesn't have anybody else. I don't like talking to her. You're all she's got. I think she's going to the library before work."

I race to the library, hoping that Jackson VanPatten isn't there, and head toward the stacks before circling up front and find her at a computer. There are fifty feet between us. I need to think of an apology and something magical to say.

To her back, all I can think of is, "I'm sorry." The words vibrate through the air, and I doubt she's heard me. Maybe my words won't reach her, can't reach her. I wish I'd brought flowers or chocolate. Something more than my words, which feel weak and empty.

"Yeah?" Aia's voice is rough like sandpaper. Unforgiving. She hasn't turned around, but she's closed the web browser. We've never fought, and I don't know what to do. Most kids watch their parents to see how an argument begins and ends, eventually learning how peace is made. I've only seen the beginning of an argument and its violent conclusion.

"I—" I try to put my thoughts into words. One hand rubs my head like I'm buffing a car. "It's just that—" I stop again. "There's just so much going on. I didn't mean to take it out on you." It's not a lie. Spencer returning, our first few months as juniors, my fear for B and who I am. But it's not the truth either. I won't let her defend Spencer. She can't rationalize what he did. He's a dangerous and violent man, and someone else will get hurt if he stays close.

She circles. "I forgive you," she says softly.

It all feels too easy, and that my apology is all that's needed. I want to tell her I don't deserve forgiveness, but after days of living in the shadows and feeling alone, her warmth is a blanket.

"I'm glad you came," she pulls only an inch away, "but I have to get to work."

"I can walk with you," I say, not wanting her to leave and

shouldering her bag, heavy with books.

It's late afternoon, and most of the students have left school, the sun nearly disappearing behind the houses. I squeeze her hand, our fingers intertwine tight, afraid she might let go. That I might let go again.

"Have you ever wondered," Aia pauses, "what happened?" I abruptly stop, our fingers still linked, pulling her backward next to me, trying to understand what she's asking. Her bright green eyes focus with a sense of wanting. We just got over this. Minutes earlier, we started moving on, and she's back at it again. Why can't she leave this be?

"During Operation Desert Storm," Aia clarifies, squeezing my hand tight.

I don't want to discuss this. Not now. Not ever. These are fresh wounds, raw. The last thing I want is to open them further. I try to sound even. "I watched TV every night. Everyone did. I saw the cruise missiles hit their targets, and the Patriot missiles intercept the SCUDs. I saw the Iraqi troops surrender at the first glance of an American tank. Everyone knows what happened during that war. It was a primetime event."

Aia pulls my hand forward, and we walk in step again. She's silent and unsatisfied with my answer. Several seconds pass, and we're almost at the hardware store where she works, and I think she's moved on and finally given up.

"Did you ever think that maybe that's what the government wanted us to see?"

"Right along with the pretend moon landing and the JFK assassination cover-up."

The lights from the hardware store illuminate Aia's concentration. No creases form at the corners of her mouth.

"I just think," Aia looks to the clouds, "I just think that maybe what we all saw on TV wasn't the whole truth, you know? I mean, nothing on TV is real. We both know that."

"Where is this coming from?" We stand shoulder to shoulder in front of the registers where she will cash people out.

"Maybe the story we learned is slanted and only showed us the side of the war the government wanted us to see. Maybe they didn't want another Vietnam where the public saw nightly body counts and pictures of soldiers stomping through the jungle blanketed in Agent Orange. Maybe the story you know isn't the whole truth." A light brightens in Aia's face. Her eyes are intense.

"I know Spencer's story. He sent me letters. Hell, he wasn't even involved in the fighting. He wasn't driving a tank or dropping bombs on Iraqi posts in an airplane. He was a quartermaster. The guy delving out supplies. Boots, uniforms, socks. He wasn't marching in the desert looking for Iraqi strongholds. He wasn't putting out the oil rig fires."

Aia's gaze is empty. "You love science. Can you reach that judgment without looking at all the data?" Her words are like a dagger pressing deep into my gut, but she softens the blow by standing on her tiptoes and kissing my nose.

CHAPTER THIRTY-FOUR

TWO WEEKS AFTER my assault on Jackson VanPatten and he hasn't doled out his revenge. He passes me in the hall with a glare but hasn't tried to retaliate. The bruise on his cheek faded, but the tip of his nose remains bent. Maybe, just like B, he'll also reinvent the truth. Create a story more to his liking and claim that his broken nose resulted from a football injury. Mo's father learned that Mr. VanPatten is planning to run for the open state assembly seat, and attracting attention about his bully of a son isn't on the campaign agenda.

Unlike Jackson, Spencer seems to have vanished. No letters, no more visits. B claims she hasn't heard from him, but I wonder if he's still watching us. Lurking in the corner at school or near B's office.

While waiting for the inevitable, I study for my AP biology and calculus tests. I barely sleep worrying about my college application to SU for next year and wake each morning with a headache, a vice that seems to tighten around my head. Coffee helps, but how long before I scream for a bottle of whiskey?

This morning, thick gray clouds blanket the sky. The once-green trees that were a kaleidoscope of color two weeks ago are gone. After last night's rain, brown leaves heap together in the corners of the parking lot or plaster to the asphalt. It's cold enough that we need jackets, and I pull my collar tight to my jaw. In agreement, Mo zips his tan checkered jacket to his chin, and Aia huddles her head at my side against the almost violent wind.

"Jesus, it's only early October." Mo's teeth chatter as he leads our single-file line through the rows of cars.

There's a white Honda and a blue Ford, each with leaves stuck to the windshield like parking tickets, but no black Pontiac.

Halfway across the parking lot, the *rat-tat-tat* of a jackhammer cuts through the air, competing with a bang from an I-beam settling on the ground.

I never see him coming. I don't see the streak of his green coat or the black baseball hat. The wet leaves and the jackhammer in the distance muffle his footsteps.

"Daniels!" a voice shouts, and in an instant, Spencer flies through the air, colliding with Mo, sliding in a heap along the parking lot, and landing on a blanket of wet leaves. I am slack-jawed and petrified. I focus on Aia, needing her to see Spencer.

"Daniels!"

This who he is. My father. A dangerous man. My arms pull tight around me in some sort of impotent hug. For all my previous bravado, I still can't defend who I love from my father. On the ground, Spencer wraps his arms tight around Mo. Mo's legs kick, trying to work free. I'm cemented in position, afraid of what to do.

Two football players pull Spencer off, and a group of students circle around Mo and Spencer, hoping for a better view. Mo leaps to his feet, but one of the football players easily yanks him back.

"What?" Mo screams. The circle grows deeper from onlookers and absorbs me into the ring. "The hell!" Mo twists his body, trying to work free. Spencer stumbles to his feet. His eyes are steel gray.

Like a rabid dog on a leash, Mo swings at Spencer but remains held in place by the football player's massive paw. The other boy wrenches an arm around Spencer's neck, "What are you doing, old man?"

This will be justice. Not justice for B. Not justice for Spencer's terror. Not even justice for Mo and the bruises under his ripped pants. But it's a start. I expect a giant football player's fist to twist into Spencer's jaw.

Spencer's eyes and mouth remain closed.

A voice echoes from behind the circle. "Let him down." The voice is urgent. From the mass of students, I expect a teacher or maybe the school safety officer. It's the crossing guard. He's limping, dragging his left leg as he thrusts toward the circle's center.

"Let him go," the crossing guard shouts. "He's sick."

The crowd collectively stares at the crossing guard leaning heavily on one leg, panting huge plumes of air, and then back at Spencer.

"He's sick," the guard repeats, as Spencer drops to the ground in a heap. Mo dances like Mohamad Ali, expecting Spencer to stand. But Spencer folds in a pile, his hands protecting his face.

The crowd groans, understanding that the spectacle is over. Aia scrambles to her brother's side, inspecting the tears in his jeans. The crossing guard lowers himself to Spencer and wraps an arm around him.

"It happened again? Didn't it?" The crossing guard speaks in a low voice.

"It's never going to stop," Spencer cries, and the crossing guard slowly lowers his head. The guard starts crying, and Mo stops shadowboxing. The air surrounding us is pulled out. I still haven't moved. I'm not sure I've even breathed. The crossing guard pulls Spencer to his feet. They're both wet and covered in leaves, and the guard, the same guy I've seen since school started this year, looks directly at me. "He's sick."

Mo is vibrating, and Aia isn't speaking. We're transfixed by

Spencer and the crossing guard anchored to each other as they walk away. Mo interrupts the silence. "I gotta change," telling the few members of the crowd who have stayed, or maybe just me.

I want to explain what happened. Try to explain that this is what I'm afraid of. That Spencer is dangerous and controls the left part of my body. Now Mo and Aia have witnessed it. Now they have to believe me.

"What the fuck was that?" Mo exhales, and in his question, a shame rolls over me like a summer storm. I've seen my father when his eyes get glassy and gray. I saw when Spencer got angry. When he nearly killed B. I can't answer. I can't explain to Mo any more than I already have.

"So, who the hell is Daniels?" Mo rubs his elbow, inspecting his jacket.

"Why did your father yell Daniels?"

My feet scuff against the sidewalk, and I nearly stumble, but my outstretched hands prevent a fall. Why would Spencer be calling for a drink now? He wasn't in the kitchen. He wasn't near the cabinet. Mo's question burns a hole in my center. Not what, but who? Who? I've heard Spencer yelling for his whiskey for years. He ran to the cabinet, both hands outstretched, needing the bottle like a drug addict craving cocaine. Who is Daniels and not what causes me to tilt.

"Your father was yelling Daniels right before he hit me." Mo flicks off another wet leaf caked to his jacket like the frosting once plastered to my shirt.

"I—" I swallow. "I—" Mo waits for me to spill it out. "I'm not sure. I thought it—"

Aia glances expectantly. Like she wants to say more. When Mo returns from the locker room wearing his gym clothes, which are at least dry, she's still staring at me.

"What do you think?" she fiddles with the ends of her hair.

I'm trying to understand. *Is Daniels a person? A friend?*

A firefighter?

"Let's go," Mo barks, pulling me away from my thoughts.

I sift through my memories, looking for one to grasp. "I don't feel so good."

"Curly, your father just tackled me, and you don't feel good?"

My head shakes, and just like my father, I run.

* * *

The public library is quiet, especially at this early morning hour. I sprint the entire way. I need a space without the school librarian looking over my shoulder or limiting my search to thirty minutes. Most patrons are older visitors reading the paper and pay no attention to the high school student, even in the early morning. With my head down, I walk toward the back of the room and the tall bookcases of reference volumes.

My elbows lean onto the cold tabletop, and my palms pull at the edges of my scalp, stretching my face. I can't believe I'm willing to entertain this idea. I find an empty computer, type *Dhahran Saudi Arabia missile attack* into the search browser and am assaulted by images from years earlier.

I vividly remember the news clip of Tom Brokaw and Jane Pauley. Tom Brokaw's gray suit, Jane Pauley's tan coat, B dropping the pasta. That tiny blip in the sky followed by absolute chaos—panic. Death. I scroll past the video link, remembering that night, and click on an article from several years ago, a newspaper story about the anniversary of the SCUD missile attack commemorating the nineteen Pennsylvania soldiers killed that night. There's a picture of each soldier and a sentence about who they were. I scroll past the first two photos, which look like high school yearbook photos, ignoring the text.

When I see the third picture, I lean toward the monitor, trying to capture all the details. The blonde hair is pulled into a bun, not flowing in the wind. Blue eyes as bright as sapphire. Beneath the photo is the name PFC Samantha Shepard. I know I've seen that name before.

I find two more photos halfway down the article, PFC Anthony Ladura and PFC Gerard Schnieder. What I'm searching for is at the bottom—the last photo. A man with dark brown hair, the top lapels of his military dress uniform folded crisply. *PFC Bryce Daniels*, and I want to cry.

"*He's sick.*" The crossing guard's voice echoes in my mind. I may not know all the details, but I can guess. Headaches, mood swings, and the inability to forget images from the past. I remember looking up shell shock and thinking it couldn't be related to Spencer. He wasn't in the trenches. He didn't suffer through months or even years of bombardments. But maybe it only takes one? He was on guard duty, far away from the blast, and he wasn't involved. But was he?

I clear the browser, typing *Gulf War Syndrome*. In seconds, the computer returns over ten thousand hits. I click on the first link and a statistic sinks into my mind. Studies show that up to 25 percent of veterans from Operation Desert Storm may have Gulf War Syndrome. Some soldiers may be afflicted with post traumatic stress disorder, or PTSD. Specific triggers, like loud noises or bright lights, can exacerbate the symptoms. It can't be that simple. It just can't.

CHAPTER THIRTY-FIVE

STARING AT THE computer for the third hour, I remember the news footage of Patriot missiles intercepting Iraqi SCUDs. There was pride, knowing that America was protecting the world. I found an article suggesting that most of the mid-air explosions resulted from SCUDs exploding too early and that the Patriot missiles intercepted only one or two. There was an article about how George Bush wanted only certain portions of the war televised to suggest our overwhelming superiority to prevent the negativity reported during Vietnam.

Standing from the computer, my legs go stiff, and my eyes dry. I leave the library, walking the two miles home against a headwind. Shuffling forward with an unfocused gaze, my feet kick at the gravelly stones by the road's edge. I try to remember Spencer before the war, before he left for Iraq, but it's like staring at a blank screen. There's nothing there. How can there be nothing there? I was eleven years old when he left for war. I should be able to remember my father from that time. But the only memory I have is of the splintered Lego. I press my hands into my eyes, wanting to see a different man, and I can't.

***

The house is quiet in the late afternoon. The door creaks, and I slam it shut, trying to imagine a time when I didn't have to worry about every decibel of sound. Still nothing.

In my room, my hands tremble, staring at the faces in the photograph, aligning them with the faces I saw on the computer hours earlier. When I flip the picture, my finger traces the blue ink on the back and lingers on the last name—*Bryce Daniels.*

Is this who Spencer was yelling for? Did Spencer see him die? Was he thinking about Daniels when he tackled Mo? Was he trying to save him? Will I ever know?

I race downstairs at the sound of tires in the driveway. Spencer is back to try to explain what happened today. Why he's sick.

My feet trip over one another, stumbling to the front door and swing it wide. I expect a black Pontiac in the driveway and my father on the porch.

My shoulders slump, and my head drops at the sight of Mo and Aia.

"Well, it's nice to see you too." Mo pushes his way inside, Aia trailing close behind. "Where'd you go?"

Aia rests a hand on my forearm, guiding me onto the couch. "You okay?"

I nod, not sure what's going on. I'm sandwiched between them. A set of fraternal twins. Two siblings who shared the same womb but are different genetically yet possess a bond stronger than science. They're still gawking at me, and I wonder if each expects the other to initiate some sort of intervention.

"I think there are some things you should know," Aia's hand squeezes my forearm.

"No." I have so much to tell them. Maybe Aia is right. That maybe Spencer's genetics don't have a tight grip on my personality.

Aia straightens her arm, pushing her palm out. "Please, Ethan, you need to listen now."

"But—" I am immediately cut off by Aia forcing her palm forward again, and her tight-eyed glare signals me to be quiet.

"I think your father is telling the truth." Her palm remains outstretched, ready for any retort.

My mouth opens but just as quickly snaps shut, and I nod for her to continue.

"When you told me about Spencer, about your father," she says, her shoulders hike to her ears and slowly fall, "when you told me that maybe I should look into the idea that he's telling the truth, I spent time in the library learning about Gulf War Syndrome. It's a real thing. I'm not saying that it explains everything Spencer did or is a reason to forgive him, but just hear me out. About 25 percent of soldiers from that war have this cluster of symptoms. Not often, but sometimes, there is also post traumatic stress disorder, or PTSD, when they remember traumatic events. Certain triggers, like different sights and sounds, can force those memories to flood back. Some soldiers have irritability, mood swings, and headaches. All of the symptoms exacerbate each other. Many soldiers were provided drugs to prevent the effects of chemical warfare, but there may have been side effects. The chemical warfare alarms went off almost daily, but most accounts describe that soldiers were told to ignore the warnings. That the levels were so low that no one could get sick." She sighs before restarting again, looking to Mo for encouragement. "That's only the beginning. Some soldiers have nausea and vomiting. Others even have a red rash that forms and then goes away."

Spencer had a rash. He said it was from the fire. It didn't appear fresh. Maybe not the fire where he rescued the SU student, but maybe a fire in Dhahran?

"I'm not saying this explains everything or even anything." Aia exhales. "But what your father described is real. It's a real thing."

Aia stares into my eyes. I wait, expecting more, expecting Mo to bolster her case. They both look at me with identical green eyes.

"I read about it today. Daniels, the name he screamed when he tackled you today—" I meet Mo's gaze. "Daniels was a soldier killed during the missile attack. I think Spencer was close to him. Maybe he thought you were him and he had to save you. I don't know. I think that's when he gets violent. I think he believes he's back in the desert. I don't understand why Spencer was there at school, but the noise and who knows what else probably triggered him."

"So we were right." Mo sits straighter. "His genetics didn't cause you to punch out Jackson. Spencer has nothing to do with it. You weren't somewhere else. You weren't in the desert. You just finally had enough."

For the second time today, Mo tilts my world. His statement hangs in the air like a floating balloon. I gasp, and there is a long silence. I stare into the kitchen. I was right here, facing the stairs, crouching years earlier before jumping to the floor.

"You're wrong." The words are a croak. Aia and Mo look at each other before focusing back on me. I breathe fast, pull out my inhaler, and take a puff. I think about my trigger. The crack and the thud. The repeated crack of Spencer hitting B and her head thudding against the counter. The sound of Jackson's ring smacking Aia's head and her hands thudding against the table. *Crack. Thud.*

"My kitchen." The words are a whisper. Mo's and Aia's eyes widen. They know exactly what I mean; my reaction had nothing to do with a missile attack. For two years, I haven't moved past the sound of B's head against his fist and then the counter. The crack and then the thud. Two percussive sounds. The same sounds I heard in the diner. Except in the diner, I was protecting Aia.

I feel like a dog chasing the wrong bone—focused on the wrong thing. I fixated on Spencer's DNA, not his medical condition. Aia wraps her arms around me as if I'm a wounded animal. Her head leans against the crook in my shoulder. "Now that you know all this, what will you do?"

"I need to talk with B. I need to tell her," I pause, looking at both of them. "But alone."

Mo and Aia are part of my family—a brother I never had and a girlfriend who is my closest confidant. But I need to talk with B about Spencer and let her know that maybe there is some truth to his letter. I glance at the clock, knowing she'll be home in less than an hour.

"You're sure you don't want us to stay?" Aia touches my arm, and I shake my head. She kisses me on the nose. "I love you," and she walks wispily toward the door.

"I just like you." Mo slaps my back and follows his sister.

***

I take the stairs to my room, still avoiding the creaks, and trace my fingers across the encyclopedia spines. I want to remember. I want to remember a time before Spencer went to war. I can remember Spencer and B fighting. I can remember him stomping out of the house. I can remember. I can remember the pencil box that sat on the shelf.

I buried that box the day I came home from the hospital—my ceremonial removal of Spencer from my life. I want those letters. I need those letters. They might be the only proof that my father, who left for the war, was different from the man who returned.

"Whatcha thinking about?" B leans against the doorway. Her hair is pulled up, and the look in her eyes extends beyond curiosity. I swallow, wanting confirmation, needing assurance that what I've put together is real.

"You and Spencer argued before he left for the war, right? I mean," and I pause, unsure what to say.

"We weren't perfect. But things were worse when he returned."

"Then how come I don't remember? How come I don't remember before?" My questions aren't a plea. It's like trying to search in a dark room. I'm convinced the memories are there, but I can't see, so my hands touch every surface, hoping they'll brush over something familiar.

"You do. It's in there. We used to take him lunch at the firehouse. You would ride in the truck."

My hands grasp that thought, and suddenly, I'm six years old, sitting in a fire truck, turning the large steering wheel with increasing vigor. My father is to the side, eating a slice of meatloaf. He's bouncing up and down as the two of us race to the fire. Spencer's smile spreads. His mustache is dark and trim, not haggard and unkempt. His eyes are a bright shade of blue. I look over to B, who is standing in the bay.

We were happy. Not just happy; we were more than happy. That's who we were. It's there, buried under years of more recent memories. But it's there.

"But I have headaches," I protest. Part of me can't give up the idea of my genetic difference.

"So do I. Does that mean something special?" B takes a step toward me.

How can she so quickly dismiss my symptom? Spencer had headaches and would get irritable. I have headaches, just like Spencer.

"I don't sleep sometimes. Usually when I'm stressed." She shrugs.

I think about the first few weeks of school, trying to maintain my grades for my application to SU next year, Spencer getting released, and my worry about Jackson VanPatten. Any one of those events would probably be enough for someone to lose sleep.

"Why are you asking about this?" B looks inquisitive, almost like she knows the answer but needs me to say it.

"I saw him today at school."

She nods, and there is no fear in her voice, no level of concern. No question.

"You know?"

"The school called me because you left," she pauses, "and then your father called me and told me what happened. He said that he likes to watch you. I think he knows that even if you don't want to see him, he needs to see you."

"He took a run at Mo." I close my eyes for just a second, picturing Mo on the wet pavement.

B takes a step back. "Is he okay?"

I wonder if she is asking about Mo. "Scared the shit out of both of us, but yeah." I look down at my left hand and then my right. "He said he was better." The edges of B's eyes turn glassy.

"I don't think he'll ever be better." She exhales, trying to force the words out. Something I know she's never been able to do. Certainly not with me.

"Does he know that?" I wonder if the two of them have spent time together. How else would she know? Was it in her letter?

"I don't know," she pauses. "It's who he is now. He's different. Not like he was before the war, but not like he was after either."

B's answer to everything has evolved over time, her words are empathetic instead of fearful. It's who we are. She used that single line to explain so much throughout my life. It's not static, unlike a series of stacked DNA nucleotides. Who we are is determined by what happens around us, not the genetic code. The genetic code is what we are. It specifies that I'm human and not a dog or a plant. It determines that I'm a chimera. That's what I am. Not who I am.

"Do you still love him?" My pointed question isn't a barbed spear, but B steps back outside the doorway. She bites her lip, maybe trying to decide whether to answer my question or hide.

"It's not black and white."

It's not an answer, but I believe for the first time that it's her answer and not an avoidance of the question.

"Do you?" she asks, and I'm floored.

For years, I would have answered no. I would have listed why I wanted nothing to do with him and hoped I could have somehow removed his influence over my genetics and my life. "I can't remember if I ever did." The remorse in my tone reminds me of Grandpa's funeral. Of saying goodbye because I'm not sure I ever did love him. Sure, we shared a meatloaf sandwich one afternoon, but that doesn't constitute love.

B pulls her hair back behind her ear. "You did. You might not remember. But you did."

Outside, it's almost dark, but I can still recognize the shed's silhouette. Part of my past is buried there, the physical aspect of my father's gifts.

"Do you remember the letters he used to send?"

"That we all sent," B corrects.

"When I came home after," I pause, not because I don't want to talk about it, but because I'm not sure what to label it anymore. I used to think it was an assault. "After the accident. I thought if I put all his things in the ground, it would remove him from me. Distance me from him. I think I want them back."

***

We walk to the raised mound of earth. Shoveling into the wet soil, the ground heaves and the blue pencil box comes into view after another two shovels of damp dirt. The top is cracked, probably from my recent dig. On my knees, my hands sweep away the neighboring soil, and the ground releases what I buried years earlier.

I comb through the letters at the kitchen table. These are the words Spencer wrote when I was in sixth grade. The picture of him in his Army uniform still smells faintly of milk, and the busted army watch is a testament to the past.

"Do you know where he is?"

B nods and I ask the question I didn't think I would ever ask or never want to ask. "Can you take me to him?"

CHAPTER THIRTY-SIX

"**H**AVE YOU BEEN to his apartment?" I turn from my reflection in the window. B's shoulders almost reach her ears, and her hands grip the steering wheel, white-knuckled like we're in a blizzard.

"No." She remains focused ahead.

Pulling into Spencer's apartment complex, gray buildings angle along the road. Passing the clubhouse, I can make out the pool where I went swimming years earlier with Mo and Aia. My head leans against the window, remembering the heat, Mo's bravado, and my panicked ride home.

B drives down several winding streets before pulling into a spot. She sighs, still gripping the wheel, staring at a unit on the second floor.

"Which one is it?" Of the four apartments, there's only one with the blinds drawn. I imagine it's dark inside, and he's sitting in a corner with a glass of whiskey. Maybe Daniels is a person, and that explains some of Spencer's actions, but Jack Daniels had been his sidekick. "Up there," and I point to the one in the corner.

B nods. I wonder how hard this is for her. Taking me to Spencer's apartment. Her husband. My father. The man who nearly killed her.

"You stay. I'll be back in a few minutes."

Her fingers unfurl from around the steering wheel. "I'll wait here for you." Closing her eyes, she takes several cleansing breaths.

Creeping up the stairs above his door, a soft white light casts a shadow over the number 259 on his door. This is a bad idea. I shouldn't be here. B shouldn't be here. Pressing my ear to his door, listening for the TV or the water running, there's an absolute void of sound. It's exactly what I would expect.

If I'm going to see him, I'm going to have to knock. Knocking makes noise, and I know what happens if Spencer is disturbed. I pull out my inhaler and take two quick puffs. I can do this. I need to do this.

I tap lightly and immediately press my ear against the door. Nothing.

Swallowing hard, I pound my knuckles hard against the steel door. It rattles in the frame, making enough noise to wake a bear. I don't need to put my ear close to the door to hear footsteps. Standing in view of the peephole, I turn sideways, ready to sprint. I'm still not sure what to say. That I read about Gulf War Syndrome and his letters prove maybe he was a different man before the war. I don't forgive him. But maybe I can understand him.

The door opens a crack, illuminating his apartment with a dull glow. Spencer stands, leaning on the door, wrapped in shadows.

I push my hands deep into my pockets. His eyes stare unblinking. Maybe he doesn't believe that I'm really here. I take a deep breath through my nose, trying to smell the faintest tinge of whiskey, but there's none.

"Hi." I roll forward on my toes, trying not to look awkward. This wasn't a good idea. I should have phoned first or written a response to his letter. Showing up without warning might set him on edge.

"I—" he pauses and swallows hard, "I didn't think you would be here." He shakes his head. "I don't think you should be here." His words are soft, quiet, like we're in the middle of a fancy restaurant. He looks beyond me and to the side to see if I'm alone. "I'm sorry about—" He stops and lowers his head, his eyes shut tight. "About today." He's barely able to get out the words. He isn't crying like earlier, but maybe he has a headache, and that's why his voice is quiet.

In my head, I say, *I understand. I get it. It's not all your fault.* My body won't comply. Won't let him get off that easy. "Why were you there?"

He coughs and lowers his eyes before whispering, "I just wanted to see you. Just to see you." His admission sounds less like a nefarious peeping tom and more like a father who knew he could only get so close. "In the letter, I said I was better." He shakes his head hard like he's trying to thrust away the demons of his past. "But I'm never gonna be better. You were right." He sniffles hard. "I don't know why you're here, but you should probably go. I won't go near you ever again. You or your mother."

He starts closing the door, and I shove my foot in the crack. The door squeezes against my sole. Spencer looks perplexed. In the dim light, real pain crosses his face, the kind that twists and distorts his features into a mask.

"Do you remember when I was six years old?" The question disarms him, and he lets go of the door, and the pressure against my sole releases.

"We brought you lunch. I think it was meatloaf or something, and you ate while I pretended to drive the truck." He looks at me intensely, but not with eyes that are cold and gray. Even in the shadows, his blue eyes are open wide. "I think you even let me wear your helmet."

Still leaning against the wall, his answer is somewhere between a whisper and a cough. "I remember." The edges of his mouth twitch, like he wants to smile but can't. Afraid that the act might be too painful.

"For years, I'd forgotten about those days. I was only a kid." It's not meant to be an apology, but it sounds that way. "I remember you and B fought before the war, but it got worse when you returned. Everything was worse when you returned, and I guess," I pause, unsure about what to say. I think about his time in Dhahran and how it altered him.

"Today, after this morning, I went to the library and read about the war and Gulf War Syndrome. I read about how the doctors don't know what causes it. Maybe it's from pills or the release of chemical warfare. Veterans can have headaches, and sometimes a rash, and all sorts of symptoms that don't seem to connect. But it's real."

Spencer stands stoic.

"For years, I've been afraid of being split." I take a deep breath. "My left side from you, my right side from B, and that your half would try to destroy everyone and everything around me. Just like you destroyed your job, your family, your friends. Everything. But maybe that's not who you were. Not before the war."

He quivers, looking at me, his voice cracking. "I was doing so well. I hadn't had an episode for months, maybe even a full year. I heard a noise, saw your friend, and—" his voice trails off, but what he's trying to say is that he didn't know where he was until it was too late.

"Lenny told me it would happen again. He told me that no matter how good I felt, it would happen again." He leans his head heavily against the wall.

"Lenny?" trying to put all the pieces together.

Spencer looks up for a moment before resting his head on the wall. "The crossing guard. He's in my support group. He still has dreams from when he was in Vietnam."

I remember seeing the USMC tattoo on the guard's arm and Lenny's dark eyes looking directly at me before he said, "*He's sick.*"

I push the door ajar, moving toward Spencer. "Can I come

in?" Both feet are inside before he has a chance to answer. From the shadows of the dark hallway, I can see into the next room. My feet shuffle along the carpet as I head to the living room's far wall. The hairs on my arms stick straight as my eyes gawk at the photos. Pictures of my father when he got married. Photos of me when I was a baby. Pictures of the three of us. They are tacked like a constellation across the wall. Each one is connected to another. A collection of what our family was like before the war. Each one is a candid print. My hand reaches toward the prints, afraid that this is a mirage. I touch the edge of a captured image from when I must have been four or five. Spencer is on all fours, and I am riding him like a horse. The two of us beam toward the camera.

Spencer shifts to the corner of the room, trying to block my view of a table and two chairs. Despite his attempt, I can see the light gleaming off the glass and the brown turbid liquid. My elation rips away in an instant, and I charge toward the table, intending to make a thousand accusations. That he isn't better. That he's the same.

Next to the glass of whiskey, fifteen white tablets fill a small plate. He's never taken any pills. It's always been just whiskey. Grasping one of the tablets labeled *AMB 10*, it rolls in my palm.

"Dad?" It's a name I haven't spoken in years. Looking from the pills to the glass. "Are you drinking?"

"I haven't had a drop in years." His voice is proud, but his head hangs low as he glances at the bottle and the glass.

"Then what are you doing?" I clasp one of the pills, confident that they are not a dish of candy.

"What I need to do to keep you and your mother safe."

CHAPTER THIRTY-SEVEN

THE PULSING WAIL of a siren combines with the frantic pounding on the front door. I'm still on the phone with the 911 operator. I've learned that AMB tablets are Ambien, a sleep medication.

The operator asks, "Do you think he's ingested any yet?" and "Does he have any weapons in the house?" I don't think he's ingested anything. He doesn't smell of alcohol, and the glass in front of him is still full and looks to be the only portion missing from the bottle.

I'm reasonably sure he doesn't have weapons. He doesn't have anything in the house, for that matter. The only furniture is a couch that seems older than ours, a red chair, and a small table that seats two. In the bedroom, on the floor, a single mattress lays in the center of the room, covered with a fitted sheet. In the closet, a shirt and two pairs of pants dangle loose on hangers. Socks sit in a pile in a corner. He's a refugee.

Still on the phone, I open the front door. B leans against the frame, breathless. Her eyes scour me, looking for injuries. Relief spreads across her face that the ambulance must not be for me, and then she arches on her toes to look around me.

"The ambulance is for Spencer." I nod in his direction and open the door wide. I put the pills in the garbage and pour the whiskey down the sink. All traces of what he was attempting are gone. Spencer, a man who towered over B, sits in the corner. His knees press tight to his chest, his arms wrapped securely against them, and he rocks back and forth. He's so small.

B tiptoes toward Spencer, her hands outstretched just like she might have done when he came home after the war. No sudden movements. No loud noises. She sits next to him, her back to the wall, her knees propped up; she touches his forearm. Gentle at first, and then a little harder to let him know she's there.

A man and woman dressed in blue jumpsuits stride into the apartment. The woman kneels beside Spencer. Her partner carries a clipboard, a white paper clasped to the front. "Can you tell me what happened?"

I don't know where to begin. That maybe there was once a time when I loved my father and wasn't afraid of him. He went to war and changed. He nearly killed B. He's not the man I remember or forgot, but I can't say or won't say that.

"He's sick."

B meets my gaze before she leans back onto Spencer. There's an understanding, an acknowledgment.

"Some bad things happened to him in the Army. I came here to talk and found a tray of white pills and a bunch of alcohol."

The paramedic scribbles notes on a sheet and asks the same questions the 911 operator did earlier.

I don't know what other meds he takes, the name of his doctor, or even if he's ingested anything. It takes several minutes, but B and the paramedic get my father to rise, leading him out the door. He hobbles down the steps like an old man and into the back of the ambulance.

"You're a good son," the paramedic says, carrying a tackle box of supplies.

Only after the ambulance doors shut do I realize that B is riding in the back, and she has the keys to the car. Without anywhere else to go, I climb the steps as the neighbors downstairs peer out their windows.

Inside, I intend to clean up, washing a dirty frying pan and putting the dishes away.

Looking around, I notice a stack of black-and-white notebooks by the edge of his mattress. They're worn, and the pages hang loosely, the weight of the cover no longer keeping them in place. I thumb through the pages, each nearly full. The early entries have sharp, angled letters.

There are no lamps, only an overhead light, so I take both notebooks into the living room and sit back in the recliner. An uncoiled spring greets me, and I shift to the left to get comfortable. There's a date at the top of the page: *10/6/1993*.

CHAPTER THIRTY-EIGHT

10/6/1993
I do not want to write anything
I do not want to write anything
I do not want to write anything

Each letter is a stab into the page, the anger etched in pencil. The defiant marks of forcing Spencer to write.

12/18/1993
The dream always begins the same way.
Six soldiers, in desert fatigues, huddled around a card table with a Trivial Pursuit Board. A single light kept the space dark. Sand scattered on the gray floor.
Shepard asked Daniels as I walked out the door. "How many seconds elapsed before the tape self-destructed on an episode of Mission Impossible?"

I focus on the name Daniels.

My arm kept the door ajar, causing sand and heat to blow into the building. After a moment, Daniels yelled, "Five seconds, and I am the champion!" A chorus of groans from five regretful soldiers filled the barracks as they each handed over their $20. After six months in the desert, poker and blackjack were just too damned short to pass the time. Trivial Pursuit was the new game of chance.

Daniels asked me to join, probably hoping to sweeten the pot. I might have put down $20 if I wasn't on guard duty with Howard, a hundred yards from the barracks. Howard was an ROTC kid just out of school. His sandy blond hair melded into his helmet, and a spot of peach fuzz always dotted his upper lip.

One of the few benefits of guard duty at night was the cooler weather. Even in the middle of February, the sun turned everything into overcooked steak. My tongue was perpetually dry despite the mandatory water breaks forcing us to chug liters of water at a time. Standing at the gate, a thin metal strip that a VW bug could plow over at 10 miles per hour, the air raid siren started emitting a one-note whine.

I remember that sound, and I want to scream at Daniels, Shepard, and all of them to get out. To run. The journal trembles as I relive this experience.

But the air raid siren always sounds. Sometimes, it goes off two to three times a day. When I first arrived, I dropped to my knees and pressed my gas mask so tight against my face that I'd have the impressions from the rubber seal later in the day. After months of false alarms, it wasn't worth the energy.

Howard fumbled with the strap of his case, glancing at my inactivity. He'd been here for a few days, part of a water purification group helping to hydrate the army during the G-war.

Unfazed by the alarm and scanning the horizon, I told him that for the first few months, I put on my mask everytime there was a siren. But we're so far away from the fighting that there's a better chance of Daniels becoming a professional Trivial Pursuit player than a SCUD missile attack.

He chuckled, placing the mask into its protective pouch. The siren continued for another ten or fifteen minutes, which wasn't uncommon. Some nights, it went on for hours.

The flash of light was so bright I thought I was staring into the sun. It looked as if the entire world detonated, and everything was on fire. Howard's face twisted, and the blast originated from nowhere and everywhere. A thunderous boom sent a shock wave, knocking me forward, my face landing hard on the ground, inadvertently breathing in the gritty sand. The bright light contracted, sucking back into its source, leaving total darkness. I wiped the sand from my nose, looking for my M-16 that was askew to my side. Were we under attack? I couldn't hear the siren anymore, but I couldn't hear anything over the ringing in my ears.

I read faster because this is the part of the story I don't know. The gap between where Tom Brokaw and Jane Pauley reported the missile attack and the details my father lived through. I focus on each letter and word, and I am standing in the desert next to Spencer.

I yelled to Howard. My lips moved, but there was no sound. I grasped my rifle, sprinting toward the burning building. The flames eating the warehouse were the only source of light. Burning insulation floated toward the ground like falling snow—soldiers from the shower ran past naked. Saudis crowded the streets, frantically trying to see what happened and what was hit. The metal frame of the barracks *screeched, bending from the heat. A Jeep, the engine still running and tires spinning, lay flipped on its side.*

Flashlight beams arced frantically through the air, searching for more missiles. Beams from searchlights hung on pieces of smoldering ash falling from the sky, momentarily thought to indicate the next wave in the attack. I ran toward the building, leaving Howard several steps behind. The rat-tat-tat of rounds fired from random directions, and I hit the ground, looking for an incoming Iraqi battalion of soldiers or tanks. The Iraqis were attacking, but from where? Where were their tanks? I couldn't find their soldiers. Next to me, a soldier mouthed, "The bullets are ejecting from the heat."

I didn't believe him. They had to be all around. I scanned back to the barracks, still burning hot. This wasn't a house fire, but Daniels was in the warehouse, and I wasn't going to let him die.

I think about the angry marks on my father's chest and back after he saved the SU student. Red skin that looked angry and dry. When I asked if those marks were from the fire, he paused, thinking about my question. Was this the fire he was thinking about? Was this where his mind went?

I pulled out my gas mask and ran through the doorway, head down, shoulders up, nearly knocking into someone trying to escape. The flames bit at my skin. The acrid smell of burning fuel filled the room. There was so much smoke that the heat forced me to my knees.

I screamed Daniels's name but couldn't hear a thing over the fire and the persistent ringing in my ears. The smoke felt like a cloud of thick molasses. I pushed it away. Crawling forward, I felt the arms of a soldier. I screamed, but he didn't respond. Pulling the soldier by his arms, I dragged him to the door; it was too hot to stand.

The heat scorched my head, my neck, and my hands. Twenty yards. I just needed seven or eight more strides. Ten yards, and I could see the barracks entrance. Once outside, I kept going for an extra twenty paces before collapsing. Turning toward the soldier, I felt for a pulse. Nothing. Unlatching the helmet's chinstrap, I pulled it back to start rescue breaths. Saudi onlookers from the street and soldiers surrounded us.

Pulling the helmet off, strands of bloody blond hair spilled onto the sand. It was a woman. It was Shepard. The top portion of her head was crushed. Blood trickled out her nose and ears, and her pupils were both blown. I leaned over and wretched.

The next page is blank. My hands paw at the pages, wanting more. What happened next? Did Spencer hunt for more victims? Did he stay with Shepard? Did he find Daniels? Where is the rest of the story? There must be more.

Two blank pages later there is an entry about the different members of Spencer's treatment group. There's no further mention of Shepard or Daniels. I imagine Spencer streaking through the house after a flash of light or heavy bang, calling for his friend and finding a dead soldier. I imagine him reliving that moment of his life over and over again. It doesn't change what he did to B. It doesn't change how he forced us to live for two years. But I understand now.

I close the journals and return them to the bedroom. In the recliner, I stare at the pictures on the wall, just like that night when I was a kid after learning about the SCUD missile attack.

CHAPTER THIRTY-NINE

MY BODY JERKS awake from a knock on the front door. Scrambling to my feet, I nearly trip over the blanket screwed around my legs. My head twists, trying to remember where I am. A picture of me riding a tricycle on the driveway catches my eye in the faint morning light.

Tossing the blanket over my shoulders like a cape, I peer through the peephole.

B wobbles, her eyes barely open.

I spring open the door. "Where have you been?" I prop the door open for her to enter, but she stays on the porch, her legs stiff.

"With your father."

Her statement crashes into my head. Conflicting emotions about how we should support him, if at all, pull and tug at my brain. I don't want him to die. I'm sure B doesn't either. But even after reading his journals, does he get to have her by his side, sitting with him while the doctors try to make him better? I remember her letter. That all she wanted was for him to return whole. He did physically come back, just not whole. But where does her obligation end?

"They're keeping him a few days. They think the dose of his meds might be too high. He's okay, though." She sighs, holding the car keys. "I grabbed a taxi to get back here, but I thought you would have called Mo."

I shut Spencer's front door behind me. "Let's go home." I wrap an arm around B, linking us together, and striding toward the car. Two peas in a pod.

It's mid-morning before we emerge from a nap and a shower. I tell B about the journals and the family pictures on Spencer's wall. During our second mug of coffee, B rummages in her room, returning with a bright orange shoebox filled with photos.

An hour later, she pulls another Polaroid from the pile. "Oh my God." She bends at the waist, giggling and shaking the picture between her fingers.

"Let me see." I grab her arm to wrestle the photo away, but she grips it just out of reach.

"You asked for it."

In the picture, a firefighter's helmet obscures most of my face except for a toothless grin. On the back, written in smudged black print is *Newest Recruit. October, 1986.* Just like the others, I look for details to jog my memory—the face of another firefighter in the background, the gray bench that Dad and I are sitting on while staring into the camera. There's nothing.

"Why don't I remember?" I'm not denying that it's me in the picture, but shouldn't the picture spark a memory?

"You were six." B picks at the scattered photos, arranging them back into stacks within the shoebox. "I don't remember anything before high school."

Squinting my eyes, I try. There's the time I burned my hand, but Grandpa retold the story so many times I might only remember the retelling. The day-to-day events when I was younger are gone. Lost. "Anymore?" handing the photo to B.

She wobbles her head. "We stopped taking pictures after Spencer came home."

"Why?"

"The camera flash aggravated his headache."

It seems like such a small thing, the loss of a few candid photos. A few pictures to remember the events of the day. Maybe an image of us at a birthday or a holiday. It's what a normal family would have, a record of the past. But the war obliterated our past and even our present. It changed our family. It changed who we were.

"I miss our life before the war." The tragedy is that those were probably the happiest times, and I can't remember them.

B pats my arm. "It's who we were."

Her cryptic answer for everything.

In the early afternoon, B left for the hospital. She invited me, but I still can't separate the father I knew, even with what I know now. She remembers the morning of the assault but also recollects the time before he went to Saudi Arabia. The day she got married, when I was born, and when they moved into the house. Those events remain cemented in her mind. Maybe over time, the forgotten memories of my father will return, or I'll find new ones.

Tucked into a pocket in the front pouch of my bag, I pull the small card and stare at the phone for several minutes. He probably won't answer. He's either teaching a class or performing an experiment.

"Hello, hello," his pleasant, upbeat greeting leaves me without words. He answers on the second ring. I imagined a secretary or a grad student would answer.

"Doctor Meyers?"

"Speaking."

In the background, soft violin music competes with the rhythmic tap of fingers hitting a keyboard.

"Sir, I'm sure you don't remember me." The phone slides in my sweaty palm. "This is Ethan Rivers. You gave two lectures on genetics to our AP bio class."

"Of course! Did you call to discuss a paper?"

I need a breath and then a second. I haven't read many papers lately. "No." My eyes snap shut, picturing my two different strands of DNA. The two different fingers twisted around one another. "I had a few genetics questions."

"Well, hopefully, I'll have an answer."

In the background, the classical music fades, and there's a squeak from a chair. I picture him leaning back behind a large wooden desk in his comfortable, austere office. He's wearing a white collared shirt but without a tie, with sleeves rolled to his mid-forearms.

My thumbs arc backward, each at a different angle. "Dr. Meyers? You know that genetically, I'm a bit different."

"I am aware that you are a *unique* individual." He stresses the word unique. "But you look very human to me." His tone is pleasant. It isn't an insult, more of the Bill Nye personality shining through.

"Well, yes, but I've been worried about which parts of my DNA come from my father and mother. I had a test that showed the DNA of my father dominated my left half. I've never been sure who I am." My voice trails off.

The silence mushrooms. I didn't provide a question. This was a bad idea. I need a script. My hand pats my front pocket for the security of my inhaler.

Dr. Meyers sighs. "I'm not sure about your testing, but I assure you that your father's DNA doesn't dominate one half of your body. There is no internal DNA battle waging inside of you. The DNA on your left side is a mixture of your father's and mother's genetics. The same is true of the DNA on your right. Maybe with just dumb luck, or bad luck in your case, a few bands suggested some kind of discrepancy. But my guess, and this is just my guess, is that you only had a few bands tested. Who did these tests anyway?"

"Dr. Taylor, my allergist, tested ten segments." I remember Ms. H. drawing the blood and mailing the photographs of the gels that came in the mail two weeks later.

Dr. Meyers scoffs. "I would place as much faith in an allergist studying genetics, as I would in myself treating patients. Plus, ten segments aren't nearly enough to reach any conclusions about paternity. At least fifteen should be tested. Yes, you have two different DNA sets, but plenty of people have two different sets of DNA. Patients who receive a bone marrow transplant will always carry a portion of the DNA from the donor."

I nearly drop the phone. *Every transplant patient is a chimera?* Maybe they're a different type, but they're a chimera. Someone with two different strands of DNA living inside. Someone like me. I think of the hours spent looking in the library for information about a chimera.

"More important, DNA doesn't define who you are."

"My father—"

"I know very well who your father is," Dr. Meyers interrupts. "I read the paper, and Syracuse, despite the university, is a small town."

"Then you understand that part of my father's DNA might control who I'll become?"

Dr. Meyers is silent again. Maybe he's collecting his thoughts, or maybe he's giving me time to absorb what he's saying.

"I can imagine that this has been an immense question for you, but there is no genetic predisposition that I know about that will make a person violent. Unfortunately, violence is more of an environmental association. Those who witness violence are sadly the ones who are often most violent."

I think about the violence I witnessed in my own home. How I saw Spencer nearly kill B.

"But my impression of you is that you are not a troubled or violent person. And although you may have witnessed things you'd rather forget, you don't have a genetic predisposition to violence. Genetics defines what you are. You're human. Genetics may even help define the diseases you'll have later in life. Who you are, though, that's not genetics. Who you become might have much to do with your father, but probably not so much with his genetics."

Tears form in the corners of my eyes. "Thank you," I say, gritting my teeth while holding back my emotions.

"Anytime. You know my number."

As I hang up the phone, our first family photo stares back. B positions me in front, presenting me for the photographer. Dad's arm wraps around B, pulling all three of us tight. It's who we are.

AUTHOR'S NOTE

By definition, a *chimera* is an organism with two different types of DNA. Although a chimera can occur following a transplant, particularly a bone marrow transplant, the most intriguing and provocative chimerism is when a twin is absorbed in utero. First described in 1946, it is commonly associated with an early trimester miscarriage. Although difficult, the current estimations suggest that a fetal chimera occurs in approximately one in every eight multi-fetus pregnancies. Many times, a fetal chimera is identified, much like Ethan's in the story, by an astute clinician who notices discordant laboratory data. Also known as vanishing twin syndrome, early notoriety for a fetal chimera relates to issues of paternity where the child of a chimera has different DNA than the suspected father of the baby and was popularized by several TV shows, including *CSI, House,* and even an *All My Children* episode.

***

Following the invasion of Kuwait by Iraqi forces in August of 1990, more than 700,000 United States troops joined a coalition—Operation Desert Shield and later Operation Desert Storm. During the six weeks of air strikes and four days of the ground war, the largest single event involving the death of US service men and women involved the SCUD missile attack in Dhahran. Sadly, nineteen soldiers were killed and countless others injured. Following the Iraqi forces' surrender, most United States troops returned home by the spring of 1991.

In the months and years following their return, many soldiers noticed a constellation of symptoms not observed before deployment. The wide variety of ailments included neurologic symptoms such as headache and memory loss, things observed by Spencer within this novel, as well as gastrointestinal disorders, respiratory ailments, fatigue, and a rash. Initially labeled Gulf War Syndrome, the complaints by these service men and women were dismissed as extraneous, and the veterans were mistakenly categorized as weak. In many instances, the afflicted soldiers were reservists and not considered true soldiers. They were prescribed Prozac or other antidepressants.

Our current understanding of what is now called *Gulf War Illness* has evolved over the past thirty years. It is recognized that soldiers were often exposed not only to low levels of chemical warfare agents during the bombing of Iraqi facilities such as the Khamisiyah Weapons Depot, but also pesticide exposure designed to protect the soldiers against insects, and untested prophylactic medications designed to guard soldiers during a chemical warfare event. Current estimates suggest that up to a third of Gulf War veterans exhibit some signs of Gulf War Illness in isolation or combination.

www.ingramcontent.com/pod-product-compliance
Lightning Source LLC
LaVergne TN
LVHW041910070526
838199LV00051BA/2571